THE CABIN SESSIONS

ISOBEL BLACKTHORN

ACKNOWLEDGMENTS

Many have been involved in the creation of this story. I am indebted to all the wonderful musicians who attended the legendary open mic at Kelly's Bar and Grill, a log cabin nestling in a mountaintop forest east of Melbourne.

I hasten to add that no character in my story bears any resemblance to all those patrons and artists.

This book would not have been written without the early involvement of the open mic's host, songsmith and Scottish troubadour Alex Legg, a passionate man with an enormous heart who furnished me with an insider's view of running an open mic.

From those early drafts emerged a story that took years to evolve into its current form. For that, I am indebted to the sharp and creative mind of my daughter, musician and composer Elizabeth Blackthorn. I extend my gratitude to Suzanne and Dave Diprose, who gave their thoughts and suggestions generously, as did Annie Dixon and Max Lees.

My heartfelt thanks to Jasmina Brankovich for her engagement and valuable feedback.

For Dave Diprose

CHAPTER ONE

ADAM

Guitar case in hand, he shut the lychgate of the churchyard, relieved to close behind him his day. Still prickling in his mind was the certain knowledge that beyond the turmoil of the skies the Moon would tonight slide into the earth's umbra and glow blood red. The day's Gazette had given over a whole two pages to the event, including a coloured photo of a previous Blood Moon, an insert portraying an astronomical explanation, and the musings of stargazer columnist, Stella Verne.

That an eclipse augurs the death of a king, the ancients observing the firmament in the deserts of Mesopotamia knew. After all, they bore witness to the happenstance, those soothsaying men of yore, they would not have reasoned otherwise. Without the benefit of modern science, the correspondence had taken root in the collective psyche, even finding its way into early Christian history. Millennia later, in those predisposed, the omen still held sway; helped along by Stella Verne and the Gazette.

In the dawn of the day Adam had been feeling in the totality of his being in balance, if precariously.

Then he'd read Verne's piece and the news lodged in the vestibule of his mind. At first a mere filament of dust on the doormat. But on his way to work the filament soon multiplied into a cloud that threatened to suffocate his sanity. By the afternoon he had to reassure himself that he knew no kings. He tried to shake his mind free, anxious not to find himself unhinged.

On the journey home, he'd managed to reason away as sensationalism Verne's Blood Moon auguring in what must have been an otherwise uneventful twenty-four hours. And in a fleeting moment of cynicism as he'd readied to leave his house for the evening's sessions, he knew that no one in the region would witness the event as the heavens would be obscured by the rapidly coalescing cloud.

Noting the warmth of the evening air on his skin, he strode down the lane, passing the Stone's weatherboard cottage: circa 1900 and tastefully restored, with a bullnose veranda and elegant finials. A house that stood in large grounds adjoining the once hallowed land of his own abode. He scarcely knew the owner, Philip Stone, but he pictured the sister, Eva, curled up somewhere inside, perhaps reading a book as she seemed wont to do. Or perhaps he'd find her with her brother, celebrating Christmas Eve at The Cabin. It was a thought that generated some cheer.

The day had been uncommonly hot and close; the time of year might otherwise have brought a light breeze to soothe the skin and a cool night for restful sleep. Yet the solstice had seen a climate so at variance with the norm, it had instilled in the residents of Burton at best puzzlement or unease, at worst a babbling hysteria. Several times in the previous few days he'd stood at the counter of the general store and found himself privy to the grim ruminations of someone or other on the topic of the weather, as if the sunny native disposition had arrested at the foot of that cleft of a valley. On Christmas Eve, the scare-mongering had been worse than ever, as the prospect of a storm of hitherto unknown intensity moiled over the plains to the south and to the west. While not yet eight o'clock, the sun had long since fallen behind the mountains, leaving Burton in shadow to be darkened further by the cloud that amassed beyond the peak.

Wafts of cool air stroked his cheeks and the bare skin of his neck. Wafts that soon became a breeze and as he reached the bottom of the lane, a fearful wind funnelled its way up the valley. Turning the corner by the gnarly sycamore tree, he faced into the brunt of it, the wind buffeting his guitar case and pressing his trousers to his legs. He battled his way to the old beam bridge, with its timber deck and iron railings. He crossed halfway and set his guitar case at his feet and leaned against the metal, feeling through his pants the hard cold against his hips.

Below, the river flowed in deceptively languorous fashion, having long before carved a deep channel through the sandstone, moving apace, undeterred by the tangle of fleabane and horehound on its banks. Whence it began in the springs of the mountains to the east, the river gathered to itself numerous tribu-taries, pressing through the confining cleavage of the mountains to emerge like a blessing on fecund plains, and wending on through the city to the coast.

In the twilight, the water appeared black to Adam, the rush of its movement unheard beneath the wind about his ears.

He stood for some moments, pinned to the rail-

3

ings by the wind, uncertain whether to head back home and survive the storm on his own, or proceed across the bridge to The Cabin where he would find company, of a sort: the regulars, locals all of them. His indecision held him fast, for were he to return home he would endure a night of relentless wailing as the wind found its way through every crevice; much of the old church, after years of renovation, still in disrepair. It was not a comforting prospect, yet were he to join the others in The Cabin he would be forced to endure wailing of another sort, the bemoaning cries of a demented crone, the sort of demented crone one would expect to find in a strange old town like Burton. Yet he was beholden, for he'd been at last invited to fill the guest spot at tonight's sessions, Christmas Eve no less, and whilst few would be in attendance on this foul night, he could not let down his mentor, the one and the great Benny Muir.

He picked up his guitar case, lifting his gaze from the watery gloom. The town, scattered to either side of the river, was obscured from view by thickets of laurel and dogwood, dwellings kept hidden by their owners covetous of seclusion. Even the general store squatted low on its haunches behind a privet hedge. From the vantage of the bridge The Cabin was barely visible, only its low gabled roof emerged from the slope of the hill. A few paces on and it would be gone.

He left the bridge as if leaving behind a watershed; so intense was his certainty that whichever path he took would somehow assure his fate.

His had not been a convivial day, riven as he was with anxiety that never left his soul. He had reached an age of slow recognition that the mess of thought and feeling that propelled him this way and that, affecting his every mood, was a fraying ball of wool. All he knew for certain was he might unravel at any moment and it was an effort to keep himself wound tight.

Yet his was angst he could make only partial sense of, the sort of inchoate angst manifesting in one who never belonged or was properly loved. He carried a gnawing sense of not being worthy, and as the world had rejected him so he rejected himself.

He never knew of his father, for his mother and grandmother never spoke his name after he absconded from his responsibilities prior to Adam's birth. Although it was mentioned that he'd laboured at the steelworks on the far side of the city. His mother, a singer who earned a meagre living fronting skiffle bands and taking in washing, had been a bony, careworn woman, the one photograph in his possession rendering her more Billie Holliday than Sarah Vaughan in spirit. She took to mothering like a cuckoo, leaving him at his grandmother's house whenever she performed, and one time she never came back. He was only two at the time. Left with no choice, his grandmother, a widowed pensioner who spent all day every day knitting and spitting platitudes by way of wisdom, raised him to be a good and honest boy. He did his best to fulfil her expectations, making sure he was well behaved, mild in manner and ever eager to please.

His grandmother lived in a plain old house in a suburb by the sea, a suburb filled shoulder to shoulder with plain old houses. While the other kids from the local school ran amok on the beach or in the park, chasing seagulls, skimming stones and building sand castles, or playing mock battles with stick swords, he sat alone in his room and read Tom Sawyer and Heidi and Little Women, in fact wading through all the classics on his grandmother's bookcase indiscriminately.

He remained a good and honest boy until his voice broke and his eyes fixed on his music teacher, Mr Hodder. Angst grew alongside his fixation and he yearned to fall into Mr Hodder's arms, kiss him passionately, fumble for his satisfaction. But Mr Hodder, he knew, was married, apparently happily, and there was never a glimmer of desire in those cool, recondite eyes. Adam had no choice but to repress his carnal urges and wait, wait until he'd escaped his grandmother's knitted prison.

After many lonely years of adulthood, Adam relinquished his virginity to the front man of a Lee Reece cover band: The Reece Effect.

It had been a balmy summer's night and the city bar full of smartly turned out, heavily scented men. The Reece Effect was crammed into a corner stage area, not much larger than a king-size mattress: two guitars, bass and drums. The singer stood on the floor in front, facing the left speaker as he talked to the bass player on the stage. He was a crane of a man, reaching the height of the guitarists behind him. His formidable stature enhanced by his hair: slickly quaffed, glossy and swept back from his face. Hair that lent him a further two inches of height. As the singer turned and Adam saw the width of his shoulders, he quickly adjusted his spindly crane analogy. The singer had a long, strong-featured face of Latin pallor, with the eyes of a hunter on the prowl, and a pencil moustache that accented his full spreading lips. The bass player struck up a pulsing groove and the singer slid into it. Holding his mike stand, he sang and those full lips parted, unveiling a complement of large white teeth. His appearance was altogether striking if disquieting, the sort that turned stolen glances into long gazes. As if underscoring the countenance, he wore black patent leather shoes with white button-down spatterdashes, an incongruent match with the red satin body shirt he wore tucked into black drainpipes. His manhood making a tennis-ball bulge in the crotch.

When their eyes met, Adam couldn't help but be dazzled by the singer's swaggering charm. Instantly beguiled, Adam left the bar, wine glass in hand, and took up a seat near the stage. At the end of the night, when the crowd had thinned and the band played their last song, the lead singer attended exclusively to this new adoring fan.

Always on the road, wooing audiences at venues far and wide, Juan Diaz was a rare breed of singer songwriter able to exist on the proceeds of his craft. With tattoos on his collarbone and a crucifix dangling from his left ear, he was ex-army fit, a man tough enough to front a drunken rabble. Yet his animal allure that could enchant the unwary from the first, fogged Adam's vision and he became Juan's partner and devotee.

Four turbulent years later, and Juan Diaz was a man Adam feared, a man too cruel, too vainglorious, too dangerous to countenance in his proximity.

Ever since the demise of this one union of promise, angst returned to become a fixture of Adam's psyche, abrading his sensitivities like thistle.

It was with a leaden heart and an ambivalent mind that Adam followed the road that followed the river to The Cabin. He paused again, this time at the edge of the privet hedge outside the general store, a ramshackle hodgepodge of a building clad in rotting weatherboards and flitches, with closed in verandas of asbestos sheeting painted a pale cream. The roof sloped every which way to accommodate a concatenation of small and narrow rooms.

A dim light shone through a small window. The proprietors, Rebekah and David Fisher, would no doubt be partaking of an unhealthy dollop of festive fare, and with luck their bellies rendered so full neither would muster the will to move beyond their threshold, though he doubted luck had the power to override habit. A habit never once broken by either party, one that found them every Wednesday night in attendance at Benny Muir's Cabin Sessions.

To his left, the northern mountaintop was shrouded in cloud. The wind pushed him on, past a vacant block where once he'd tried and failed to stave off Juan's wrath after a night of heavy drinking, Juan in a frothing rage and Adam placating that he hadn't, truly hadn't flirted with Philip Stone. Seconds later, Juan abandoning him in a bruised and bleeding heap.

The flashback stirred in him another recollection, one he hastily pushed back under the trapdoor, where it languished in an interior space he named his oubliette, an appellation appropriate for its contents.

He turned up the track to The Cabin, now in full view: a log cutter's cabin constructed from ancient trees that once towered in the forest. The logs of the walls were heavy and dark. In the wall overlooking the river, the square-eyed windows set wide apart, the long nose of brick chimney flaring between, and the low hat of roof, altogether lent The Cabin a menacing visage. A visage worsened when the proprietor of this lonely hostelry, Delilah Makepeace, had, in a whimsy of faux vintage, replaced the window's glass with trellised panes.

The wind, much colder now, curled around his calves and coursed through the thin jacket he'd slipped into on his way out his bedroom door thinking at the time he might find himself overly warm. His guitar case swung about and slapped his thigh. The cold propelled him on and as he approached, The Cabin took on a softer feel, for the small amount of light that emanated from the trellised panes looked warm and inviting.

He came to a sudden halt as he rounded the front wall. Penetrating the howl of the wind were three sharp crashes as if something heavy and dense had slammed into metal. He listened, straining, unable to move, the wind hard on his side. The door to The Cabin not three strides thence, but a courageous impulse quelled apprehension, and he stepped on, cautiously, and peered into the gloom of the yard.

Beer kegs were lined up against the wall like fat men's paunches. Otherwise the veranda was empty. He made out the elements of Delilah's garden, the stone birdbath poised on its pedestal, the gnomes dotted here and there, and the clipped bushes of herbs. Beyond, where the garden petered, a woodpile and a corrugated iron incinerator.

Familiarity took hold and he relaxed at the sight of a figure heaving into the incinerator what looked like lengths of sawn branches. Beside the stranger, a barrow piled high with leaf litter. This was no time to be clearing debris but Delilah was a fastidious woman who had surely required of one of her patrons he clear away the remnants of a fallen tree.

Berating himself for his fearful sensitivities he

made to turn when the figure straightened, and a quick burst from the headlights of a car flashed into sight a face of such unpleasantness Adam felt himself cower. He couldn't recognise its owner. The light vanished and he heard the thud of a car door in the distance. Without wasting another moment, he turned back, desirous of the comfort of The Cabin, no matter who was inside.

He pressed the latch and pushed open the heavy old door, ready to greet Benny setting up the stage. A rush of hot, heavily incensed air belted his senses as Delilah called to him to close the door fast and tight. The Cabin's ceiling was low, and the incense formed a dense haze anyone standing was forced to inhale. Wall lamps gave forth a subdued glow through crooked tasselled shades. Walls of logs piled one atop another and varnished brown mahogany sucked into themselves much of the lamplight. Delilah had yet to light the table candles. Adam was slow to realise there was no one seated at either of the two tables of polished oak—small and round yet still they took up much of the available floor space—and no one in the nook right beside him. The open-hearth fireplace with its carved timber mantelpiece was the main feature of the room. No fire had been lit in the grate, the heat source a column heater positioned over by the old oak barrel in the far corner of the room.

Delilah was standing at the mantelshelf in regal pose, bedecked in the full-length gown of deep purple she wore on Wednesdays. Her performance gown she called it, velveteen, with a plunging neckline and ruffled cuffs. Her lips were painted an equally deep red, her glossy black hair tonight swept back in a topknot bun with braided wrap, and she was holding her head imperiously high as if attempting to lengthen her neck. She looked as she always did, markedly handsome, yet she appeared distracted, the incense in her hand hanging from her grasp. Her gaze shifted from Adam to the stage to the bar, where it remained, leaving Adam to take in for himself Benny's absence.

Where every Wednesday by seven o'clock a microphone stand and Benny's Domino amp would be centred on the small dais of black carpet, there was an empty space. Adam turned, scanning The Cabin, absorbing the solemnity, opening his mouth to speak and closing it again when he noticed Nathan Sandhurst, bow backed on a bar stool, pretentious in his Ray-Bans, his head so low it might at any moment fall in his cider; and Rebekah and David's daughter, Hannah, eyeing her sop of a boyfriend derisively from behind the counter.

'There's been a tragedy,' Delilah said, directing her statement to Adam, a statement all the more ominous conveyed in a timbre uncharacteristically high in pitch, and not at all that deep, husky voice she had.

'Benny?'

She made as if to answer when Adam's neighbour, Philip Stone, came through from the kitchen, entering the room via the bar. He seemed out of sorts and Adam speculated that he, too, might have encountered the figure with the phantasmagorical face. For coming from that direction, he must have passed by the incinerator and it puzzled Adam why he had entered in such a manner, when he said, addressing Delilah, 'The old gal' pipe's rusted through and needs replacing.'

'Oh dear,' she said indifferently.

'Not to worry, I've fixed it,' he said, rolling down

his shirtsleeves and buttoning his cuffs. Seemingly not cognizant that when it came to the finer details of plumbing no one in the room gave a care, he went on, 'The bitumen spray and tape is only temporary so you'd better put a bowl underneath to catch the drips and avoid using the sink. Should hold over Christmas. Then I'll replace it with nice new PVC. And a waste trap.'

Delilah expressed her gratitude. Of course, Adam thought with some relief, Phillip was her plumber, he was everyone's plumber. Standing there by the bar in a stark white shirt, tailored fawn pants and polished leather shoes, Philip Stone must have been the most well-groomed plumber the world had ever seen. Adam couldn't fathom how a man who spent his working hours crawling under houses amongst blocked or leaking drains could present himself so impeccably, a practice that had instilled in Adam an inexplicable unease from the first. A reaction shored by a rumour Benny had given voice to, that untoward things had occurred in the Stone house. Then again, untoward things were said to have gone on in every house in Burton and Adam made every effort to dismiss the whole of it as gossip. Besides, although they were neighbours, Philip was to Adam virtually a stranger, Adam having had no recourse as yet to acquire his services. They'd not exchanged more than a sentence, save for that one occasion when they'd engaged in light-hearted speculations about the goings on of Nathan Sandhurst, the exchange that had resulted in Juan's pummelling.

A self-contained man, when here for the sessions Philip generally maintained his reserve, talking almost exclusively with Delilah, or sitting alone waiting

12

for his turn on the stage. He wrote soporific ballads, delivered in soft baritone, and Benny always put him on before or after the guest spot, a safe slot, for anyone present would either remain focused in anticipation of the main act or still be bathing in the afterglow of a dynamic set. Benny had let Philip perform the guest spot only the once, on a low-risk night years before Adam had moved to Burton, when the usual crowd was at the funeral of Rebekah's older brother.

Adam shifted his weight, his guitar case heavy in his hand. Philip glanced around, hesitating at the sight of him then pinning him with his china blue eyes. Phillip had fine blonde hair cropped to within an inch of his skull, a cut that accentuated a receding hairline, giving his wide forehead prominence and hiding nothing of his elfin-like face. His mouth, small and irregular, the bottom lip thicker than its counter-part, looked pinched. Adam felt instantly discon-certed. He smiled and, thinking he'd hid his reaction well, steered his gaze back to Delilah.

'You were about to tell me...'

She caught her breath. 'Quite dreadful. You better sit down.'

Despite his guitar case pulling on his arm, he didn't move. He detected beneath the fog of incense something sour, fetid: if he were not mistaken, the odour of rotting flesh. 'What's happened?' he said in a low voice, mindful of the foreboding the ancients as-cribed to an eclipse. The Blood Moon was still to occur and whatever had happened to Benny did not strictly align, but as Stella Verne stressed in the Gazette, the ancients allowed an orb of potentiality. At the very least, Adam sensed Delilah's news would cohere with the tightening of his abdomen.

'So sudden,' Delilah said, her voice now modulated. 'So terribly sudden.' She tugged at the large green stone hanging from her neck, drawing it back and forth along its long gold chain. 'One week a small growth on his back, the next,' she clicked her fingers, 'he's gone.'

'Gone?'

'The funeral's next week.' She gave him a pitying look. And with that she crossed the room and joined Nathan and Philip at the bar.

Adam found his legs weakening and made for the nook. He put down his guitar case and sat side on at the end of the seat with his elbow resting on the table. His mind a tumult of memory, he sunk his head in his hand.

Last Wednesday, Benny had seemed in fine spirits. Adam had been on his way to The Cabin when Benny swung his Volvo estate into the patch of dirt that served as The Cabin's car park, pulling up beside a pile of roughly sawn logs—the remnants of the tree that had fallen across Burton Road East the previous day, slamming into Rebekah and David's garage and narrowly missing a passing car.

Adam waved from the footpath and Benny waved back, cheery as ever. He went over and leaned against the passenger-side window, watching Benny roll a pinch of pipe tobacco in the palm of his hand and tamp it in the bowl of his Peterson, tobacco falling like sawdust to join the scatterings of scrunched paper bags, loose CDs, empty coffee cups and unopened letters littering the car floor. 'You're nae gonna ask to get on early?' he said. Adam laughed and told him no. He'd never pressure Benny.

A hefty man with a pork-belly paunch, Benny

was not the sort Adam would normally consider a friend, for Benny looked as he was, forthright, in the tradition of rural Scotland: a farmer's boy of sixty. He had thick wiry grey hair framing a large strong-boned face, with bottom-heavy lips, eyes small brown dots beneath thick angled eyebrows. He dressed casually in a plain white shirt and brown trousers buttoned below the belly, and ever since he'd taken to wearing a pair of fawn cowboy boots he had the look of the wannabe but well-past-it rocker. He was a Muir, an entertainer and an entertaining man at that, and Adam found his friendship restorative.

Benny sucked on his pipe, indifferent to the gurgling of the tar-slurried stem. When he'd had enough he plopped the pipe, still alight, in his shoulder bag and got out of his car. Refusing Adam's offer of help, he opened the boot and heaved to shoulder and to hand his microphone stand, Domino amp and guitar case, along with his red tartan vanity case full of his 'Only Muir' and 'More Muir' recordings; all his own compositions, inspired by the Bothy ballads and cornkisters he grew up with.

Every Wednesday he would open the sessions with songs of lost loves, songs of protest and songs of victory; lyrics of suffering and heartache sung with the power of conviction. Adam always maintained Burton was lucky to have Benny. He'd even had a couple of minor hits back in Scotland. The first was his Jacobite battle song, Bonnie Prince No More, which he claimed reached Number Five in the Scottish regional charts, a song that hoisted him on the folk wagon to tour all over Scotland, and even as far as Norway, Holland and Germany. On the wagon himself, his second hit was a love song which did modestly well on the regular charts. Then Benny replaced 'you' with 'Jesus' and the song took on a new life and became a number one church hit. Thankfully, by the time he came to Burton he'd dropped the 'Jesus' in favour of the original.

Benny was fond of telling of his successes to anyone who paid attention but there was much doubt in Burton over the validity of his claims. Delilah was equally fond of saying when Benny was out of earshot that if he hadn't seen more value in a bottle of whisky than his own talent he might have found enduring success. Instead, in a dramatic fall from sobriety, after turning up to the final gig of a tour drunk and stumbling off the stage, his career was cast aside by the industry like yesterday's bread, stale and well past its use by.

Poor Benny, too self-effacing despite his braggadocio, too humble, too kind. Gone? To have avalanched off this mortal coil within one week? It was Benny who'd helped him with his stage craft, Benny who'd taught him the aerodynamics of a song, Benny who'd stood by him the day he asked, no begged, Juan to leave. And Benny who'd soothed his shattered heart.

Adam lifted his head. Needing a distraction, he stood, blinkering from view Delilah in conversation with Philip at the bar, and Nathan, still slumped on his stool in his Ray-Bans. He wandered the room making pretence of studying the photographs dotted about the walls, plain-framed sepia images of log cutters with crosscut saws wearing their pride from boot to hat, standing erect beside felled trunks of magnificent girth. Tough men, hard men, log cutting men, Burton's pride. Above the nook hung twin photographs, one of the general store, all spruce with

'Fisher's General Store' written in bold lettering on a rectangle of board nailed above the entrance doors, and one of The Cabin sporting its original rickety veranda. Both buildings set in a wide sweep of cleared and dusty-looking ground. Absent from Delilah's collection was a photograph of the church, built in 1885 in modest chapel style. It had never before occurred to Adam odd that his own home, a building of much local significance, didn't feature in Delilah's display. Perhaps no adequate photograph had been taken. Or if one had, for surely one had, Delilah had not the fortune to acquire it.

He crossed the room. Through the window to the left of the fireplace he watched the wind tearing ribbons of bark from tree trunks, and he doubted anyone, even the Fishers, would venture out. He lingered by the window until Delilah and Philip left the bar, there being little space with Nathan spread-eagled on his stool. Once they'd taken their drinks to the nook he crossed the room and greeted Hannah with as cheery a smile as he could manage. She returned it with an even weaker one of her own.

'What'll you have?' she said.

'A glass of sauvignon blanc please, Hannah.'

The telephone sprang to life and she turned to answer it, tapping a lacquered pink fingernail into the number holes as she listened, and issuing a moue before setting down the receiver in its cradle without a word. Then she reached for a wine glass and the half-empty bottle nestling in an ice bucket and poured generously, shooting a cool look in the direction of Delilah before returning the bottle with a flourish. She was a plain and slender girl, large-eyed, her looks marred by a smothering of ill-applied makeup and lank, dyed-blonde hair. She had on high-waisted skin-tight slacks and a baggy cropped jumper of cobalt blue. Her demeanour was at once sour and sleazy. She did nothing to endear herself to anyone, leaving Adam convinced that some unhealthy creed had corrupted her at a young age. It was the vacant stare that had Adam persuaded, the sort of vacant stare worn by someone whose beliefs, however tightly or loosely held, formed a wall where a window should have been, a wall through which she would never see.

He took a sip of his wine and paid with a large bill. While he waited for his change Nathan stirred, slugged his cider, removed his Ray-Bans and slid from his stool, making his way in unsteady fashion down the room and on outside.

When Adam looked back, Hannah had disappeared. Delilah and Philip were in the thick of a conversation that appeared to Adam private. Not half an hour had passed since he'd stood on the bridge, pressed against the railings by a determined wind, and gripped by indecision. A lifetime might as well have gone by since, and he leaned his back against the bar, sipped his wine and, holding the glass by its stem, took in the room, at last settling on the incense sticks smouldering on the mantelpiece and the festive gold tinsel draped in unevenly spaced arcs beneath.

The wind gathered pace outside and he felt a compulsion to leave before it was too late, battle his way back home, a lone figure clutching a guitar case to his breast. And as if in response heavy spats hit the windowpanes, spats that grew rapidly into a torrent and his impulse vanished, replaced by the certain knowledge that he was trapped.

Delilah and Philip appeared unmoved, their

conversation, conducted in low voices, obliterated by the downpour. Adam found himself privately watching the door, wanting it to open, hoping Nathan would reappear. As the minutes passed he grew concerned for his welfare—the stranger by the incinerator could still be out there—and he was anxious too for any sort of presence to ease the sombre mood that seemed to be pervading the room in the absence of Benny and his Sessions. He pulled his eyes from the door. It was then he noticed Philip's guitar case propped against the barrel in the back corner of the room. So the sessions were to continue, or had Philip, too, come here in ignorance and anticipation?

He glimpsed Delilah eyeing her watch. The distress she'd displayed in speaking of Benny's death replaced with an assured calm. Nathan entered with a rush of cold air and she told him to shut the door hard and fast as if in this single command she asserted her authority and anyone inside The Cabin would thence know it was hers. She was a presumptuous woman; a parvenu Benny had called her. Her father had been the local pastor, a miser who'd left her mother scratching about like a half-starved hen for every morsel she could find.

Nathan swaggered back to his stool, acknowledging Adam with a slight tilt of his head. Dressed in a tight short-sleeved shirt of blue with red buttons, and matching thin blue pants and red plimsolls he must have been bone chilled but showed no sign of it. The wind had tousled his hair, the neat asymmetry of his side-swept bang a shaggy mess resting on the wedged undercut beneath.

'Dreadful night to be out,' Adam said.

'I haven't been home,' he said flatly, returning his Ray-Bans to his face.

'It was hot in the city earlier.'

'I wasn't there either.' He gave Adam a smug smile.

Adam took the hint with disappointment. He had no idea why Nathan was in such a costive mood. His was not the manner of a grieving man. Besides, he wasn't so close to Benny to suffer his passing. Perhaps an altercation with Hannah? Whatever the cause Adam was left alone to muse.

The conversation in the nook continued apace, Delilah and Philip furtively drawn together save for the occasional moment when Philip leaned back in his seat, put his hands on his thighs and nodded sagely.

It was with irritation that Adam turned to the bar and downed his wine, convincing himself the storm was abating as the rain eased, and if he were quick, he'd make it back to his house before it came heavy again. Then a frisson of guilt rippled through him that he was about to abandon the Sessions, which were set to proceed it seemed, for Delilah was surely waiting for someone to appear, a replacement, not that Benny could be replaced. Still, he ought to go home. In solitude he could take in the loss of his ally and begin to grieve. Not exactly a comforting thought but he didn't relish spending the evening with the present company, and as the minutes ticked by there was every chance no one else would come. Rebekah and David were the only contenders. Joshua and Ed lived too far out of town to make the journey in foul weather and Alf was unwell. Eva, Philip's sister, although again back in town, would without doubt have arrived with her brother if she was coming. At least Cynthia hadn't shown up, for he'd be forced to keep her entertained by virtue of the circumstances in the room, providing him further impetus to leave before she burst through the door.

A titter of laughter in the nook and Philip flashed a look in Adam's direction. Nathan emitted a rumbling belch. Adam turned to the bar.

A pendant light illumed the kitchen. Hannah was nowhere to be seen. The sink cupboard was propped open by a large plastic bowl. The back door stood ajar, the key swinging in its lock, and storming into Adam's mind was the figure he'd seen by the incinerator, no doubt still lurking outside along with whoever had pulled into the car park, their headlights illuminating the scene for the briefest moment.

A forceful rush of wind and a distant groan of thunder and he made up his mind to stay despite feeling alone and exposed. He had no idea how he would fare. Already he felt choked by the incense and the rank odour lurking beneath, an odour that emanated he knew not whence, an odour the others seemed determined to overlook as if it didn't exist, as if it were a stench he alone could smell, causing him momentarily to question his olfactory responses even as he applied himself, by way of distraction, to ascertaining the source.

Pointing his face in the direction of the kitchen he took a discreet sniff. Then he spied Hannah standing on the far side of the room, head bent down, her posture—she was side on—an appalling blend of sway back and hunched shoulders, her buttocks, flattened by her slacks, two side-on saucers atop spindly legs. A fold of belly flesh hung over her waistband. She was so caved in as to be bereft of dignity and Adam might have pitied her were she not supercilious with it. She appeared listless and adrift, yet she had an occupation, two in fact, tending the bar and attending the phone. One might say she was flat out, engaged as she was in activities that required little of her.

Adam straightened, lifting his chest. He was a man who spent five days of every week talking smoothly through his headpiece to a never-ending series of callers at Chattergulls, the largest telephone company in the outer suburbs of the city. Gainful employment and he prided himself on being good at it.

He took another sniff of the air and decided the smell was not emanating from that direction, for which he was grateful. Casting an eye about the room he could see only one other possible location, the chimney, and he recollected a tale, oft told by the Fishers to newcomers at the general store, and he hadn't believed it upon first hearing several years before and he had all but forgotten it as a result. That once a possum had fallen down the chimney and become trapped in the soot about halfway up. Some say they heard its cries, but Delilah maintained the first she knew of it was the smell, although anyone close to the chimney breast would report a low buzz. It wasn't until the maggots fell that she dealt with the poor dead thing and arranged for Joshua to sweep the chimney. Apparently, there was a remarkably high population of blowflies in The Cabin for weeks.

That smell must have been as rank. When he'd listened to David's possum tale, Delilah's negligence had seemed to him so astonishing as to be implausible, but with the passing of the years, nothing of that sort surprised him living here. Neglect was an accurate summation of Burton. Whether it be the paucity of street lights, sealed roads and storm water drainage— provisions other towns took for granted—the old weatherboard huts left to rot on their stumps, or the abandoned spot mills and caravans in the hinterland, Burton was pretermitted in favour of more amenable locations.

The town reached its pinnacle of progress a decade before, when a subdivision of acre blocks on the sunnier, drier, north-facing slope, was gazetted and approved, with buyers and builders to the ready. Buyers and builders quickly frightened off by a ferocious bush fire that razed that part of town, while the rest of Burton, the soggy boggy rest where the sun strained to reach even in summer, was spared.

Languishing at the bottom of this deep and narrow valley, fed by a single road that turned to dirt half a kilometre on before snaking its way through the mountains, Burton was not a town for the fun loving, the open-minded, or the innovative. Residents and their dreams stagnated, the river carrying away not their anguish, or their troubles or their woes, but their hope.

Adam had despised Burton from the moment he moved with Juan into the old church on the sunless side of town, and was met with hostility when he entered the general store, Rebekah all but refusing to serve him once he revealed where he resided, although he had to admit that Juan's provocative behaviour hadn't helped.

In their first week in Burton, Juan had gone to help Adam with the groceries. Adam wished that he'd remained in the car as agreed, Juan expressing a desire to listen to the news on the radio, for it would have made his life in Burton much easier thereafter. Adam was at the counter checking out his purchases when Juan breezed in and, in front of an incredulous Rebekah, put an arm around Adam's shoulder, cupped his face in his free hand and planted a wet kiss on his lips. 'What's keeping you, sweetheart?' he said. 'Not flirting with the staff, I take it?'

The only reason they were not barred after that was the Fisher's obligation to deliver them their mail.

Rebekah ignored them both from then on until Juan moved out and then she ingratiated herself into Adam's favour by offering to clean for him. He supposed it was her way of exerting control over a building that would always be for her a house of god.

It was Juan's dream to renovate an old church, and the Burton building was all Adam could afford. Juan's contribution was to be physical, in helping to carry out the renovations. Yet he contributed little, stopping once he'd fixed the plumbing, plumbing which caused a ripple of consternation and much disapproval amongst the locals for failing to employ Philip. Eva had divulged the gossip during one of her infrequent visits to Burton to see her brother. Adam was passing by and found her resting against the front gate of Philip's property with her elbows on the top rail, and she'd called him over all small smiles and hesitations, nevertheless eager to bestow upon him an air of caution and Adam had been cautious ever since.

Three years passed and Juan became intolerable, his departure forcing Adam to fend for himself. He couldn't rent or sell the church in its partially renovated condition without incurring a hefty loss and he was reluctant to abandon the only home he'd owned. So, he'd stayed.

Benny had been his deliverance.

A great sadness welled in his heart and he again toyed with the thought that he might after all head home when the phone rang. Hannah shuffled in and answered it, and when she hung up she said, 'Hey, this is a killer storm that's comin'.' Her eyes widened. 'It's a freakin' monster.'

Delilah paused to shoot her a cool stare then continued talking to Philip. Nathan didn't move. Adam felt compelled to respond.

'How so?'

'My friend Tracy says half the city's without power. Trees down, roofs ripped off. Ocean's flooding shops.'

'It'll miss us,' Nathan said without looking up.

'What would you know?'

'Lightning never strikes in the same place twice.'

'You reckon?' Hannah said through curled lips.

'Yeah. And we had that storm last week. Someone else's turn this time.'

Hannah's glare was contemptuous.

At the sight of her, of Nathan, of Delilah and Philip, suffering the nausea he now felt inhaling the vile stench barely masked by the incense, a sudden burst of bravery swept through him and he made to leave despite the imminent weather, heading for his guitar, planning to grab it on his way by with the briefest of farewells.

He was reaching for the handle of his guitar case when the door of The Cabin opened with a rush of cold air.

Adam paused and looked up, curious to see who, out of the Session regulars, had arrived, anticipating two lardy behemoths to corner the door for it had to be the Fishers, Rebekah and David.

Delilah leaned forward in her seat. A look of relief appeared in her face as the figure of a man closed the door behind him. She stood and walked round and greeted him with a warm smile. 'So pleased you could fill in at such short notice.'

'It's good to be back.'

Adam straightened and waited, clawing back what little equanimity he had, forcing his face into a bland expression.

Juan was slow to notice him. When he did, a grin spread across his face.

CHAPTER TWO

EVA'S DIARY – MONDAY 15TH DECEMBER

There's a lone loose thread in my pink quilted bedspread. I can't help picking at it, worrying it free. As the stitching unravels I desist, and smoothing out the satin fabric, I sit up. Facing me is my own image, reflected in the winged mirror of my white-painted dressing table. I look to the row of dolls lined up on the high shelf above, legs dangling. The dolls of my childhood, staring straight ahead with their big doll eyes. In the centre is the odd one out, a rag doll, with woollen hair in bunches, a floppy doll leaning on the shoulder of the big mamma on its right.

Good or bad, omens come in peculiar ways. I wonder what the rag doll would think about that. This omen is surely good; my first day back and I've achieved a new personal best. All the better for I had not been expecting to manage so long after the labours of yesterday.

There'd been the packing, and then the moving and the goodbyes. I felt no sadness bidding farewell to the house share, tired as I was of petty nonsenses: whose dishes were still in the sink; who was hogging the bathroom, again. Always me. There's only so much blaming and nagging a person can take and the women in question shall remain locked from my heart as though strangers.

It is true that I spend long periods in the bath, for where else am I to train! Holding one's breath in the air of a room or outdoors isn't the same. It's a question of focus. The very act of submergence intensifies the experience, rendering it far more confronting. It's my sport and today I achieved a spectacular result.

Breath holding may seem an unusual pastime, especially for a non free diver like me, but so is bungee jumping in my view, a pursuit my housemates raved about after a holiday overseas. Leaping off a bridge with a rubber band tied round your middle—where's the challenge in that? You bounce around a few times and someone in a boat comes along and unties you.

Whereas breath-holding, well, there is nothing to compare. Not a pastime for the daredevil. It requires endurance, persistence and an ability to resist the desire to exhale. There's something satisfying in dwelling at the brink of panic and not allowing it sway. So thrilled was I when I finally raised my head this morning and saw the time that I leapt out of the bath, dizzy and gasping, rapture coursing through every cell of me.

I came straight to my bedroom to record the feat: Nine minutes and twenty-three seconds.

Half the world record for a woman but then I do not partake in lung packing or hyperventilation. The new Buddhist meditation technique I've been using is beneficial and I'm finding that I enter the zone far more quickly as a result, but I put down my triumph to my remarkably relaxed state of mind now I'm here.

I must also attribute some credit to my brother, Philip, for creating a spectacular bathroom.

He has converted Aiden's old bedroom, which adjoined the original bathroom, knocking through a large section of the wall. The result is palatial. There's a window set in the eastern wall overlooking the magnificent, tree-filled valley, with glimpses of the river at its base, and there's not another building in sight. No need for curtains, although a feminine touch wouldn't be amiss, and I've already conceived drapery of the finest chiffon in yellow or pink. Possibly both.

The notion came to me while I was in the bath. And what a bath! Large enough for Rebekah and David at once, and lacquered in the deepest sapphire. It was as though when submerged I was in the ocean itself. And looking up at the wall tiles I was beholding the sky on a lovely sunny day.

It was very clever and imaginative of Philip to create a space evocative of the vastness of the ocean and the heavens, especially here in Burton, a village that bears witness to a grey slit of sky, way up above the mountains. Mountains that clip the wings of all Burton's inhabitants. For it is a universal truth that you are where you live, not what you eat. Food may affect physical matters, such as weight and health, but location affects the psyche.

Desert people, mountain people, river people, they all see the world differently, think differently, know differently and experience differently. Holidays, those happy changes of environment, are respite from all that one is. I have oft heard it said that when you move house your old self relocates with you, which explains European gardens in far-flung climes, but these are merely vestiges of an old self clinging fast, resisting the emergence of a new one.

Then there are the city dwellers, those indecisive vacillators whose psyche is at odds with the habits of millennia, somewhat uprooted from the fundament, aimless butterflies dancing hither and thither in their cars.

And of course, there are the home-comers, those who go back. It's always to complete unfinished business—isn't it? —a task to be undertaken before once again one leaves, this time never to return. Even if one has no idea what that unfinished business might be. Perhaps compelled by an inner need, the task at hand an exhumation of a memory. A felt pressure, as if deep below the earth, captive in its coffin, a body bangs and yells, 'It's time!'

I've come home after ten years and four months toiling at the post office of a small coastal town right on the river mouth some thirty minutes by train from the city. My workdays spent in the sorting room while the proprietors, Jacob and Ruth Cartwright, attended to customers out front. A satisfying job made loathsome by the Cartwrights. I loved to hold the light, crisp envelopes from places abroad, run my fingers over the address on the back, or gaze at postcards with their images of castles and cathedrals and old ruins. Best of all, were the stamps themselves, stamps of birds and butterflies and flowers, boats and buildings and famous paintings. Marvellous stamps, with their marvellous franks from places I've never heard of like Cape Verde and the Azores. But my philatelic interest didn't gel with the stuffy old Cartwrights and their fussy old ways. They were forever, hurrying me along to meet an arbitrary deadline, reprimanding me for dawdling when I was smiling at some foreign letter in my hand. To make matters worse, every day there was a new address to remember. Don't put Michele Brown in box thirty-three; they've split up and she's collecting her mail from the counter. Or Bill Platt's no longer on the estuary mail run; he's moved in with Louise Quant of box forty-nine. Then there were the new arrivals to contend with, and the redirections. The deaths were never a problem as some family member or friend always seemed to take charge of the drop point, the dead man's mail redirected to the box of a son or daughter, or remaining in its own box relabelled 'deceased estate.'

The stamps lived on and that's all that mattered to me.

So, I was sacked. Or rather, 'I'm afraid we have to let you go,' Ruth had said, with Jacob standing beside her.

I'd been let go and it did feel like a release for it's wonderful to be back among the mountains.

Mountains are special. The mountains that trap also protect and this is why I've returned. To relax and be still after the vicissitudes of the post office and the house share, to retreat to a place where the non-senses of modern life can't reach. Yes, this is surely why I've come back. This, and nothing more.

Not surprising then, that I was as eager as a child before a Christmas tree when I saw the bath. Philip's glorious sapphire bath that sits on its claw feet in the centre of the room, a watery throne on a dais of fine Italian tiles of taupe and indigo laid on the diagonal, perfectly edged along the one step that follows the curve of the dais. The tiles on the floor itself indigo inlaid with iridescences. It's like walking on night.

The shower, tiled with a large showerhead, is re-cessed in the wall opposite the window. The basin, matching the bath in colour and size, mounted on a stone pine slab. Towels of luxuriant Egyptian cotton neatly rolled and stacked four high on a freestanding rack. The toilet remains in the original bathroom, ac-cessed through a door beside the shower.

This morning, with much anticipation, I placed my stopwatch on the side lip of the bath in easy reach and moved the large, elegantly cushioned wicker chair to face the window. Having disrobed in the bed-room, I was adorned only in a white sarong.

I let the bath fill from the gold taps, set to a slow drizzle, allowing ample time to alter my state of mind. The view, for I meditate open-eyed, and the slow steady splash of the water, were perfect inducements and before long I felt heavy and my heart rate slowed and I descended into relaxation as deep as sleep.

In Philip's bath I can lie on my back with my legs extended and neither my head or the soles of my feet touch the sides. The plug has a golden chain and I wrapped it between my toes as a precaution. I can empty the bath if I feel myself at risk of blacking out. At the share house, I used to tie string to the bath plug, not that blacking out is the worst that can happen.

The worst that can happen is an interruption. Happened often enough in the share house, someone hammering on the door, or yelling. Here that is never going to happen. Here, during the day, there is only me.

I got in and took five deep and slow breaths to clear my lungs, then as I clicked the stopwatch, I took one enormous inhale and slid beneath the water.

It's easy at first. As time passes the urge to exhale intensifies. I steadied the reflex, held my mind calm and still, lulled by the tranquillity of the space. I imagined as I always do that I was submerged in the clear waters of a tropical sea, watching fish scamper and cavort, the coral, the whorls of sand kicked up by a friendly crab.

I see paddletails with their mournful mouths and sad black eyes; bi-coloured angelfish, all wide-eyed innocence; bottom-feeding goatfish, inquisitive and watchful; salmon-pink squirrelfish with their tragic, grief-stricken eyes; and bright and happy clownfish, spotty groupers and intricately adorned sea horses of every hue. One or two swim closer, curious, and I see their gills, their mouths, their fins, their scales.

Desperation is never far from view. It might take the form of a shark or a ray, a dark menace lurking almost beyond my field of vision and should I see a spreading shadow, a sharp fin or tentacle, I erase it from my safe and sheltered underwater world where nothing bad can ever happen. I am a magician holding a spell, a shaman navigating an interior reality through the force of my will.

It is all too brief, it cannot last, such beauty, such peace, such unimaginable poise, and the dark menace crept up behind me and wrapped me in its embrace and I had no choice, my time was up, and just as I glimpsed the last little fishes of my ocean paradise I tugged free the plug with my toes, raised my head and reached for the stopwatch, and breathed.

Ecstasy consumed me. I was transfigured, euphoric, tingling, all my senses sharp and alive. My heart beat faster, I panted as if from strenuous exercise. It was an ecstasy made all the better for seeing the time on the stopwatch.

Nine minutes and twenty-three seconds.

It's an omen; of that there can be no mistake. An omen of good things to come, and a decision well made. I have returned, to Burton, to my dear brother Philip, to finish my business; and it's perfectly clear that providence will be on my side.

CHAPTER THREE

PHILIP

I n my side vision I watched the rise and fall of Delilah's bosom. A sagacious woman, once she'd cottoned that Benny Muir would fill an otherwise dead night she trapped the sewer gas that was Burton's musical congregation for the sake of his Sessions, persuading anyone with a ukulele and a functioning voice to come along. With the blandishments and honeyed words of the devoted mother, Delilah had cultivated loyalty from a pack of talentless no hopers. Impressive, but I doubted her shrewd nature extended to the booking of Juan Diaz to stand in after Benny's untimely demise. Untimely, for it was Christmas Eve after all, and no proprietor wants tragedy looming over the festive season. It isn't good for business.

There wasn't much she could do about the weather, although I dare say she would if she could. Pity she didn't apply a similar resolve when it came to her abysmal plumbing. She had the audacity to ask me to deal with her leaking drain the moment I'd set down my guitar, as if I were a servant on call. A servant kitted out with all the necessary tools. Fortunately for her I never go anywhere in Burton unprepared.

I managed to patch up the leak but I told her the entire system needed replacing. As expected, she took umbrage, so I placated her with a jocular, 'That's the trouble with all the old buildings in Burton. Been keeping me in full employment for decades.'

As I'd re-entered the bar and observed Delilah standing all imperious by the fireplace, I knew I was assured of an interesting night. A storm was muscling its way into the valley and already the wind was lashing hither and thither. Burton always had more than its share of storms, as if the mountains were a lure, the valley the repository for the ire of punishing gods. And who should have walked in on the fore of it but my Davidian neighbour, Adam, all tousled and shaken by that vicious weather only to be further shaken by the news of Benny's death.

Delilah had put on a good show in the telling. She wasn't so close to Benny Muir. She tolerated him for his trap seal role at The Cabin, preventing any of her flock from seeping out. Privately, she considered him an interloper.

Once seated in the nook, Delilah had much to say to me about Benny's blocked gooseneck, and the alien lumps riddled right through him. I recoiled as she spoke, speculating that she'd most likely embellished the truth of his malaise. She spoke in confidence, naturally. She seemed to believe she could trust me. Like all the women in Burton, she was half in love with me. A half love that was inappropriate and disgusting since she was seventeen years my senior and not only old enough to be my mother, she had been Mother's closest friend. To go there would feel like betrayal and incest all at once. Besides, she was not at all my type. The raven had a way of narrowing her eyes and tightening her lips when she spoke of others, rendering gossip conspiracy that only she was privy to, conveying by means of an authoritative manner she had inherited from her father, Pastor Makepeace, the unquestionable veracity of her opinions. She liked nothing more than to hold court with her poisonous vignettes, and since I was content to listen for want of more interesting company, she felt no restraint in the telling. Yet her misplaced affections and equally misplaced blether privately repelled me and I was thankful when she at last rose from her seat and took up her post by the fireplace.

Freed, I could relax and focus on enjoying the scene. Adam hovered nearby with his hand to his throat, watching Juan exit and enter with his sound equipment. He'd propped open the door, letting in a rush of cold damp air; a welcome freshness, for the incense-laced odour of rotting corpse was a touch overwhelming, even for me.

The only other presence in the room was that contemptuous excuse for a man, Nathan Sandhurst, busy pickling his every organ. He would turn into a living preserve before long. I could only presume he was wallowing. I have no time for wallowing. I don't wallow. If he had a right to wallow, then so did I since we have both lost our parents in tragic circumstances. Six years my junior and he'd turned himself into a coxcomb. His visage was personable enough; although bland, his features were arranged in good symmetry. If he would only lose the frown and that affected tilt of the lips he'd verge on good-looking. But his eyes were always cloudy. Come to think of it, his wallowing wasn't grief. He drank from the trough of self-pity at having never made the big time, all the while beefing himself up with stories that no one believed. I doubted he was working. Boasted to Rebekah whenever he went to the general store that he was waiting to learn the outcome of an interview with a record company but we'd all heard that before, many times. Delilah said he did a lot to keep the general store afloat with correspondence to potential record companies with whom he hadn't a hope of success. He should have looked around Burton for options, not the city where he was a nobody from nowhere. Here, he would have been the only applicant. The sooner he realised he wasn't going to make the big time any time and set about learning a few more complex guitar chords the better off he'd be. I had no idea how Hannah put up with a sop like him. Then again, she was devoid of self-respect as well. That those two constituted Burton's youth, augured ill for its future.

Nathan roused himself into a sideways lean to observe the goings on through his Ray-Bans, and Hannah was staring too. All eyes were on Juan ferrying in his sound equipment. A machine of a man, six foot six and ex-army fit which was plain to see through his body shirt that revealed the chiselled muscles of his chest. His jet-black hair was slicked back around his ears, doing nothing to soften the angularity of his face: straight nose, square jaw, thin pencil moustache. Even his plump lips were straight. Anger was the only emotion that sort of face could portray, in the eyes that smouldered, in the lips that reared, in a jaw that locked. The charisma that others saw in him was fake, a mask that made passion of wrath, from my purview stuck on like a sticking plaster on a gash. People see what they want to see and most prefer to find in others something comprehensible and cultured, not animal and base.

We all watched on while, with much huffing and grunting, he set about arranging his sound equipment, lifting speakers onto large metal stands, positioning others on the front edge of the dais for foldback, and trailing leads to plug into the monster thirty-two channel mixing desk bolted to its own table, a table he'd hefted onto the back-corner edge of the dais.

Delilah seemed nonplussed. She made no comment, which was unusual for her, but I supposed she was at a loss. As no doubt, we all were.

Adam was clearly off kilter but then who wouldn't be when their boyfriend turned nemesis shows up. I can admit that at that point I felt something like sympathy for Adam, although I held no great affection for the man. He wasn't suited to Burton. He didn't understand how things worked here and without Benny to protect him I wondered how he'd manage. Still, I caught his eye with a beckoning gesture and he joined me in the nook.

'Can I get you a drink?' I said because he looked like he needed one.

He was an exceptionally attractive man, sculpted like a Greek god, cupid lips, elegant nose, eyes all black and innocent, jaw a little weak. He wore his thick wavy locks in a side parting, feathered about the forehead. It was a contemporary yet timeless coiffure, one that set off his features, and I decided he paid too much attention to his image.

I saw him naked once. He was standing in his living room, framed by the window, as I happened to pass by. His body was enough to turn a man to his own gender. He was illumed from behind by an interior light, posing like a sculpture, and proportioned perfectly. He had a swimmer's body, thighs like seals, thick about the shoulders, softly arcing pectorals. His manhood an adequate feast. I could scarcely believe Juan would throw that away.

Adam modelled for a life-drawing class and straight away I couldn't help picturing Cynthia scurrying in when she couldn't paint a stick, the lascivious hag.

Adam didn't seem to have heard my offer of a drink so I asked again.

This time he graced me with a weak smile and said, 'Thank you,' and I went to the bar.

Hannah had already put my low carb beer on the counter. 'And a glass of dry white,' I said, watching her turn. She wouldn't even look at me.

That's all the gratitude I got for comforting her yesterday when I found her blubbing out on Delilah's back veranda. It had taken some time before she could tell me through all her sniffling that Nathan was cheating on her. She wouldn't say with whom.

She had been hard to look at. Eyes puffy and red, black makeup streaking down her cheeks, lips flaccid and quivering, tears, snot and spittle wet on her cheeks and her chin. I gave her all the sympathy I had as the thought came to me that she was a hypocrite to gush tragedy when she'd happily straddle anything in trousers.

There she was, shuddering and needy, with me sitting beside her, a comforting arm round her shoulder. Then, in some astonishing flip, she came on all simpering and wanton, throwing her head back and holding my gaze through half-open eyes as she fondled her nipples through her top. Heat surged through my loins at the sight of her doing that, and despite my knowledge of the self-loathing I'd felt after the other times she'd tempted me, I devoured her, right there on Delilah's veranda, in a scramble of un-zipping and tugging.

Thrusting my member into her loose and sloppy gash, an image of Adam, statuesque, unexpectedly flashed into my mind before I realised Hannah was staring at me open mouthed. Keen to finish, I looked down at those lacquered pink fingernails circling those hard nipples through her top.

It didn't take me long and the animal in me was done. Filled with that all too familiar self-contempt, I pulled out of her and zipped away the culprit.

I'm not proud of what took place. Yet again, an unbidden lust had overridden the revulsion I usually felt at the sight of her. That I was a victim of her de-sire for revenge only served to further cheapen the incident.

I took the drinks back to the nook. Adam was fixed in his seat like an exhibit. He left untouched to warm on the table the wine I bought him, which I thought no way to show gratitude. I told him to relax but he didn't respond. 'You're getting yourself too worked up,' I said, and extended a friendly hand and placed it lightly and briefly on his arm.

He turned to me then, as if awoken from a trance.

'I should have gone home.'

'What? And miss all this?'

I was trying to make him feel better. I could see it wasn't working. Aside from his discomfiture at Juan's presence, he was making too much of Benny's death. Frankly, he displayed a tendency towards the melodramatic and my sympathies waned. I understood they were close, Benny and Adam, and that he'd received a shock when Delilah related the news, but it doesn't do for a man in the third decade of his life to wear his emotions like they were adornments. He was too sensitive. No one would survive in Burton being that sensitive. No one in Burton welcomed arbitrary emotional displays. I only had to look at Nathan to confirm the veracity of that.

At last Adam reached for his wine, which I could only hope would benefit his manner.

Juan plugged into his sound desk the last of his leads and, after a steely glance in our direction, took himself outside. He had no legitimate reason to go outside, at least, none that I could think of. But if this was the same man as the Juan of old, then I knew what he was up to. I didn't understand how he could let addiction get the better of him like that. To stand out in the brunt of a raging storm to fill your body with poison. Had Burton always attracted degenerate types? Although, unlike Nathan, Juan had made something of himself, and was not without talent. But he had a side to his nature that only the brave-hearted would confront. Life for Juan was war and he seemed the sort to go into battle over every ordinary chore.

When he was still with Adam up at the church, on any afternoon that was clear and warm, out he would come with all manner of gardening tools, from pruning shears, spades, shovels, forks, hoes and rakes to his leaf blower, whipper snipper and his wheelbarrows—not one but three—along with the lawn mower and his chainsaw. He would line them all up beside the house ready for the attack. And he would set to with bullish determination, storming through foliage, shouting expletives, while Adam watched on from the safety of the back deck. It might have been comical were it not obvious to me, the discreet onlooker, that his was an unnatural fury born of some intoxicant.

How had Adam coped with all that throbbing gristle charged up in a frenzy? I pondered this question when The Cabin's door opened wide. I could see from Delilah's manner that it wasn't Juan. Her eyes shot me a wry look before she arranged her face in a welcoming smile, failing to tell whomever it was to close the door fast and tight behind them, which I found surprising knowing how much she resented using the column heater. The door remained open for a goodly while as Rebekah and David Fisher lumbered in with their arms full, and The Cabin got another dose of cold damp air, which was no bad thing considering the smell in there. I'd told Delilah when I arrived that she had a possum in her chimney, but she hadn't wanted to talk about it.

Rebekah and David Fisher were as repugnant a pair of God-fearing gluttons the world has ever seen, both in their forties and not a wrinkle to share between them, skin stretched drum tight atop their blubber. Rebekah had a round and sallow face with a button nose and squint eyes that darted about like small fish behind black-framed glasses. The whole ghastly visage ensconced in greasy lanky hair. And to make the visage even worse, she sported a hairy upper lip.

I think a fine down of moustache has to be the most unbecoming feature on any woman's face, the mark of one whose hormones listed to the male side, evidence of some deep perversion in the makeup.

All the daintiness of Rebekah's being was reserved for her feet. Small and so podgy she tottered when she walked. No point going to the general store if you're in a hurry. If not her, then you'd suffer David lumbering and wheezing behind the counter. Every movement of both appeared laboured and ineffectual. It was painful to watch.

David carried his weight as if it were a curse. Had it never occurred to him to simply stop eating? He, too, had a round face, his of florid complexion. He wore his hair—all sandy curls—short and tidy about the ears and hairline, accentuating his low forehead. Thick-rimmed glasses sat high on the bridge of his nose. His cheeks merged with his neck fat, enveloping his chin. I watched as he went to put his guitar on the floor where Adam's sat. Rebekah put down their music stands and waited beside him.

'Philip, Adam, good evening,' she said without warmth. 'How are we going tonight?'

'Good,' I said, speaking for the both of us.

'Praise be.'

I leaned back in my seat, making as if to survey the room. David's patience gave out, and without so much as an 'excuse me', he shunted Adam's guitar case out of his way and put his in its stead. Adam just sat there clasping the stem of his glass. Rebekah brought a hand to her mouth and gave out a sharp cough. Then David looked at me meaningfully. I took a slow draught of my beer and put the bottle down in front of me, teasing them both, forcing one of them to speak.

'Come on then,' David said, as if to say, leave so we can sit down. They had a hard job squeezing into the nook but Delilah wouldn't let them sit anywhere else for the sake of her furniture, antique oak she claimed, not to mention the space the pair took up in the room.

Not waiting for us to move, David hefted along the bench seat adjoining the bar, his favoured location in full view of the stage.

'We'll be leaving you to it then,' I said, grabbing my beer, happy to get out before I was hemmed in on both sides.

Adam collected his guitar and took it to the back of the room, depositing it against the wall by mine. He didn't seem to know where to sit so I hailed him to the table in front of the stage. He hesitated before sitting down, looking back at the table behind: Cynthia's table. No doubt it would have seemed the lesser of two evils to find himself all the closer to Juan, taking what small comfort Delilah's proximity might afford.

No sooner had we settled in our seats than Juan walked back in, smiling maniacally at nothing. He caught Delilah's eye and made for the stage, but she stopped him mid-stride with a censorious palm. So he swivelled on his heels and came to us instead. This time, his smile he directed at Adam. He took up the remaining chair and bent his head for a discreet sniff, as if to accentuate what he'd been up to outside.

'I could murder a scotch,' he said, loud enough to be audible in the kitchen.

'Hannah! Get Juan a whisky,' said Delilah. 'On the rocks.'

'Yeah, yeah.'

The storm exhaled in a forceful gush and The Cabin shuddered. Plainly untroubled by it, Juan leaned back in his seat, thrusting out his chest.

'So, Adam,' he said. 'How've we been sweetheart?'

Don't answer that, I thought. There was more oil in the man than a deep pan fryer.

Adam inhaled to speak so I butted in with, 'All the better for not seeing you, I'd say.'

'It can speak for itself,' he said in slow staccato. 'Or is mousy not playing with the cat today?'

Neither of us responded. There was a touch of colour in the poor man's cheeks, which was no bad thing considering he'd looked ghost pale earlier.

Hannah came with Juan's drink and he slugged it in one, slamming down the glass with a fake laugh and saying, 'I was only kidding.' Then he nudged Adam with his elbow, so hard Adam flinched. 'Still can't take a joke eh?'

I can't recall ever meeting a human more obnoxious. There was no grace in his manner. Beneath his pencil moustache, his smile smeared across his face, lips parted, revealing that straight line of oversized white teeth: I could scarcely look at him.

I couldn't look at Adam either. It occurred to me that he was tainted, that Juan had been all over him, that there had to be something corrupt inside his nubile form for him to have fallen for such a miscreant. A fall to a very low depth. Lust probably. It's always lust. A twisted lust. And there they sat, the perfect couple, the cheese and the chalk, aggressive and submissive, and all that time up to god knows what in the old church. Rebekah's church, for she was the most devout of all of us former Kinsfolk of Burton, or had been before Pastor Makepeace was hounded out of town and the building sold.

Nothing had been done to the church building for decades and maybe that was why the elders had offloaded it so fast. No building inspector would have passed it. A new roof, new stumps, re-wiring, and that was just for starters. The place needed every conceivable repair. I would happily have done the plumbing but Juan thought he could do that himself. Any fool can plumb, he'd said, all around town. Another thing that doesn't bear thinking about.

Juan stood up abruptly and went back outside. Adam slumped forward in his seat for a few moments, before picking himself up again. Juan's presence was affecting him badly. He reminded me of someone I couldn't recall, of a small child in dire need of his mother's succour, a babe in the woods too vulnerable for his own good, a limpet in search of a passing ship. Something you'd rather not have latched on to you, something stuck fast that you would prise off at the earliest opportunity. And then I felt sorry for Juan, for succumbing to the charms of a leech.

The wind blasted the front wall but no one took much notice, except Adam, who had yet to get used to the way storms roiled in this valley. Delilah lit more incense and went about lighting the candles on the tables. I looked around the room. The Cabin looked cosy but the atmosphere was strained. Rebekah and David were crammed in the nook like two bushels. Nathan was slurping his umpteenth cider and Hannah's attention was fixed on her fingernails. With Delilah preoccupied there was no one to talk to but Adam and he was proving unimaginably tedious company.

We exchanged brief remarks on the storm and speculated as to whether anyone else would turn up. Then I offered a sympathetic non-sequitur on how difficult it must have been for him with Juan.

And in the next moment Adam drew close, lowering his voice so I had to lean in as well, and I could smell the wine on his breath. And to my astonishment he began to spill. His divulgences confirmed Delilah's suppositions and despite not wanting pictures of blindfolds and chains, and clamps and whips in my head, I was attentive and intrigued. Stuck fast in my mind an image of him bent like a dog with his tail in the air, an image that had replaced the vision of masculine loveliness I'd seen through his living-room window.

As he spoke, a torpid look came into his eyes. It seemed to me part terror, part lust. He dramatized his sordid accounts with pregnant pauses, as if wanting to impress. Some way in, I found his entire rendition little short of theatrical and I sensed he was exaggerating. I tried interjecting with general comments, such as 'each to his own', or 'I'd seen something of the sort in a magazine', but he insisted on keeping himself the topic of conversation, if one might call it that. Save it for the priest, I kept thinking, keen to block out his words the more base they became. Had the man no pride? He didn't know me. Now he was telling me he felt he could trust me and expressed how relieved he was to have finally broken through the reserve. 'I'm not normally like this,' he said, something I found hard to believe. Then, as if he were explaining away all that he had just revealed of himself, he said, 'It's just the shock of Benny's passing, and then Juan.'

'Two shocks in the space of half an hour is rather a lot to take,' I said with false concern.

'Three shocks.'

'Three?'

He was about to say more when a blast of cold air caused him to stiffen, and his gaze turned to the door.

I looked over as Alf Plum walked in, paunch first, the rest of him following on behind. Alf had lived in Burton all his life, in the same house in fact, the house he was born in. A few decades back he'd turned the front room into a guitar repair shop. How he made a living out of that here in Burton I couldn't imagine. Delilah told me once he had another business on the sly but she wouldn't tell me what. Then his health had faltered and he'd retired.

Paunch aside, Alf Plum, was a neat and compact man, always smartly turned out in a three-piece suit. His tight curls of salt and pepper hair framed a lack-lustre face, eyes bloodshot and tinged yellow, fleshy lips held in a downward arc, the curve of his face rendered a gibbous moon by a chin curtain. He was a Bluesman, harp and slide, evidenced in the four twists in his crescent-moon beard, twists that hung down to the collar of his shirt. He looked more unwell than usual, as though he'd stoically dragged himself out on this Christmas Eve, a diehard who would never miss a chance to play his songs. He was harmless enough, if somewhat puzzling, for he kept his own counsel and revealed so little of himself even I couldn't fully work him out. Still, I was grateful that someone in the room was halfway to being decent company. In his presence, Delilah never descended to calumny, which was as strong an endorsement of his character I could find.

He went to the old oak barrel in the far corner of the room, propping his guitar case against the wall near mine and well away from the column heater. Then he made for the bar.

I was thinking that would be the complement on this wild Christmas Eve; Rebekah and David had just fifty metres to traverse from the general store, and Alf not much further. Nathan might as well be nailed to the bar. And then there was Adam who had crossed the river on foot, an act of the prima donna or the hysteric I couldn't decide. That, along with Hannah and of course Delilah, more or less completed the local contingent of musicians. And as for Juan, he'd drive through a bush fire for a packet of potato chips.

The wind blasted against the windows. When it abated, I heard a faint rustle of something shifting in the chimney then the pitapat of soot falling into the grate. 'You got a possum in there again?' David said.

Delilah tightened her lips. She looked askance as if daring anyone to mention the smell.

The room fell quiet. Before long the door opened and we were all waiting for Juan to reappear when to my amazement, battling their way in with their instruments were Joshua Thorne and Ed Smedley. Juan, close on their heels, slammed the door behind him.

Rebekah caught Joshua's eye as he passed the nook. 'How are we tonight, Joshua?' she said warmly.

'Good.'

'Praise be.'

'Amen.'

Joshua said it to be polite. Ed Smedley, the heathen, was ignored.

Joshua and Ed lived on neighbouring blocks in the rugged mountainous hinterland where only the criminal, the insane, or the criminally insane chose to dwell. Joshua had been out there the longest. He was a burly hairy giant of a man with a smoky grey beard that covered most of his face and upper chest. He'd built a mud brick house when there was still some old growth about, and money to be made from timber. He hailed from dry river country on the other side of the city, but no one knew exactly where. Delilah was convinced he was one of the Thorne boys who'd had their way with a backpacker and left her for dead on a remote strip of highway. It was only luck that someone pulled up to relieve themselves and stumbled on the body before the dingoes found it. I was not convinced, there being nothing to suggest Joshua was capable of defiling women. Delilah was adept at putting all the pieces together and solving the wrong puzzle. Although it had to be said that in his case, not all her suspicions were without foundation. As soon as the mud brick house was built, he installed his wife and his spot mill and neither have left the property since. Joshua supplied Burton with firewood and venison, mowed lawns and did the odd job. He made a tidy sum out of Cynthia, who wouldn't climb more than two rungs of a ladder and was forever needing repairs to her dilapidated old shack. And his venison trade did well in the winter when Delilah put on a special menu for the locals and the occasional hunting party.

I couldn't take to Joshua. He might have been a believer but he was, to put it bluntly, a murderer. He murdered trees and he murdered deer. That's not an honourable way to live. Too much destruction hardens a man. Besides, there was something cowardly in the human killer armed with a chainsaw or a gun. Using machines to do his work, work he'd shy from if he had to do it with his bare hands. It's logical to say that bare-handed killing is a pure and honest act. There's no intermediary device. To my mind, the moment machines were invented, killing machines, something in the human spirit was lost. A moral descent took place from that point and now we are a corrupted species. Taking in the room on that wild

Christmas Eve only confirmed my theory. I felt a familiar contempt moil in my abdomen. Immediately, I pulled myself up hard. It didn't do to entertain macabre thoughts, especially someone like me who would find it hard to kill even a fly.

Joshua must have had his demons but he wasn't a criminal or insane. Rumour had it his wife, on the other hand, was deranged. Delilah said that once she'd pulled a shotgun on an unsuspecting stranger who'd gone out there for the census. Women, too, are far from incorruptible.

Everyone knew that Ed Smedley was a criminal with a crop. Lived in a shack on a rocky bit of bush, his only company a pack of under-fed dogs. Slipped a disk many years back and had been on the disability ever since. A small, wizened man, Ed Smedley had a thin, rugged face, bad teeth and long wispy white hair tied back in a ponytail. I had everything against stoner wastrels, addling their brains with chemicals that do nothing but stupefy. Once, I went out to his place to fix a crack in his rain water tank's inlet pipe and for the duration of the repair I had Ed on one side of me, reeking of dope and messing with his violin, and on the other side, his mangy dogs baying and slavering and scratching their flea ridden backs. It was the fastest repair on a burst pipe I'd ever executed.

We all had our preferred spot in the room and Joshua and Ed took up their positions at the back. They liked to stand, leaning against the wall by the column heater, the barrel in the corner serving as their personal drinks table. Joshua's guitar and Ed's violin case adding to the growing collection of instruments nearby.

Alf eased himself into the spare chair next to

Adam. One of us would have to move soon, for when the music started Delilah would want her seat at the table and Juan was already on stage adjusting the microphone stand to his height.

It was a pity Eva was missing the night. She'd have found cheer in the festive mood, marvelled at that gold tinsel Delilah had draped beneath the mantelpiece. Eva loved tinsel. And I'm sure she'd have enjoyed herself, or at least have been kept entertained. That had been the nub of her problem all along; she would scarcely leave the house. I doubted she'd ventured past the bridge since her return. It was hard to understand why she'd come back if she didn't care to engage with the community. No one should remain a stranger to the place where they were born and raised. People would talk. Delilah had already begun her contemplations on the matter and every time I entered the general store, Rebekah looked at me inquiringly as if to say, where is she?

I had begun to wonder if something unpleasant had happened to her while she was away in the city, something she wouldn't talk about, even to me. She'd been all smiles at breakfast since her return, and when I arrived home from work she would greet me at the door and quiz me about my day and ask if chops were fine for dinner. All of which was uncharacteristic of her. She behaved like a newly wedded wife. She even ironed my shirts.

I did worry about her. For days, she'd been behaving towards me in an ingratiating, syrupy manner. It was a front, almost a game she played to hide her fear. For as long as I can remember she'd had that raw fear, an oil slick of fear that spread right through her, coating in its sticky black her finer sensibilities. Fear that rendered her immobile, a prisoner in my house. Rendering me a slave to her obsequious ways. And what was that terror in her? Whence had it come? It was guilt's creation—of course it was—the sort of guilt that brought hell into the soul. She was furtive with it too. Terrified I'd discover her secret. So she coated me in her sugar.

We'd always been close, Eva and me, and I couldn't help reading much into her behaviour. She was a beautiful woman and for the most part it was pleasant to see her smile at breakfast and when I came home from work. Her eyes would sparkle, always watchful, sensitive, taking everything in. Light blue eyes, like our mother's. She had our father's chin, small and receding. She was a pixie, petite and youthful, thick fair hair kept short, her movements fast and furtive, always leaping from her seat or darting into a room. I found her endearing, if a little tiresome.

I was sure the evening would have turned out differently had she been in a position to attend. Although I suppose she wouldn't have enjoyed the sessions any more than Adam. Her aversion to Juan was beyond irrational and seemingly without foundation. Although in the light of Adam's recent revelations of Juan's predilections I found her revulsion entirely appropriate, if misplaced, since she was female and Juan attracted only to men.

The fact remained that if she had been present she would have been good company for Adam and I'd have been relieved from the burden of mollycoddling. They could have comforted each other, dwelt in their shared abhorrence and Adam's confession would have fallen on more receptive ears.

Or she could have brought her knitting and sidled

up to Rebekah in the nook. They would have had a merry old time, clicketty clicking. Then again, I don't think I could have tolerated that.

Eva had purchased the wool via mail order from a woollen mill out west, without consulting me as to colour, pattern or size. Wanted it to be a surprise she'd said when I came home early one day and caught her mid row. She went all sheepish and was momentarily disappointed, quickly clapping her hands together and announcing she would make a pot of tea.

Once she'd left the room I examined the knitting and the pattern. It was to be a polo neck—I hate polo necks—a tight fitting affair covered in little knitted balls. Worse, she'd chosen an emerald green that clashed with my eyes.

A sudden burst of rain hammered the roof. No one spoke above the din. Juan stood behind a microphone with his big-bodied guitar, two foldback monitors at his feet, the top of his head level with his speakers propped high on their stands and almost brushing the ceiling. Hannah had turned on the single stage light that was shining on his face, flattening his features, and without shadow his charm shone through, and as he smiled he appeared harmless. He scanned the room before playing an open G that reverberated around the room. 'Ladies and gentlemen,' he said, 'It's a privilege to be here tonight. Thank you all for coming.'

Delilah moved forward to claim her seat and since neither Alf nor I shifted in ours, Adam was left to make way, retreating to the back table. At last I was released from the burden of him and could focus, unhindered, on the entertainment.

Juan went on. 'We've all had a terrible shock with

the passing of Benny Muir. I know to many of you Benny was a dear friend.' He paused. 'And to some, a mentor.' He directed his gaze at Adam. I glanced behind me and saw the look of unease I anticipated. 'Gone from Burton. Benny's generous spirit,' Juan said in a shift into parody, hand on heart and eyes raised, 'But I don't doubt that the river, the mountains, the valley will vibrate to his tunes forevermore.'

Delilah cleared her throat, and Juan adjusted back to his standard stage banter. 'I'd like to dedicate this song to Benny's memory. It's called Carla.'

He delivered the song with verve, and his playing was undeniably good, if edgy. But he was too loud and his guitar playing too convoluted. He took over the room, leaving no space for anyone else. The only good thing about him was we couldn't hear the storm.

I did my best to stop listening after the chorus, upon hearing, '*hit me like tragedy, the road forever bare...*' Instead I watched his mouth round out his vowels. His left hand moved deftly along the fretboard, his right finger picked, and he was just like any other musician doing his job. Then I watched his eyes, still fixed on Adam, so venomous they were, and I saw that he was still charged up. As the song rose to its climax so did his aggression. It was then that I began to feel grave concern for Adam's welfare.

Still, some get what they deserve and it had become clear that Adam took playing the victim too far, arousing in me a deep mistrust. His confession had revealed a sickness of soul. To debase himself in such a manner, taking role play to that extreme. Knowing this, how could I believe in the sincerity of his distress? Wasn't histrionics just part of the game? At best attention seeking, at worst some elaborately orchestrated ploy to win back Juan's affections. Or his debased lust.

I didn't have a chance to think further. Juan was into the first verse of his second song, a frenzied number and I couldn't make out the lyrics, when the door opened and in scurried Cynthia, drenched and shaking herself free of her coat.

Cynthia was a scrawny old spinster, slightly stooped. Her face incongruously large, with eyes set wide apart beneath invisible brows, and thin lips that stretched from ear to ear, revealing small and crooked teeth. No doubt The Cabin was a superior location for her to ride out the storm, leaving her cats to cower in that hovel that Joshua was forever patching up.

Cynthia was a Morgan, and the Morgans had always been Burton's non-believers. They were impure to their core and there were times we all had believed they were doomed. For only true believers would be swept up into the next life when the divine moment came, and the Kinsfolk of Burton were as devoted a flock of believers as could be found, adhering tenaciously to the words of Delilah's father, Pastor Makepeace. The Morgans were ignored, shunned, passed over, non-recipients of all the support the Kinsfolk had to offer. When the awful revelation of our pastor's impropriety came, our flock scattered and Burton was thrown open a crack, although one not wide enough to accommodate Cynthia.

My enemy's enemy is my friend is the stupidest notion I've ever heard and Cynthia remained a human I would never stoop to pity.

She mouthed something to Delilah, lips moving in over-pronunciation, then shook her head, raising her gaze to the ceiling and giving forth an inaudible laugh as if to say, 'Thank heavens I made it.' So assuming was her entrance, that not even Juan's musical attack on our senses could compete with her, for all attention was focused on her movement to her seat at the back table, joining the beleaguered Adam, who everyone knew couldn't abide the mad old bat.

CHAPTER FOUR

EVA'S DIARY – WEDNESDAY 17TH DECEMBER

I felt the motion of Mother's old rocking chair. Back and forth it swayed beneath my shifting weight. I sipped my tea. The morning air was warm and damp and infused with the musty mushroom smell of decomposing leaf litter. I kept thinking how strange it was to be back in Burton living in my dear brother's house, and not at all what I'd expected. It was a weatherboard house built in the late 1800s in Colonial style, with double hung windows, the bullnose veranda along the façade a perfect setting for Mother's old rocking chair.

Inside, a central hallway leads to high ceilinged rooms of Baltic pine lining boards and mountain ash floors. Large, airy, and high on its stumps on Burton's northern rise, the house has a superior feel. Situated next to the church, it claims status.

I felt sure I'd had many happy times growing up here. I must have done. All children have happy days, even the most beleaguered. So it puzzled me why I didn't recall those times.

There are black spots in my memory where there should be sunshine and cordial. Hoping to trigger some sweet recollection, I stand in doorways staring into rooms, or sit on the front veranda like I did yesterday, catching brief patches of morning sun. I remember nothing.

Pushing back on my heels I enjoyed the lulling motion of the rocking chair. Although I admit it could have done with its cushion. Relaxed after my breath holding, I wasn't too bothered that the chair was a bit hard, as I was feeling especially euphoric.

Seven minutes and eleven seconds.

Using the euphoria to strengthen my resolve, I stood up and went inside the house to ready myself for a walk. I headed down the hallway to the kitchen to deposit my cup, my pace slowing as I passed the door to my bedroom. Ahead, on my right, was my parents' bedroom door. Philip's between. Just two walls of separation. I willed myself on, the muscles in my legs tensing, my feet leaden. I'd developed an aversion, not apparent for the first hours and days of my return; an aversion that seemed to worsen with each passage down the hallway. I knew if I narrowed my vision and kept going I would soon reach the kitchen and the sick feeling in my stomach would fade. I told myself, as I did every time I passed by, that Philip keeps that door locked, and the curtains drawn so I can't peer in from outside. I have no idea where he keeps the key, not that I'm keen to enter. Even passing the door I feel a chill, as if their cold spirits emanate through the keyhole.

In the kitchen, I rinsed my cup and set it down on the draining board. Everything in the room spoke of Mother. The kitchenette with its green Formica bench. The matching table. The cupboards painted off-white. The linoleum with its impressionist effect, all rectangular splodges in varying shades of green, overlaid with red and yellow brushstrokes.

I stood by the window. The sun shone and shone, the mists in the valley slowly dissipating as I watched. Since my return the climate has been humid and misty, and I haven't wished to venture into Burton, allowing the weather to excuse my avoidance, for I find I am disinclined to leave the house, there being enough inside to adjust to. That morning, with the weather so fine, I felt compelled by an inner force rising up in me to venture forth. I about faced and marched down the hallway to my bedroom, keeping my gaze to the floor.

I quickly changed into a long-sleeved cotton dress and left the house before I changed my mind.

I stood on the veranda by the rocking chair. I was to re-enter the world of Burton, a world I had spurned in favour of the city, a world of secrets, few wondrous, most ghastly, a cossetted, oppressive, rule-bound world, for that is surely the only way to view growing up in Burton.

Just then I heard a rustle in the undergrowth down the side of the house and a loud mournful call that sounded very much like the cry of a distressed woman. I kept still, my breathing light and shallow. The call came again. This time it sounded less mournful and more like a scream. Thrice the call came, the long, slow, mournful call followed by a sharp scream. A lyrebird. I knew it was a lyrebird, but hearing that scream all the joy bottomed out of my being.

I thought I might have heard those sounds before. I tried to recall when I had first heard the lyrebird make that particular cry, but I couldn't. All I knew for certain, standing on the veranda poised to walk through the front garden and down the lane, was that the dream would return that night.

One step off the veranda, and in an effort to keep steady I had to force myself to appreciate the effort Philip had put in to stylizing the garden, moving soil from here to there, levelling flat areas of slope, gouging into clay and sandstone, and terracing with large rocks, the result a zigzag path to the front gate that passed by garden beds filled with tree ferns and clumping grasses and the occasional flowering shrub.

When the house belonged to our parents, this patch of ground followed the contours of the hillside, high at the northwest corner of the house and fanning down towards the lane. Back then the yard was un-fenced and contained a few straggly oleander and rhododendron bushes. Bracken unfurled fronds in a buttercup lawn.

Philip's undertakings do impress me greatly. I would never have found it in me to create such ele-gance out of that hard earth. There's just three years between us and we've always been close, but we're very different in our approach to life. I often think his determination to stay in Burton, where he clearly doesn't fit in, and make good the old family home is nothing short of dogged. Although I doubt he'll ever finish it. He'll spend the rest of his days fixing other people's plumbing, and attend to this old house in his spare time. Judging by the work that's gone into the bathroom and the front garden, he'll make a grand job of it too. But he won't finish it.

I was still feeling courageous, so I headed down the lane to the bridge. The air was hot and muggy and with each step of my descent I wished a little more that I'd had the presence of mind to slip on a sleeveless dress. I quickened my pace, thinking to cool my body heat with the waters of the river, cornering the bottom of the lane by the gnarly old sycamore tree which afforded some respite of shade. Then I approached the bridge.

A narrow shaft of light shimmied on the river as I went by. The water lapped and gurgled at its banks.

The bridge was low and narrow with a footpath on the western side flanking a single lane. Leaning on its railings in the shade cast by a towering ash situated on the riverbank nearby, I was soothed by the river, and I felt a curious peace and the heat began to leave my flesh. In that moment I had no distinct memory of ever having stood there before, but I knew I had, a thousand times. It was here that Philip and I would play Pooh sticks. Philip and I and sometimes Aiden as well. I do remember doing that, but I had no mental image of it.

It seemed I'd forgotten Pooh sticks along with everything else in my childhood, and as the water flowed under the bridge I didn't try to remember.

I started to feel hot again. I wanted to go all the way across the bridge and walk to the general store, but my feet wanted to about turn. I could see Alf's house on the corner and the waney line of roof that was Cynthia's. Perhaps that's why I wanted to go home there and then. Cynthia. The bad old witch.

Why do so many children's tales of yore contain a bad old witch? To scare the children into obedience or to satisfy the need to keep a woman in her place: submissive, subservient, undemanding. It was Mother who read me those tales, Mother who was herself submissive and subservient and undemanding, who always bowed her head in Father's presence, who upheld the rituals of family life as if her very existence depended on it.

Growing up in the deep valley of Burton, *Hansel and Gretel* was the most terrifying of all, for the woods were all around us and there was no escaping the fact that the town had its share of crones. That's how it appeared to me growing up here.

And suddenly I did remember that story. Every page of it. We would say our night time prayers, and before she took me off to bed Mother, a willowy darkhaired woman, would smile her wan, closed-mouth smile as she put down her knitting, and she would sit me on her knee and read to me from a large bound volume with colour plates. And she would scare the life out of me with thick descriptions of the cruel deeds of the witches. Then she'd tell me to look out for Cynthia Morgan, who appeared to me old and wizened even then, and through my child eyes wicked and sure to curse me with a terrible spell or chop me up and eat me.

Looking back, Cynthia would have been about forty. Her parents had died long before I was born, and after their death she'd cared for her much younger sister, Joy. I never discovered the full story of the tragedy that befell their parents. Rumour had it there were suspicious circumstances leading up to the deaths, and I once heard Delilah insinuate that Cynthia herself had driven that knife through her parents' hearts while they lay asleep in their bed, but there was no evidence to support Delilah's claim and nothing was proven, no motive found and no one was ever charged.

Cynthia, they say, was never the same.

For years after, she would stand at the crossroads opposite Alf's guitar shop and stare at the bridge, always in the same crocheted shawl and headscarf. Suspicion had it she was contemplating suicide, but I think she was making a statement, as if one day the real killer would pass her by down Burton Road East and she'd point and say, that's him.

It was a sad and lonely vigil.

Yet when I was five, I didn't see it that way. When I was five she was the most terrifying of all the old hags of Burton, and there she'd be, waiting at the crossroads, whenever Philip and I went down to the bridge.

And I suddenly remembered more than I wanted to, more than it was possible to hold in the cradle of my mind. For that's where Philip embellished our mother's grim tales with curses of his own. He would get me to stand in the exact centre of the bridge and then he'd say, 'If you cross to the other side, Cynthia will get you.' And of course, there she'd be, standing motionless and facing in our direction. She never waved or turned away. There was nothing in her manner to suggest what Philip had said was false, that if I were to walk no harm would befall me. So I stayed put. And the one thing I do recall about Pooh sticks was that I was careful always to stay on the near side of the bridge.

I didn't really believe him but I didn't not believe him either and it was that very apprehension that had me in its grasp yesterday as I stood on the bridge in my long-sleeved dress, and I could do nothing but leave the shade of the big old ash tree and retreat like the child I once was.

Defeated and deflated, when I turned the key to

Philip's front door something of the prisoner in me subsumed all my earlier courage.

It's a challenge remaining poised and I'd pushed things too far. A walk to the front gate may have been sufficient for the day. There is always the next day, and the next, to venture forth into the heart of Burton.

I went to bed last night with too much on my mind. There were the Pooh sticks, the bedtime stories, and Cynthia. Any one of those remembrances might have been enough to cause a restless night.

I awoke in my parents' bedroom. It was night. I was standing over their high old bed. Mother and father were lying on their backs with their hands by their sides. They looked peaceful, at rest. I found I was holding the only lamp in the room. I drew closer. Mother, with her long black hair arranged neatly about her face, the creamy patina, the slant of her mouth, the soft dark down on her upper lip. Father, with his pock marked skin, the dark bags beneath the eyes, the large nose and the eyebrows that all but joined in the middle. I felt nothing except a strange curiosity, as if they were artefacts or specimens in a museum. Then I noticed that no part of them moved. There was no rising and falling of the bed sheets upon their breath. The larger part of me wanted to pull away by I was compelled by a pure filial love to lean over the bed and reach to stroke my mother's face. She'd never looked so pretty. As I touched her cold cheek with the back of my hand she opened her eyes, holding my gaze with a look of immense satisfaction.

I jolted awake and scrambled for the bedside lamp. I was trembling. I drew the covers up to my chin. Then an extraordinary sadness washed through me. I lay awake in a turmoil of fear and grief. I noticed my mouth was dry and I had no water in my room. But I couldn't countenance the walk down the hallway to the kitchen. I sucked the saliva from my cheeks and swallowed. I reached beneath my pillow for my diary. It was a long time before I went back to sleep.

CHAPTER FIVE

ADAM

Fate may come in large or small doses and tonight Adam felt he'd already had quadruple his share. Forced by the circumstances of this tempestuous night to remain in his seat, beholding Juan in Benny's stead; he saw his dear friend eclipsed, not by an affable moon but a maverick planet from a galaxy of hate. Would that he could fix him to the stage with his gaze but he knew that soon enough Juan would relinquish the microphone to the next act and make his way to the only remaining seat in the room. The torture of this inopportune night set thence to intensify, once he found himself betwixt his rejected lover turned foe and that hideous creature, Cynthia, who'd just entered the room.

If only Delilah had remained standing. Then again, he was relieved to have a modicum of distance from Philip after confiding in him his sordid past. What in the heavens had compelled him? More likely some childish desire to tell someone, anyone, in Burton how bad things had been. He hadn't reigned himself in soon enough for he could see Philip looked uncomfortable even as he spoke, and he knew then he'd made a mistake. He was his own worst enemy. Fancy attempting to foster an ally through the portrayal of those base acts! As though he'd been keen for Philip, of all people, to take his side now that Benny was gone and he had no one. He had little to do but rue the perversity of the impulse that had caused him to open the trapdoor of his inner oubliette and give his secrets to this misplaced choice of confidant, knowing that his capacity for self-censure, lazily ambling behind, had come in much too late to save him from himself.

At least now that he had moved to a different table, Juan seemed less ill-disposed, as though the jealousy that had taken hold seeing them seated together in the nook, and reinforced when they'd both moved to the front table, had eased, and Adam thought it might be prudent to avoid Philip for the rest of the evening, something he made a mental note of and repeated to himself several times.

Before Cynthia had appeared and he was seated alone at the rear table, he'd felt somewhat comforted by the presence of Joshua and Ed behind him, two good strong men sure to act if Juan became untoward. Even Nathan, inebriated as he was, provided comfort, the sort derived from the company of another human.

Cynthia was anything but. He knew that it was mean-spirited to think such a thing but irrationality always got the better of him when it came to Cynthia, and as far as he could tell, the fact that she inhabited human form was the only evidence the world had to authenticate her humanity. On the inside she was undoubtedly some sort of witch.

A witch with a propensity for intruding on his

life; her latest, he thought with a certain embarrassment, little short of violation.

Adam was under no illusion concerning his physique, although he would never have considered himself vain. Nudity came naturally and he found he enjoyed holding a pose. There was something deeply satisfying in remaining statue still to the limits of endurance. That much Juan had taught him.

One morning, on a stroll down the lane, Adam had encountered Philip's sister Eva leaning on the Stone house gate, and after a brief exchange she'd asked if he'd heard about the new life-drawing class in the village hall, suggesting with much spontaneous enthusiasm that he might model for it. He assented with little hesitation, marvelling over the changes occurring in the village and how a few new arrivals could make such a difference. They both agreed that Delilah's decision to lease three small cottages, that had been uninhabited ever since he'd lived in Burton, had given the area a lift. Especially since the tenants were from out of town.

Five sessions in and he'd been deriving much satisfaction from the experience. The attendees were all women of about his age: gregarious when together yet when apart they were serious and dedicated artists. He'd begun to feel he was coming to terms with Burton and even envisaged deepening his shallow roots. Until one cloudy Saturday afternoon when Cynthia walked in with a hessian bag clutched to her chest and a wicked glint in her eye.

She took up the only vacant seat in the hall, directly in front of him, and not three yards away. It was a hot day but a quick chill brushed his skin. He was standing on an old wooden table in full view of all and could do nothing but ignore her as she scrabbled through her bag and extracted a sketchpad and a pencil case.

With only a wooden chair and a walking stick for props, he adopted the pose of an old man bent over his stick, one arm held fast behind his back; a pose he'd seen in a portrait hanging in a city gallery; one of the galleries he'd frequented in his lunch hour when he'd worked for Chattergulls' head office; his first job after he graduated from high school and long before he'd met Juan. As he posed he focused intently on the walls of Baltic pine, painted a light cream; the raked ceiling of identical cladding; the windows set high, their moulded architraves a rich green. He cast his eyes down to the bare boards of the floor, rough and stained in places, then to the high stage at the back accessed on one side by a flight of wooden steps, five treads in all. The heavy black curtains, the plastic chairs stacked against the stage rear, along with several wooden tables. For his second pose he became a younger man, foot on the chair, elbow on bent knee, head jutting forward, fingers of one hand pressed to the chin. He took in the double doors leading out to the foyer. Another set in one of the sidewalls, which had a fire exit sign above the jamb. He focused on every chip and scuff and blemish so as not to be tempted to glance at the artists huddled together in a tight knot in the centre of the hall, in case he accidentally caught the eye of Cynthia.

Despite his best efforts his nakedness stuck fast in his mind, the shaft of his manhood nestling in curls of brown hair, normally his pride, so horribly exposed.

In The Cabin, with her presence soon to be right beside him, he couldn't bring himself to imagine the images she had sketched, no doubt adorning the walls of her house.

A vintage dresser, for Christmas Eve she was regaled in a voluminous, ankle length chiffon skirt of vermillion hue, and a tight black lace-trimmed cardigan beneath an ivory, tasselled shawl. Copious beaded necklaces jangled about her chest. Her hair was long and thin and wavy and grey, the sort of hair an observer secretly wished would find its way into the hands of a competent hairdresser. Hair that accentuated a broad, finely wrinkled face with lips that were thin and had a cantankerous turn about the corners, and eyes, set widely apart, more fitting on the visage of a turtle—wary, slow and sly. As she approached, carpet bag dangling in her grasp, she raised her other hand in a vague gesture of a wave at Joshua and Ed, then caught Hannah's gaze with a nod. She sat down in the chair beside him, and smoothed her damp skirt about her legs. Adam drew himself in. An odour of sweet violets mingled with stale sweat added to the stench of the room and it was all he could do not to heave.

'I'm pleased to find you here,' she said, leaning sideways and turning to speak in his ear, dousing him in her halitosis.

'How so?' he said, pulling away.

'After Benny's passing I thought we'd never see you.' She stared at him, grinning wickedly.

His stomach tightened, the insinuation itself a defilement.

He dismissed upon its arrival the thought that it may have been her at the incinerator, for she was too small and light of frame. Besides, he was certain the person in question had been a man. The image of the stranger still at large exacerbated the distress he felt at having to endure the familiar ghouls in the room, all through his own wrong choice of direction on the bridge.

Fixing his gaze on the back of Philip's head, he gathered his wits. He detected the wind's howl in the brief moments of nothing in Juan's third song, 'Where the rainbows go...' It was a song he'd heard a hundred times or more and he still had no idea what the lyrics meant. He took in snatches, ...*the wells of time*... and ...*life's a grind*... and thought it probable the song was about him.

In the guitar solo, when he knew Juan would be watching his fingers on the fretboard, Adam snatched a quick look at the stage. There was little room for Juan to move. He was wedged between his speakers, holding his guitar side on. Adam puzzled over why he'd brought along his full personal address, replete with thirty-two channel mixing desk, when the single amp he used for his solo act would have sufficed. Adam could only assume he'd come straight from a Reece Effect concert.

Keen to avoid eye contact, as Juan's solo came to an end, Adam shifted his gaze. On the tables candles, glowing in small glass jars, cast soft shadows on faces tilted at the stage. Adam allowed himself the briefest moment of wellbeing, although he knew it wasn't anything of the sort. More like relief pressing through torment. He took in the forms of the others in the room, their various shapes. David, partially silhouetted by the kitchen light, consumed the width of the nook. Rebekah, facing into the room, all prim in her retro navy and fawn striped dress, was knitting. An extraordinary feat considering the lack of light, but she used large needles and chunky wool and it looked like a scarf in the making so he assumed she could knit without looking, as his grandmother used to do. Directly in front of him, Alf, Delilah and Philip formed a human shield behind which, if he sunk down in his seat and shifted to his left in alignment with Delilah's bun, he was hidden from Juan's view.

Every note brought the inevitable closer.

When Juan's song came to an end, Delilah led the applause, raising her clapping hands high and enthusing with her usual, 'Bravo! Bravo!'

Adam glimpsed in his side vision Cynthia's face. Her gaze seemed fixed on the candle flickering in its glass, and she was uncommonly quiet. When Hannah arrived with her drink—it was the brandy and lemonade she always imbibed—she didn't stir to offer thanks for the service, which Adam found ill mannered.

'Thank you very much. It's great to be back,' Juan said from behind the microphone as he pulled the jack from his guitar and draped the lead in the stand's clutch point. 'Next up, ladies and gentlemen, is Nathan Sandhurst.' He took the microphone from its clip and held it in an outstretched arm. The screech was intense.

Delilah cupped her ears.

'For heaven's sake,' she said and the whole room started complaining.

'All right, all right. Can't stand a little feedback, eh,' Juan said, drawing the microphone close to his chest. There was a long pause. Then he snapped, 'Nathan!' so sharply everyone jumped.

Delilah and Philip both turned their gazes to the bar. Rather than catch Philip's eye, Adam did the same, realising as he did that he'd been betrayed by Philip, who had demonstrated, through his unwillingness to move seats when Delilah had made to sit down, that he cared nothing for Adam's welfare, and if things turned nasty would no doubt afford him no protection. In the stark light of his earlier confession, and the fracas that inevitably lay ahead, the contents of Adam's mind pitched forwards and he felt momentarily light-headed.

Nathan slid from his stool and straightened before setting off for the stage, one foot in front of the other in carefully measured steps. Outside, the temperature must have fallen dramatically, for the room had suddenly turned cold, a circumstance exacerbated by Joshua and Ed, who were blocking the warmth of the column heater. The only thing keeping Nathan warm in his short-sleeved shirt and thin pants must have been the cider in his belly.

Cynthia remained transfixed, affording Adam a reprieve from her usual cackling repartee, and he thought he might order another wine. But before Nathan had mounted the stage Cynthia's body suddenly jerked, and she emitted a low moan. Adam eyed her cautiously as she again jerked and moaned. The spasms were sporadic and he couldn't bring himself to ask if she was all right. No one else was taking any notice. All attention was fixed on the stage as Nathan edged his way into the confined space between the speakers, and made to take the microphone from Juan's grasp. Juan pulled his hand away with a grimace and returned the microphone to its clip. Nathan staggered in response and held out a hand for balance. He used the speaker to steady himself, and had almost regained his equilibrium when

Juan yanked his other arm. Nathan stumbled forward, his shins colliding with a foldback monitor. The room held its breath. Nathan looked disoriented. There was a collective sigh when he at last managed to gain a stable footing behind the microphone. Juan curled his lip and sidled round, gesturing for him to proceed.

Nathan grasped the stand with both hands. 'Thank you. Thank you,' he said, stifling a belch. 'Unfortunately, the great Lee Reece couldn't be here tonight so Alf, would you do the honours?'

Alf rose slowly to his feet and went to retrieve his guitar. Juan took the opportunity to go to the bar, walking across the room and round the back of Adam's seat. When he reached Cynthia, he leaned down and told her in a voice loud enough for the whole room that she was on next. She didn't seem to take it in.

Adam returned his focus to the stage, watching Nathan trying not to sway, but he could sense Juan, wherever he was in the room. Adam knew, too, that when Juan finally sat down he would choose the spare chair at his table, for he had no cause to join Philip and Delilah and he wasn't the bar propping type.

The telephone burst into life. Delilah flashed a look at the bar. Adam did the same. Juan had his back to the room, hands against the counter, fingers tapping impatiently. On the third trill Hannah picked up the receiver. She listened attentively, eyes widening, a slow smile appearing on her face. When she hung up she said, addressing Joshua and Ed, 'You two won't be going home tonight. A tree's down on Burton Road East.'

'What about your wife?' Delilah said to Joshua. 'You haven't left her alone out there?'

'She'll be fine,' Joshua quickly. 'And I'll make it back. Never leave home without my chain saw.'

'Whisky on the rocks, Hannah,' Juan said, slapping a hand down on the counter. 'When you're free.'

She stared at him, blank faced, before reaching for the whisky bottle.

'For Benny,' Nathan said through the microphone and the room looked to the stage.

Alf was penned in behind Nathan, the neck of his guitar angled at the sliver of space between Nathan's hip and the speaker. He strummed an open G and Nathan, one hand on the microphone stand, the other raised with open palm beside his face, closed his eyes.

'*Where were you when I needed you last night,*' he sang in nasal falsetto. Then he pulled back and waved his hands. 'Stop. Stop.' Alf stopped playing. 'I can't hear myself in the foldback.'

'You want me to turn you up,' Juan yelled from the bar.

'That would be nice, actually.'

Juan barrelled his way to the mixing desk.

'Any better?' he said, nudging a slider.

'One. Two. One. Two. Maybe a bit more.'

'And now?'

'One. One. Two. Two. Yeah, perfect.' And Nathan began the song again, a Blues ballad of his own making, although strongly reminiscent of a song Adam had heard before but couldn't place. The melody was so familiar he strained to recall the song, until he felt something brush against his back.

Juan drew up close the vacant chair and sat down, sliding an arm along Adam's backrest. Adam cringed inwardly. Juan leaned forward and looked about to speak to him, when Cynthia let out a piercing cry and swept her hands to her cheeks, the tassels of her shawl sending her brandy and lemonade careening to the floor.

Nathan stopped mid-flow and gestured to Alf.

'Adam!' Cynthia wailed, as if she'd been waiting to claim the spotlight. She reached for his hand, which he duly withheld. Grasping at the air she said, 'Something terrible. Oh, oh, I can't bear it.' She kept grasping so he held out his hand and she clutched it hard between cold trembling palms.

No one spoke. The wind abated, leaving in its wake an uneasy quiet.

'Adam's in mortal danger,' she said, her voice now low. She scanned the room as if to reinforce the truth of her words.

As if on cue the candle on their table sputtered in its jar, and there was a rustle in the chimney and a puff of soot fell into the grate.

'You see!' she shrieked.

Alarmed, Adam snatched back his hand.

'Oh, shut up Cynthia,' Delilah said. She turned, gripping the back of her chair as though poised to stand and slap a face if she felt the situation required it of her. She went on, addressing Adam. 'Take no notice of her. She's having one of her turns.' She called to Hannah. 'Get her another drink.' And with a determined set to her mouth she turned back in her seat.

As Delilah reached for her glass, Philip looked round, his expression bland. His eyes darted from Cynthia to Adam to Juan and back to Cynthia, before he paused with a slight smile before shifting round to face the stage.

Something clenched in the depths of Adam's belly. Why hadn't he seen before what was now transparent? —That Philip was a cold-hearted man. Although he admitted to himself that the others in the room appeared as dismissive: Joshua and Ed were shaking their heads, their faces spread with wry smiles; Rebekah had returned to her knitting, a look of mild annoyance in her face; David hadn't moved a jot; and Hannah was resting her elbows on the bar, face cupped in hands, eyes agog with incredulity. Under Adam's gaze she straightened and went to pour Cynthia another brandy and lemonade.

Adam didn't know what to make of Cynthia's outburst. His thoughts raced. The wind was again gathering pace, framing that brief moment of stillness, an interlude like a backstage curtain parting to reveal a matter of great significance, a crack opening into a secret universe. The falling soot on cue in agreement, the sputtering candle, even the glass falling upon the brush of a tassel, it was as though the elementals themselves were in concord, reinforcing the drama of the moment, and its import. When the elementals had been summoned to lend their weight to a premonition, surely then it would be foolish not to take heed?

Did Cynthia possess such power or were those occurrences—the wind, the soot, the glass, the candle —pure happenstance? If so, then surely that too imbued the prediction with potency, for the chances of all those happening at the same time had to be remote. Or perhaps it was simply that he had paid attention, his senses acute, and most of the time such moments, continuously taking place in the stream of life, would pass him by without notice.

Or was it that Cynthia had contrived the situation? It was hard to conceive how. All that remained was her assertion that he, Adam Banks, was in danger of losing his life. He fought against his rising alarm, reassuring himself that she was a charlatan, a mean-spirited woman who took pleasure in the distress of others, never missing an opportunity to practise her histrionics. All that jerking and groaning; as if she were a medium possessed by a demon, not a clairvoyant experiencing a portent. And of course, she was neither. The whole of Burton thought her episodes a contrivance, for she had them often enough and had never once been proven accurate. Delilah, in fact all the others in the room, viewed her apparent altered states as shenanigans designed to play on the fears of her chosen victim. When she had walked in the room and seen Juan on stage, she would have observed Adam's demeanour, seated alone as he was, and she would have seen a chance to make trouble. For she had a conveniently keen eye, and she seemed to recognise immediately the weaknesses of others. How opportune she must have found that vacant seat! And, he noted, she wasted no time launching herself into a trance.

For Juan, her display was a plentiful source of ironic quips and snide teasing. 'Tell me Adam,' he said, once the room had settled down to its own unique semblance of normality, 'How does it feel to have your welfare cared about so much? Making you squirm, is she?'

Adam didn't think the comments worth an answer. Juan's arm was still straddling the back of his chair, and when Adam reached forward for his drink, he received a slap on the shoulder.

'Like being on death row, I suppose.'

'Stop it,' Adam said under his breath, aware of Cynthia, still quivering quietly to his left.

'You never could take a joke.'

'It isn't funny.'

That was typical of Juan. There was only one way Adam knew to counter Juan's teasing and that diversion arose as Nathan resumed his set, having taken the microphone from its clip and moved aside to allow Alf prominence for his solo. Straight away there was a sharp high-pitched whine.

Juan shot forward in his seat and shouted at Nathan, 'You're in front of the speaker you goon. Move!'

Nathan moved to the centre of the dais. Juan leaned back in his seat and again slid his arm along Adam's backrest in a gesture far removed from the protectiveness it might have implied.

Adam sucked in his being, the strain of remaining where he was, feigning an easy poise, exhausting. He had to steel against bolting, the storm outside in all likelihood better than the one brewing in The Cabin. But he couldn't leave, not yet, not in full view of the room. So he held his focus.

On the stage, Nathan replaced the microphone in its stand and picked up more or less where he'd left off, about halfway through the second verse. Alf followed in a solid twelve-bar groove.

After a brief applause at the song's end, led by Delilah, Nathan commenced his next number, much the same as the last. When he was about five lines in, Juan leaned to Adam and said in his ear, 'He's easily the worst songwriter I've ever heard.'

Adam found himself laughing softly to himself,

for he couldn't help but agree, and the relief he felt that Juan had returned to near if acerbic normal was little short of beatifying.

Juan went on. 'If he crammed less words into his lyrics he might be able to deal with the phrasing.

I didn't intentionally break the banister

That caused you to tumble down those seventy-seven steps

Like a half full canister...'

What a contrivance of a rhyme. Banister and canister. Who the hell tumbles like a canister?'

His face creasing with laughter, Adam pressed his lips together and stared at the table in front of him, hoping Delilah and Philip obscured him from Nathan's view.

'Great to see you happy my friend,' Juan said, and again slapped him on the back. Which might have ruined the moment, were it not that having found a pocket of conviviality on this dreadful Christmas Eve, Adam was determined to hold onto it.

When Nathan came to the end of the song, he took a step back and bowed long and low to what little applause there was. Not even Delilah's 'Bravo!' roused the others. Nathan cast an eye about the room and, stifling another belch he said, 'Thank you so much. You're the best audience I've sung for today.'

'He's taken that phrase from Benny,' Adam said under his breath.

'Probably hasn't sung all week.'

'I last sang that song on my national tour,' Nathan said, puffing out his chest, though Adam doubted he'd overheard Juan's remark.

There was a brief pause.

'National tour? He's never been on a national tour,' Juan said in a raised voice.

'He has,' Delilah said over her shoulder. 'He's just returned.'

'Oh yeah? And what'd he do? Rock up at all the open mics?'

Nathan held his head high. That time, he must have overheard. He wasn't a large man, and standing there in his shirt and light pants he belonged at a school recital, not a public house. Adam thought he was too young to be an open stage regular, yet too old to be dressed like a designer schoolboy. Worse, he seemed to want to hog the microphone and Juan was in no hurry to stop him. 'It was an honour and a privilege to perform alongside this country's greats,' he said, stumbling over his words. 'Billy Franks, Peter Curry and of course the one and only Lee Reece, who sends his apologies for not being here on this special night. Instead, please put your hands together for our own Alf Plum.'

This time the applause had vigour, Delilah's so emphatic her flesh trembled beneath the sleeves of her dress.

'This next song is a classic. Gravy Train by the great Peter Curry.'

Nathan mouthed the letter 'C' at Alf, who looked bemused and repositioned his fingers.

'Seriously? He's changed the key?' Juan said.

'He'll have his reason.'

'If he can't handle the original key, then he should pick a different song.'

'Probably suits his voice better.'

'Shutting up suits his voice better,' Juan said, loud enough for the whole room to hear.

'Will you be quiet. We're trying to listen,' Delilah hissed with a sideways tilt of her head.

Adam, too, had tired of Juan's denigrations and he began to feel some sympathy for Nathan. He knew the subtext well, the ridicule serving to preen Juan's own feathers: the successful, performing, professional musician that he was. Adam hadn't even managed to catch himself from falling in step, an accomplice in the shredding of others. He felt duly chastened.

They endured the Blues number, then another. Each of Nathan's songs had convoluted lyrics and awkward rhymes. The set's redemption Alf's assured guitar playing, for he was an adept, his parents having moved from the swamps of a far-off land to reside in Burton, rumour had it escaping the bonds of servitude. Benny said Alf's musical talent was so innate he must have been born playing slide. Adam was drawn into Alf's steady complex rhythms and momentarily lost awareness of his surroundings.

A few sharp thuds on the roof jolted him back, thuds that soon became a thunderous roar and Alf's guitar was lost to the din. Despite hollering his melody down the microphone, Nathan's voice disappeared as well.

Alf stopped playing and Nathan, visibly rattled, marched sulkily from the stage to the back of the room to resume his seat at the bar. The hail bulleted down on the roof and Delilah and Juan both stood at once. Delilah went and peered into the night through the window beside the fireplace. Juan made for the stage, first going round the table and accosting Cynthia with an abrupt, 'Come on. You're on.'

She made no response.

The hail soon eased and as Alf passed by Juan's

vacant chair with his guitar, Adam touched his arm and said, 'Great playing, Alf.'

'Thanks.'

'Is that a new guitar?' He knew the dangers of the question. Alf was prone to long guitar monologues, but he thought it safe since Cynthia was about to take the stage.

A quick look around and he realised Juan had slipped outside and Cynthia hadn't moved. Adam was forced to listen to Alf's long-winded explanation of how he had acquired his new instrument from a friend who'd moved out of Burton long before, and then turned up unexpectedly one day in his shop. He went on to describe the instrument's sonic virtues, pointing out the finer details of its construction, the head and tuning keys, the sound hole and pickguard, the saddle, the neck, the fretboard, even the strap pins. Adam tried to listen but lost interest too quickly and hunted in his mind for a polite way to cut in. Eventually he said, 'I think I'll recharge my glass Alf, if you don't mind.'

'Right you are.' And with that Alf took his guitar and himself away.

Hannah poured Adam his wine as he approached. She looked bored and already keen for the night to end. It couldn't be easy for her in Burton, any more than it was for Nathan. Shunting herself between the general store and The Cabin, under the thumb of a disapproving mother and an exacting employer.

He paid and was about to take his wine to his table when Nathan said, addressing Hannah under his breath, 'How *could* you?'

'Same as you,' was her curt reply.

Adam had no idea what was going on between them and was grateful when Delilah said to the room, 'Shaping up to be quite a night.'

'Want me to check on the roof?'

'Leave it till the morning, Joshua.'

'Christmas Day?' said Ed.

'Oh, yes of course,' Delilah said vaguely, and she turned her attention back to the weather beyond the window.

Another rush of cold air and Juan bounded onto the stage.

'Cynthia!' he bellowed through the microphone. He must have turned up the volume, for everyone in the room gave a little start.

Rebekah had set down her knitting and was looking expectantly at Cynthia. Delilah had her arms folded across her chest and was watching with raised eyebrows. In fact, the whole room was looking on. Philip had shifted in his seat and even David had made an effort to turn around.

Cynthia wore a look of astonishment, shaking her head this way and that, on the search for some sort of confirmation. 'I had no idea,' she said, directing her words at no one in particular. She raised her hands and went on, speaking with that annoying cackle that ran behind her words. 'I'm not ready. I need notice, a lot more notice than that.' And she waved a dismissive hand at Juan. 'After what I've just been through too. Has that man no awareness. Benny would never...' and her voice trailed off.

'I'll fetch your dulcimer,' Joshua offered.

'Where's the music stand?'

'On the stage.'

'I need my music.' She rummaged through her carpetbag and extracted a sheaf of sheet music.

'He should have told her,' Philip said, catching Adam's eye.

'He did tell her,' Adam said, thinking he couldn't have been the only person who had heard other than Cynthia, who'd chosen not to hear, because it suited her to create another palaver.

On her way to the stage, her long chiffon skirt snagged on a corner of the nook, and when she plonked down her sheaf of music on the table in front of Rebekah and fussed to free her skirt, she managed to sweep the sheaf off the table. She then spent a good few minutes collecting her music. All the while Juan stood wearing a look of stony impatience.

The storm raged outside, the fetid odour emanating from the chimney seemed to worsen by the minute and Adam knew that once Cynthia had taken the stage the night would deteriorate beyond imagining.

CHAPTER SIX

EVA'S DIARY – THURSDAY 18TH DECEMBER

Beastly is a curious word, childish and old-fashioned, the sort of word you would find in an illustrated children's book. Beastly. The word has been corrupted. For the original meaning, like a beast, would surely have packed descriptive punch. Instead, 'Oh, you beast!' sounds diminutive, feminine, weak. I hold to its original power: literally having the attributes of a beast. What sort of beast? A lion? A Bear? I can't decide. Both seem apt when I think of Juan. Then again, considering his height, he's more giraffe-like, but that isn't what I mean either. He's a mythical beast, an evil beast, a hellhound.

Two years have passed since I last locked eyes with him and I would have preferred never to have thought of him again, but Philip mentioned him at breakfast for no reason that I can recall, except that we had been discussing local characters and I suppose he stands out, though I would never have considered him a local. Now it's late in the afternoon and I must set about preparing for Philip's return. There's a chicken to roast—Philip loves roast chicken—and I haven't even prepared the stuffing. I've been too distracted. Knit, knit, knit. That's all I've achieved today. No meditation. No bath. Nothing. I can't erase Juan from my mind.

Juan comes from a town on the coast and when he moved with Adam into the old church four years ago, Burton shuddered. Delilah insisted it was a minor tremor the result of an earthquake in the south, but it felt to me as if Dracula himself had landed. Not that Juan has a vampiric air. He's too unctuous, too crass, for the comparison to hold. Besides, he wears a crucifix in his ear and Dracula would never have coped with that. Yet Juan proved for Burton the wisdom of maintaining a collective apprehension of outsiders.

For a hundred years Burton's inhabitants were cosseted by the mountains, and by the Elders of the Kinsfolk. A church-abiding community, hardworking and obedient; sharing in an unshakeable belief in the wisdom of the faith, until six years ago, when Pastor Makepeace was caught with his pants down.

A meeting was held, and Burton told in terms plain and harsh, that they were all culpable one way or another. The pastor's daughter, Delilah, was especially held to account. She was taken to the church and made to stand before the Kinsfolk, or so I heard. She was told the death of a child was a common punishment for the sins of the father, and she would do well to expect this to happen to any one of her own children, should she have any. It was, after all, God's own will.

Poor Delilah. Her father had brought such shame to the town that the district Kinsfolk Elders came to the conclusion that it was best to purge the whole valley of the sickness by selling the building. That way no new Pastor could fall foul of what was clearly a well of evil. A well so potent as to corrupt the heart of as pure a man as Makepeace. He died not long after, leaving Delilah, the only beneficiary after the loss of her mother some time before, with a tidy sum.

After that, most of Burton's flock shunned the Kinsfolk, just as the Kinsfolk Elders had shunned them, with the exception of Rebekah, who switched to the Assemblies of God who had a church in the next town. Bereft of a faith, many Burton residents felt exposed, so they closed ranks and remained unduly fearful of outsiders, certain that the devil himself would one day walk down Burton Road West, and pause at the bridge to pull off his boots. When Juan arrived, it was a dread confirmed.

In truth, such fear is generally unfounded. Having lived beyond the confines of the mountains for ten years and four months I would reliably say the world at large does not produce many Juans.

I concluded long ago that his is a psyche at variance with the norm.

I'm surprised venues book him for performances but then he can be charming and the ladies are drawn by his charismatic larger-than-life stage persona. He was always too big for Burton. At The Cabin the force of his delivery pinned listeners to the back wall like so many flies.

I'd been a regular of a sort, attending whenever I came back to visit Philip after Benny Muir fortuitously moved into town, falling from the sky like a bright star into our laps. Benny had been keen to start up the sessions in homage to those he'd hosted back home in Scotland, and after persuading Delilah to at least let him host his sessions for one night, he'd gone to Alf's guitar shop and put it about and all the musicians of Burton turned up wanting to play. It was an instant success. I enjoyed the music and the cosy atmosphere and it was a chance to mingle with Burtonites who had never been part of the Kinsfolk. Until Juan started attending and then I stopped, for even back then I couldn't endure his presence.

I've learned from Mother that it pays to be cautious, to exercise restraint, to consider with care before making a decision, and to reflect on your actions. And this is what I believe. How else is the human race to grow? I confess I am one of Burton's lapsed believers, but I am spiritual, and now that I've found Buddhism, I seek betterment for all and know in my heart that each and every one of us must learn goodness and forgiveness and grace. So lacking in these qualities is Juan, he's a veritable husk of a man, the nut extracted long ago and left to wither and rot.

Written on the page, my judgement seems unduly harsh. I must qualify such negative passion, for it compromises the values of my own heart. Otherwise, what sort of mealy-mouthed guttersnipe am I?

Philip's old bathroom window didn't face the verdant splendour, which was then the privilege of the back bedroom: Aiden's room. Oh Aiden! Sometimes it pains me to recall that little life. I have only a vague recollection of how my younger brother's room used to be. Philip cleared out the contents eight years ago, long before he converted it into the new bathroom.

In the old bathroom, the window looked north at the side fence and at a tangle of ivy that was choking the life out of a large elm in the grounds of the church. The grounds were large and wooded and on their upper reaches sat the church itself.

One sunny afternoon on a previous visit, while

Philip was at work, I crammed my body into his small white bath positioned beneath the window. To lay back flat I needed to bend my knees, calves pressed against thighs. I was as relaxed as I could manage, with my knees parted and rested against the lip of the bath. It was an indecorous pose but one entirely necessary considering the confines I was forced to endure.

It was not one of my better sessions. I had just managed to focus and immerse my mind in my underwater world, and I was marvelling at the antics of a shoal of clownfish, when, not two minutes in, a black mass cast a distant shadow that wouldn't be dismissed. The mass approached, slowly at first, then gathered pace and there was nothing I could do to push it back, so I reached for the stopwatch and emerged from the water.

Three minutes, twelve seconds.

Imagine my chagrin when I found that what had intruded on my peace stood right there outside the bathroom window! A black mass indeed, secateurs in hand, for ostensibly he'd been pruning. Only his gaze was directed straight at me and it was filled with lust, or so it had seemed, and he didn't make to move when I stared back. He stayed there, leering at me with his grin all toothy beneath his pencil moustache.

What a lecherous grin he had!

There was no curtain on the bathroom window. Under that lubricious gaze, I had no choice but to scramble from the bath and grab my sarong. I left the room without a backwards glance.

I have no idea how long it took for him to go away. I did know that I would never again practise my craft in that bath. I could have asked Philip to hang some curtains or a blind but he would have dismissed the request as a waste of time since he was about to renovate.

And of course, I could not divulge the reason for my request. It does not do to cultivate animosity between neighbours and, sensitive as he is, I'm not sure Philip would have coped with the knowledge that his sister had been violated, in a fashion, by the gay Latino next door.

Knowing my brother as I do, that was sure to have led to a confrontation. A confrontation sure to have led to the revelation that I had lain submerged in the bath for quite some minutes. For Juan would most likely have used this fact to explain away the situation, rendering himself the hero of the piece, poised to rescue the tragic woman from her attempt at suicide. A defensive move on Juan's part, yet a slick way to re-apportion blame and deflect Philip's ire, for his ire can be incendiary.

If Philip thought for one moment I had been trying to drown myself! It would be an unbearable burden and I couldn't put him through it. And I wasn't about to explain my breath-holding habit either, for he wouldn't have understood and might have cast me aside as insane.

I was left with no choice. I would have to return to the post office.

I didn't relish going back to Jacob and Ruth Cartwright. They were former Burton residents excommunicated over daring to speak with their excommunicated son Carl, who had fouled the Kinsfolk's name by associating with Sam Briggs who had been excommunicated by Pastor Makepeace for failing to show remorse after being overheard making penis jokes in Bible study.

Excommunicated or not, the Kinsfolk was a sort of prison in itself, a prison comprising a web of contacts, lapsed and shunned, and however far you travelled the prison boundary extended that much further. And so it was that back when I was planning to make my own escape by moving to the city Delilah, who had managed to cultivate a surreptitious means of staying in touch with all and sundry who hailed from Burton, had put me onto the Cartwrights.

After Juan's transgression, the danger of heathens seemed suddenly too close and I was keen to return to the city and the coast. I cut short my holiday without offering Philip any explanation and returned to the city the following day.

I really shouldn't allow one ghastly memory to spoil my whole day but like the chicken sitting on the kitchen bench waiting for a turn in the oven, I find I am frozen. I try to reason away my distracted state of mind by reminding myself that Juan has left Burton for good but it's of little use. Yet I must do something with that bird or Philip will arrive home all suspicious and I don't like it when he's suspicious. I might leave the chicken untouched, return it to the freezer and prepare a fricassee with some leftovers. When he arrives home I'll retire to my room feigning a headache.

Today I need to be alone. It isn't just the memory of Juan that troubles me. I've been out of sorts since I awoke. The dream has returned.

It was the same dream as before. My parents were both lying on their backs in their bed. Only this time, I was outside in the hallway and the door was locked. I rattled the handle, pushed against the door, called out their names. Desperation had me in its grasp. I called to Philip but there was no reply. Yet I sensed he was there in his room. I banged on his door. Nothing. I went back and rattled the door handle. The sound echoed down the hall. It was dark, so dark and I couldn't look down the hallway to the kitchen or up to the front door. I couldn't look but I had to look, so I did. And I saw a slick of black oil seeping in from outside, seeping in under the door, oozing its way towards me. I rattled and rattled but I knew I wouldn't get inside.

I awoke in a cold sweat. And I realised as I pulled back the covers of my own bed that I had to find the key to my parents' bedroom.

CHAPTER SEVEN

ADAM

The wind gushed up the valley, roaring through the trees. It sounded from inside The Cabin like a stampede, and Adam half expected a thousand buffalo to come charging through the walls in a charnel frenzy. He pictured the missile-laden air, glass shards and splintered timbers impaling flesh, beasts crushing and trampling, all that was left of those gathered there a mess of bone and blood. The air thick with its metallic odour. He shuddered. The image became vivid as the wind charged on, and he wanted to shrink and disappear beneath the floorboards. Then he recalled seeing a painting in a gallery in the city that had depicted something similar and he felt instantly relieved. Horror, he decided as the stampede abated, had its source in the imagination and in the capacity to dread. In the real world, carnage was simply what it was, a bloody mess for someone else to clean up. Perhaps it was his olfactory sense that had helped invoke the image, for beneath the incense the stench of rotting flesh intensified as the night wore on.

He took comfort knowing he wasn't the only one concerned about the storm. An atmosphere of uncer-

tainty grew in the room. From her station by the fireplace Delilah called to Hannah to locate the torches
that were somewhere in the kitchen—on a shelf, possibly in a drawer or under the sink—and to check their
batteries. She told her to take the packet of household
candles from the cupboard beside the back door and
put them behind the bar. 'And fetch a box of matches.' Delilah's tone was sharp and sarcastic like that of
an irate headmistress and it must have been humili-
ating for Hannah to receive orders in that manner in
front of everyone, but she appeared accustomed to it.
Compliant, she disappeared through the kitchen
door.

Taking advantage of Cynthia's lengthy sound
check, Delilah went and snatched the matches from
Hannah's hand as she returned; lighting yet more incense, as if the room were not thick with it already,
before returning to the bar.

A scented fug wafted Adam's way, and he realised
he was developing a headache. No one else in the
room seemed that bothered by the smell, something
he found bizarre, for he would have considered it the
primary topic of conversation. He couldn't be the
only one with a functioning nose. Or was he imagining it? Was it possible to imagine a smell so potently
rank? He sat, frozen in his seat. The capacity to smell
something that didn't exist would define him a crazy
man, akin to those who heard voices or saw gas. A
paranoid. Yet he would never consider himself paranoid. Besides, he was sure he spied Rebekah wrin-
kling her nose earlier. He wanted to ask her, but it
would be too obvious. He'd have to cross the room and
sit in the nook and everyone would be wanting to
know why, including Rebekah, and were he to ask

that question of her, and she told him no, she couldn't smell a thing, then everyone would hear and he'd be left knowing he was mad. But if she said yes, she would be the one questioning why on earth he would ask such a thing when it was as plain as day, and she would have no choice but to conclude that there was something wrong with him in the nose or in the head. Besides, hadn't David mentioned the smell earlier?

There was another gush of wind.

Behind him, Joshua and Ed were discussing the last time they'd chain-sawed their way past a fallen tree after a similar wild night at The Sessions, joking light-heartedly over Benny's attempts to assist, for the tree had fallen in the path of his house. When Benny broke the nail of his right thumb and downed tools to light his pipe, they'd caught him in the flashlight toying with his shortened thumbnail, the cause of much amusement in their recollecting, but their laughter was controlled.

Adam pictured the scene, the tangled limbs, the debris, Benny sucking on his Peterson, taking that chance to stand aside. And a wave of sadness washed through him. Benny would have made light of the storm. He would have recalled his childhood. 'Och, ye want a real storm? Get yersel te Scotland,' he would say. He would have bantered and joked and wrapped an affectionate arm around the women in the room in turn and Christmas Eve would not have been this dour.

Everyone, with the exception of Juan, was subdued. Rebekah and David, who rarely held animated conversations with each other or anyone else, were even more self-contained, and so far, Adam hadn't seen their usual private exchanges, Rebekah leaning to let David in on a thought that had just occurred, and the slow rise of his shoulders when he laughed. She persisted with her knitting, stabbing at each stitch the way Adam's grandmother did when she was upset, occasionally looking up to shoot Adam a pointed stare. He quickly looked away if she caught his eye. She must have been still annoyed with him after discovering some literature in his house. Harmless, but she'd found it offensive.

With Juan by his sound desk and Cynthia squashed in between the speakers fiddling with her dulcimer, Adam found himself alone at his table, although it wouldn't be for much longer, and he thought he might use the opportunity to find another place to be in the room. But he soon determined that wherever he went, Juan would join him. He felt trapped, too, by the strictures imposed by the regulars whose seating habits were not to be broken. There was only one person who might have sat elsewhere, who usually never sat at all, in fact stood at the back with Joshua and Ed, or over by the fireplace with Delilah, or took up a stool at the bar, leaving for others who might swing by the free seats at Delilah's and Cynthia's tables: Philip. And tonight, he showed no sign of relinquishing his seat.

Adam took a sip of his wine, resigned to Juan's imminent return, when Delilah, upon leaving the bar with a fresh gin and tonic, forewent her usual seat and sat down beside him. Adam was taken by surprise for he couldn't recall a time when she'd done such a thing. Was this a show of solidarity? Or was she worried he might be upset over Benny and wanted to demonstrate her sympathy? It was impossible to tell for she just sat, tall and dignified, her bun high on her head, that purple gown she always wore on Wednesdays falling at her feet. Knowing Delilah, all his suppositions were unlikely, but he found he was able to relax in her company.

At last Cynthia plucked a few strings of her dulcimer. Juan rolled back the treble and stood, hovering over his mixing desk. 'I'll start off tonight,' her voice trailed away. She shot Juan a quick look and said, 'I'm too loud.'

'You sound fine to me.'

'Not to me I don't.'

'Roll back the foldback,' David said.

Adam watched Juan mouth something like, 'Prick.'

Cynthia adjusted her shawl. The wind had dropped, exposing the stirs and murmurs about the room. Adam's gaze settled on the back of Philip's head, the neat down of fine hair cut into the neck with scrupulous care. It was then that Adam noticed Alf's chair was still empty. He ran through his mind to when he saw Alf leave The Cabin. A sweep of the room and, concerned for his welfare, he inquired of Delilah.

'He isn't well.'

That was obvious. Rarely did he look in fine mettle. Ever since they'd met, Adam couldn't recall a time Alf had looked well. 'He should have stayed home.'

'Been having digestive problems I believe,' Delilah said, warming to the topic. 'Eats too much fried chicken if you ask me.'

Which he hadn't, and he didn't want to be drawn into a conversation about Alf's health. Besides, Delilah had a way of blaming everyone for whatever condition they found themselves in, no matter if it pertained to their health, their relationships, their work or extraneous circumstances. Benny would quip behind her back that if a wayward boulder came tumbling down a mountainside and crushed some unsuspecting man to death, she'd blame him for being in its way.

The crisp tenor of Cynthia's dulcimer broke the silence. At first the music sounded charming, it always did, too soon descending into a rambling series of notes that lacked rhythm, the sense of the composition lost to incoherence. Then Cynthia inhaled and out of her widely open mouth came the high-pitched, throaty wail Adam had anticipated. Seated behind her dulcimer in her long chiffon skirt and tasselled shawl, with her thin grey hair trailing about her shoulders, she might have been a banshee, feeding on the sadness in listeners' hearts. His headache took a sudden turn for the worse.

Yet he was unexpectedly drawn into the lyrics of Cynthia's song. A song of love lost and never again found. He wondered if it were true. The way she laboured over every drawn breath, panting syllables as though overcome by emotion, aspirating her aitches and issuing long breathy ohs at the end of the chorus. He was made aware that she was once young, possibly beautiful, though he found that hard to picture, and perhaps she'd nursed a broken heart for all those years, doomed forevermore to spinsterhood.

It was a brief interlude of speculation. The song went on and by the fourth verse Adam no longer cared if she had ever been attractive. Listening was a chore. Juan, who had hovered by the mixing desk for much of it, strode past the nook and Philip's table, drink in hand, and plonked himself down in Cynthia's seat on the pretext of telling Adam he was on next. He promptly splayed his legs, his knee resting against the table. Adam took in the length of thigh, the bulge of his manhood, and he was back home in the church, enduring the weekly indignity.

The bench press draped with the white towel, the cleated leather, the clamps, he saw them all laid out for him like an altar. The hand at the back of his head that pushed him down and made him kneel. The searing pain radiating from his tension as Juan thrust his way in. The blood-smeared towel left for him to launder.

He had to resist an urge to stand up and put as much distance between him and Juan as he could in the confined space of The Cabin. He knew better than to even shift in his seat. All he could do was take comfort from Delilah's presence to his right.

Juan slugged his whisky. 'The daft cow needs to get her ears syringed,' he said without preface.

'Cynthia?'

'I told her she was on next.'

'I heard you.'

'Yeah, she heard too.'

Adam didn't respond. He found himself with nowhere to place his sympathies.

After what felt like an hour, Cynthia brought her song to a close and Delilah led the applause. Cynthia looked on at her audience in a self-satisfied fashion, waiting to the very last clap. 'Thank you,' she said and took a breath. 'As we all of us know, we've lost our dear Benny Muir in the most tragic of circumstances.' She paused and peered at the room, squinting into the stage light. 'One loss triggers the memory of another. Fifteen years ago, as many in Burton will recall, I suffered a terrible, terrible loss.' She strummed a chord and waited, for dramatic effect.

'Here we go,' Delilah said under her breath.

Adam observed the arms folded under her bosom, the hard set to the mouth.

'I dedicate this next song to the memory of my dearly departed Joy. May you rest in peace.'

'Joy?'

'She's delusional,' Delilah said.

'I don't follow.'

'She believes she has a dead sister. Listen.'

There was the long and laboured introduction full of rambling sequences and wayward melody, then came the lyrics and he was on the verge of zoning out when he noticed a change in Cynthia's manner. She'd become focused, intent on her delivery.

You went for a walk and you didn't return
Though your body was never found
I know, I know, I know
I lost you to the river
It was a path you knew so well
You knew every stone of it
I know, I know, I know
I lost you to the river
You wore your blue cameo necklace that day
The Victorian woman you were
I know, I know, I know
I lost you to the river...'

Adam's mind halted before another recollection. He hadn't even heard of Burton when Joy supposedly died. He certainly couldn't have known a thing about it. Until that moment he could have had no idea that he had in his possession something that might be related to the matter. Had Cynthia sung this song before and he'd paid no heed?

He listened closely and realised he was familiar with the section of the river in Cynthia's song. It was on the way out of town to the west, where the river widened and curved against a low cliff, the near bank flat and grassy, the water languid and deep. An idyllic spot ideal for picnics and fishing, accessed via a narrow muddy path that began at the bridge, although the path was neglected and overgrown and full of brambles. A haven for resident snakes.

Three years before, Adam had taken that path. He'd been upset after an altercation with Juan that had left him sore and bruised. Still new to Burton, when he discovered it, the path along the river seemed an obvious choice, affording the remoteness his heart was searching for.

About two hundred yards from the bridge, walking clumsily in a fog of battered flesh and dented pride, he slipped and lost his footing. To avert sliding into the river, he grabbed a clump of grass. It was as he scrambled to his feet, his pants and shirt smeared with mud, that he saw something glinting in the weeds. Just then the sky darkened and rain came slow and fat, hesitating then exploding in a watery blast that pummelled his skin. With the necklace firmly in his grasp he made for the bridge.

The bust of a Victorian woman set in a blue cameo suspended on a gold chain. The necklace matched perfectly the description in Cynthia's song.

'You left my side all dressed up

Sweet perfume on your skin
I know, I know, I know
I lost you to the river...'

No one goes out dressed up and perfumed, only to drown themselves. It didn't make sense. Unless she was meeting someone. Yet as far as Delilah was concerned, no one in the town believed Joy had even died. They were convinced she had left Burton of her own accord to reside in the city, comfortably away from Cynthia. A view no doubt promulgated by Delilah, who tolerated Cynthia as she did the rest of Burton's drinkers, cutting her no shrift when it came to her shortcomings.

The song petered out to a smattering of half-hearted applause bereft of Delilah's usual vigour and cheers, and Cynthia applied herself to re-tuning the dulcimer. Adam turned to Delilah and said, 'What if she's right?'

'I don't follow.'

'About Joy.'

Delilah frowned. 'She can't be right. There was an investigation at the time and the police didn't even bother putting her on the missing person's register.'

'They didn't look for a body?'

'Why would they do that? Philip saw Joy with a suitcase getting on a bus.'

It was the staunch way she'd said it. As if Philip's sighting closed the matter and there was nothing to discuss. Adam sensed he should leave well alone but the combination of the necklace, still in his possession, and Cynthia's lament demanded scrutiny. Could the necklace have belonged to someone else? Possibly but unlikely. It was evidence of a sort and his mind scrambled to piece together a picture of what might have happened.

'And no one ever thought to re-open the investigation,' he said reflectively.

'Don't be ridiculous. You know what Cynthia's like. If you were the police, who would you believe?'

'What if I told you...' he broke off when Philip turned in his seat.

'Told Delilah what?'

The expression on Philip's face stalled further inquiry, any suggestion that he may have been mistaken, curtailed. When Philip sighted Joy it may have been dark, the weather inclement, or he may have been at some distance, able only to make out her form. All those possibilities would remain unspeakable fancies in the face of that indomitable look and no one would ever know the truth.

Adam had kept the necklace hidden in a shoebox at the back of his wardrobe and after Delilah's dismissiveness and Philip's cool hostility that was where he planned to leave it. Cynthia would have to go to her own grave, whenever that day might be, in ignorance. The town had done her, and her sister, a disservice on the strength of a single eyewitness. There should have been doubt, especially since Philip would have been a teenager at the time.

There was no question in Adam's mind that Joy had died as a result of foul play. It was true that she may have dressed up to leave Burton for the city, but that could not account for the necklace on the river path, which he had decided without equivocation belonged to Joy. Cynthia may have invented the recollection of Joy wearing it that day. She may have lost it on a different occasion. Even so it was too strong a co-incidence, too compelling to dismiss and his mind wouldn't rest. Rather, his speculations galloped on.

More likely Joy had gone to the river to meet someone, perhaps a lover. And she'd taken the river path and met her fate. She couldn't have fallen in the river for how would the necklace have ended up on the bank if she had? There must have been a struggle. And now, somewhere at the bottom of the river, lay Joy. How much did Cynthia know? It occurred to him she might know the secret lover, turned killer. Then why, if she knew or even suspected, had she not revealed the information at the time? Or did she fear a similar fate? Perhaps she revelled in the insinuation buried in her song, taunting the perpetrator with veiled knowledge. If that were the case, then the killer would be known to all, a regular at The Sessions, and judging by the pointed way she had delivered the song, right there in this room. A killer also keen to discover the whereabouts of that necklace!

Necklace. Lover. Killer. It occurred to him there were too many assumptions in his thinking. His head ached all the more. He reached for his glass.

The door opened and Alf walked in, looking more haggard than ever. As he approached, Adam saw gobbets of vomit lodged in his beard. He'd been gone so long Adam had forgotten he should have been seated next to Philip, blocking his view of Cynthia's dulcimer. He took up his seat in laboured fashion, smiling apologetically at Delilah who leaned back and called to Hannah, 'You better get him another dark ale.'

'Looks like he needs it,' Juan said.

'He'll be fine,' Delilah sounded emphatic.

'Nothing a beer won't fix.'

Her single-minded remark on the curative virtues of dark ale seemed cruel in light of Alf's condition. Whatever was wrong with him—a stomach ulcer, a gastric infirmity, cancer—would not be assuaged with beer. Still, when Hannah set down his glass, he took a long steady draught, slaking an apparently powerful thirst, and when he was done he turned to Delilah with a nod and a smile.

Cynthia gave her dulcimer strings one last tweak and after riffling through her sheet music, she cleared her throat. The room hushed. A break in the clouds allowed the moon to shine its soft luminescence into the room, casting a latticed silhouette on the table and imbuing the Sessions with unexpected calm. Adam checked his watch. It was not yet a quarter to nine and the Blood Moon would not occur until ten thirty.

'I'd like to dedicate this next song to Benny.'

She peered into the room. On cue, Ed went to the stage with his violin, Philip leaning slightly aft as he passed him by.

Ed cut a spindly figure, his trousers hanging from his hips without hindrance, there being no flesh of consequence about the buttocks. His long white hair, tied at the nape of his neck, fell between his shoulder blades like a limp snake. The black of his clothes accentuated his runtish build. His gait was stiff and the step up to the stage clearly an effort.

Lit by the stage light and the cool glow of the moon, Cynthia and Ed took on the visage of a pair of aged sprites.

Ed positioned his violin on his shoulder, gripping it beneath his jaw. He waited. Cynthia played a bar. Ed was close on her heels with an improvised melody that bore little resemblance to the bones of her tune. When Cynthia sang, he continued on with slow whines, out of joint with her throaty wails. Occasionally they met in an accidental harmony. Then drifted apart in a cacophony of plucks, warbles and abrasions, the song, meant to be an ode to the wassailing of olde England, a time of Christmas cheer, all cider and hot cakes and songs sung loudly to ward off evil spirits, delivered with such ineptitude it was impossible to listen to. The dulcimer, Cynthia's voice and Ed's violin altogether a wall of grating treble and Adam vowed to ask Delilah for some headache medication the moment it was over.

Alas, it was set to be another ten-minute song. Adam drained his glass. He noticed David tilt his head back and open his mouth in a protracted yawn, his neck flesh bulging past his chin. Eventually he brought his hand to his mouth in a show of stifling it. The performers appeared oblivious. Ed had closed his eyes and Cynthia was staring vacantly into the room. Adam couldn't be sure but it appeared she was gazing right at him. He thought she might be about to have another turn, so unstable was her nature, the alarm in her eyes seeming to grow with every bar.

When the last notes were played to a flutter of applause—Delilah didn't manage a single clap—Ed promptly left the stage, leaving Juan to help Cynthia pack away her dulcimer. Adam felt himself relax as the room made for the bar, Rebekah, Joshua, Alf and Ed inundating Hannah with orders. Nathan was slumped where he'd been all night, and Delilah went and stood between the end of the counter and the nook, blocking the entrance to the kitchen.

Adam stood as well, hoping for a chance to approach Delilah for some headache pills. She seemed preoccupied. Feeling the effects of the wine he'd already consumed, he decided against another until after his set. Besides, there was no time to place an order. He was about to fetch his guitar when Philip looked around and asked him how he was bearing up. 'I saw you sandwiched between those two earlier. Lucky for you the hag went on after Nathan.'

'She isn't too bad,' Adam said cautiously.

'You're kidding,' he said in a voice so quiet Adam had to lean down to hear him. 'How can you say that, after she predicted your death?'

'She is a little crazy.'

'A little!' he said, with a quick glance in her direction. He went on, lowering his voice even further, so that Adam had to offer his ear to hear. 'That hideous song about her sister. Did you know Joy despised her? Told me she couldn't wait to leave.'

'You knew Joy?'

'Small town like Burton, everyone knows everyone.'

Which was true, but not enough to confide in a teenager. In small towns like Burton, it was more likely residents would keep their own counsel, especially regarding their attitudes to members of their own family.

'How's Eva,' he said, eager to change the subject.

'Terrific.' His face broke out in a wide grin.

'I thought she might have come tonight.'

His smile faded. 'Live music isn't her thing.'

'Not even for Christmas Eve?'

'She's better off where she is.'

'The comforts of home.'

'Something like that.' He reached for his beer.

Adam straightened. He was puzzled by Philip's remark. Eva had come to the sessions numerous times and always looked like she was enjoying the music and the company.

Juan was lifting Cynthia's dulcimer back into its case. He caught Adam's gaze and his face morphed from focused concentration to a mix of unwarranted lust and loathing. It was a look Adam had seen too many times before.

He swung round and went to retrieve his guitar. Before he reached the back of the room there was a sudden roar followed closely by a boom that shook the floor, the walls, the entire structure of The Cabin. Glasses trembled, frames slapped the wall, tinsel shimmied and more soot fell down the chimney.

'You see!' Cynthia shrieked, turning abruptly and knocking into the microphone stand, which wavered before regaining its poise. 'You daft cow,' Juan said to her back but she paid no heed. Pointing a wavering finger at Adam, she said, 'It's an omen.'

Disbelieving eyes met with disbelieving eyes around the room.

Delilah caught Joshua's attention. 'It'll be a tree down.'

'I'll check the damage.'

'Hannah, fetch a torch.'

'*The* torch. I only found one that worked.'

She slid it across the bar.

'I won't be long,' he said, mainly to Adam, who hovered, waiting, guitar in hand, for Cynthia to leave the stage.

Adam was surprised to see Philip follow him outside, narrowly missing bumping into Cynthia as he made for the door. Adam told himself he was being ludicrous, and marched his suspicions back down the carefully crafted chute he used for all his defective thoughts. Philip, he told himself, was merely going to the toilet.

But he had no opportunity to restore himself to calm. The moment the door closed Juan crossed to the front of the stage and leaned down towards him. 'I know your game,' he snarled. His breath stank of whisky.

'Juan, please. There is no game.' Adam held himself fast, all his muscles tense.

'I'm a liar now.'

'You're mistaken.'

'I'm never mistaken.'

His tone left Adam in no doubt that he would not escape tonight without enduring the brunt of that wrath. He was a powder keg, his fuse shortened by the powder he snorted. Adam could already feel the blows. That he had no right to be possessive couldn't get through the fury sparking in Juan's mind. He never did have the right, but in the complexities of togetherness Adam had let that jealousy ride. He'd let a lot of things ride. It was easier that way. Now Juan seemed propelled by some warped notion that Adam was rubbing his nose in the breakup, a notion that in his crazy universe sanctioned his infernal state.

Yet again Adam suppressed an urge to leave. Even though he knew it would be the only way to diffuse Juan. Yet it would look absurd to suddenly pick up his guitar and walk out into the blinding rain and, in full view of Joshua, scramble over the debris of that fallen tree to head off into the dark, hoping that another didn't fall on him as he battled his way home. The small voice that was pride laced with doubt that he could trust any of his instincts, along with the entity within that told him his paranoia was fogging up his senses and deceiving him at every turn, altogether prevented any movement towards the door. 'Don't make a fool of yourself.' He heard his grandmother's voice; one he'd absorbed and replicated, some part of him having deemed those cautionary words useful. He'd been making a fool of himself ever since.

He moved away and leaned his guitar against the wall between the window and the fireplace: Delilah's sentry. In his side vision he noticed Juan had gone to stand at the rear of the stage beside his mixing desk. Cynthia had taken up her chair. Behind her, Rebekah, Ed and Alf formed a huddle beside Nathan, with Delilah still as if on guard at the end of the bar. David hadn't moved all night and showed no sign of doing so. Together they looked set to ponder the location of the fallen tree.

No secondary crash was heard, no sound of anything collapsing under the load. Rebekah mentioned the car that was almost hit last week, and they all agreed the driver had no business heading out this way on such a foul night. No one had any sympathy in Burton for recklessness.

'I hope the store is all right,' she said.

'The crash was close by,' said Alf. 'Too close to have hit your store.'

With a slow turn of his head, David insisted that the sound had indeed come from that direction. 'If it's God's will.'

Rebekah pressed together her hands.

The Fishers launched into tedious speculations on all the trees between the store and The Cabin.

'How could it have fallen of its own accord like

that?' Hannah asked. A question Delilah immediately waved away with a dismissive hand.

'The wind would have loosened the roots,' Ed said. 'It was only a matter of time. Would have been that diseased tree I've been warning you about, Delilah. The one on the corner of the car park. Eaten hollow by termites.'

Nathan left his bar stool and went to the window on the other side of the fireplace. He peered out one of the trellised panes into the dark. 'Can't see a thing,' he said back to the room, stating the obvious. Clouds had closed off the light of the moon and the wind was roiling up the valley once more.

The room settled into murmured exchanges.

Before long Joshua rushed in, hair wild, eyes bright, breath heavy. Closing the door behind him, he said, 'Sorry it took so long. Batteries in the torch died on me.'

Hannah shot Delilah a facetious glare.

Joshua went on. 'She's a big tree. The one on the corner of the car park. Missed the power line by a whisker.'

Ed smirked.

Delilah ignored him. 'Any damage?'

'Fell on my utility, Delilah.' He showed surprisingly little emotion. 'Chainsaw was on the back seat. Tree crushed the roof like a soft metal can. Saw's finished.'

'Your wife.'

'She'll be fine,' he said, taking off his jacket. 'Our house is built to withstand a hurricane. It's us I'm worried about, penned in here.' He looked around with an expression that suggested he thought the solidity of The Cabin no better than his utility.

'We'll call through for help,' Delilah said, turning to Hannah.

A room of anxious faces were directed at the telephone. Hannah held the receiver to her ear and waited for some moments before putting it down in its cradle, her expression alone conveying that the line was dead.

No one spoke. Hannah tapped her fingernails on the bar in slow succession. She inhaled as if to speak when Delilah cut in with, 'Joshua needs a beer.'

'We all do,' Juan said, his voice landing on the others like an intrusion. He jumped off the front of the stage and made his way to the bar.

'Beer?' Delilah said doubtfully.

'Whisky.'

The storm kept on surging up the valley. Adam craved a drink as well but he held off, even though he had no idea how he would get through his performance without it. The delays and interruptions of the night so far had resulted in the latest guest spot slot he could recall. Benny would have had him up long before now.

The door opened again and Philip came in wearing a look of slow fright, announcing to the room that it was best everyone stayed inside. 'No one,' he said in a low voice, 'is safe out there.'

Juan guffawed and said, 'Someone will come.'

'Who?' David said.

'No one will come,' Delilah said matter-of-factly. 'They'll have enough of their own to contend with.'

Joshua raised himself to his full height. 'We're survivors. Been through a lot worse.'

'Amen.'

'Amen.'

Cynthia drew her shawl closer round her shoulders. 'It's all coming true,' she said in a whimpering voice. Despite himself, Adam felt inclined to agree.

'For heaven's sake, Cynthia,' Delilah said. 'You predicted Adam's death and his alone. Not all of us.'

Adam didn't find her comment in the slightest reassuring.

Alf took a slug of his ale and shifted round. 'There's a Blood Moon tonight, Delilah.'

'Not you as well.'

'I'm just saying.'

'This is not the Rapture. For heaven's sake!'

'God be with us,' Rebekah said and crossed herself.

'It's just a storm,' Hannah murmured without conviction.

'We'll hunker down,' Joshua said. 'Delilah, you've got food out the back.'

'Plenty.'

'Then we don't have a problem.'

'Remember the great storm of '89?' Delilah said. 'When that ash fell across Burton Road West down by the bridge? Missed Alf's by inches. The whole of Burton was without power for days. No one came. Joshua, you and Ed shifted that tree.'

By now Adam viewed the tree another harbinger, and Cynthia's prophecy took on a more realistic hue. Somewhere out there lurked the mysterious figure by the incinerator, although it occurred to him too that the figure could just as well be inside The Cabin.

'Ladies and gentlemen,' Juan said through the microphone, sending a jolt of surprise through the others. 'Welcome to the stage, Burton's own Adam Banks.'

CHAPTER EIGHT

EVA'S DIARY – 19TH DECEMBER

The dawning sun sent an orange glow through my bedroom window, brightening the curtains. I'd opened my eyes on the day in good spirits, having had a dreamless night. My gratitude for that reprieve catapulted me into a familiar anxiety. For I can't pass by my parents' bedroom without thinking of the dreams, a nagging compulsion replacing the fear I felt passing that door. Although I doubt I would have had the courage to enter that room if it were not for the dream. Lying on my side taking in the sun's warm glow I decided Mother and Father were sending me a message. In the first dream I was in the room, standing over their bed. But in the second dream I was in the hallway outside and the door was locked. It was obvious they wanted me to unlock that door. There could be no other explanation.

It must be a matter of atonement. I am consumed with feelings of guilt, some part of me convinced that I am to blame for some awful misdeed, but I have no idea what that might be.

I turned over and faced the wall, my good spirits already fading. A resident frog, attracted to the damp earth outside my bedroom window where a downpipe let loose the roof's rainwater on the garden, knocked out its arrhythmic mating call, knock, knock...knock. The sound, reminiscent of drips on a drum, penetrated my being, synching with my own pulse.

Life back in the family home has proven more challenging than I'd anticipated. I have begun to miss the Post Office, even the Cartwrights and their incessant reprimands over miss-sorts and dawdling seems preferable to my almost solitary existence, incarcerated as I am by my own trepidation. There was every danger I would ignore the purpose of my return and slip into a mothering role, my life centred exclusively around Philip and his needs.

I know he needs me. I've known all along. He couldn't know it but he also needs me to find that key.

Hearing him crossing the hallway to the bathroom, I threw off the covers, slipped on a robe and went to the kitchen to prepare his breakfast. He liked his bacon crispy, eggs flipped and toast buttered. When he entered the room, I poured his coffee, strong and black, and stood back, watching. He's a dainty eater, so particular over every forkful, his focus set on his food. Sometimes he's animated at breakfast, taking time between swallows to talk to me of his day ahead or to relate a titbit of gossip. But today he was markedly reserved. I didn't like to inquire as to what was on his mind.

Minutes passed and he drew together his knife and fork on his empty plate, and said, 'Thank you.' His tone was measured. Avoiding my gaze, he drained his cup and left the room.

I was somewhat nonplussed, but I shrugged off his mood and went about cleaning the kitchen. Keen to restore my equanimity, once he'd set off for work, I ran a bath.

Seated in the wicker chair in that palace of a bathroom, my mind consumed with the slow steady splash of water, and with the feast of greens and greys beyond the window resplendent in the silvery mist, I relaxed. When I was absolutely calm and my heart rate good and slow, I left the chair and turned off the taps and entered the bath. Three deep breaths and I inhaled all the air my lungs could hold and sank below the surface.

The fish were glorious. Some had stripes of iridescence, others bright yellow spots. They swam about in shoals, or in twos and threes. There was coral to behold, all filigree stemmed, or sporting foliage of soft yellow and pink, and sea horses with their extraordinary appendages. Ribbons of seaweed wavered in the current and the fish darted in and out as if in a game of chase.

I watched the fish weave back and forth, fascinated by their lively display, tails swishing, mouths gobbling, gills flapping, when a figure swam towards me from the deeps. As the figure came closer I saw the torso of a woman atop the tail of a fish. She was a mermaid, a mermaid of exquisite beauty, with locks of fine golden hair, captivating blues eyes and lips spread in a knowing smile.

I recognised her immediately as the mermaid in the picture book Delilah gave me on my birthday one year. I must have been very young. The book had an illustration on every page and the mermaid was in all of them. I would try to stop Mother turning the pages so I could gaze for longer at that wondrous creature, who only ever did good things and cared about everyone's well-being.

The mermaid in my underwater world hovered in front of me, beckoning, then with a swish of her tail she swam through the seaweed and was gone.

The urge to breathe overcame me and I emerged into the cool light of the bathroom.

Nine minutes and fifteen seconds.

Eight seconds shy of my personal best and amid the gasping breaths and euphoric haze I felt a twinge of disappointment.

As I dried off, the mermaid began to trouble me. She was, on reflection, nothing like the mermaid in my picture book. Maybe she was the foreteller of fortune, but good or bad? Was she granting me a wish? Offering healing? Or had she come to warn me of imminent tragedy? I wrapped my sarong around me, suddenly chilled.

By mid-morning the mists in the valley below had cleared, leaving the air bright and warm, and once more I decided to venture to the bridge. Despite the rising heat of yet another unseasonably muggy day, I waited until the sun had reached its zenith and the shafting light between the mountain peaks brooked few shadows.

I put on a sleeveless dress and left the house, the sun hot on my skin. I strolled down the lane, taking my time, glancing around at the fat trunks of the trees, the tall summer grasses, the wildflowers in bloom. It was so sunny and pleasant that I welcomed a shard of memory, which broke into my awareness unexpectedly. A memory of walking with Mother down the lane.

Every sunny day at this time of year, we would set

off together on the lookout for special flowers. They were all special, she would say, but some more than others.

Without Philip and Aiden and Father, it was a glorious time, just Mother and I, the two of us with sharp eyes and bowed heads, scanning the under-growth all around. Feigning a nature walk, we were furtive and nonchalant all at once, whispering to each other, pointing at butterflies flitting from flower to flower, or birds, twittering or squawking, flapping about in branches, gliding down to peck at the ground. All the while we would keep a wily eye out for onlookers as we picked the flowers of Mother's choosing that grew along the laneways and the edges of our neighbours' gardens. Tansy, lavender, St John's wort, borage, periwinkles and marigolds were her favourites.

I wasn't allowed to tell of our flower harvests. It was our secret. Mother said Father wouldn't under-stand. She told me her family hadn't always been members of the Kinsfolk. In fact, there was a time when the Kinsfolk didn't exist. A time when her great grandmother held other beliefs. Mother reas-sured me that she was a Kinswoman to her core but even then I could see she was less bound by the rules as she carried on her family's tradition of gathering herbs and flowers. For their medicinal properties, Mother said.

Plants could cure all sorts of ailments but there were those that were poisonous. She would point out the ones that were toxic, warning me away from the deadly nightshade, foxglove, daffodil bulbs, angel's trumpets, wolfsbane, rhododendron flowers that were everywhere in Burton, and away from every bit of the oleander bushes that were dotted about along the lane.

I spotted many deadly flowers on my solitary walk down to the bridge. It must have triggered the alarm in me, for when I reached the corner by the gnarly old sycamore tree I had to blinker my vision to avoid looking at the river.

Blinkering my vision was a reflex, hearing the flow of water alone enough to arouse in me an intense mix of wonder and fear. That time I thought I might glimpse the mermaid in the tawny depths, her curls of golden hair glistening in the sunlight, tempting me to join her, grabbing my hand and pulling me away.

There was birdsong coming from the trees all around. A pair of dragonflies danced above a small patch of grass that had been clipped short by ducks, a landing pad in the otherwise overgrown riverbank, at a point where the river widened, the waters away from the main current, calm.

And there I was, standing on the soft grass, looking at the river, drawn by lulling ripples splashing on large pebbles, the sun shining through the trees and dappling my skin.

How easily I slip into trance. Years of practice but I suspect I'm predisposed. For my imaginary under-water world is as real to me in my recollections as the mundane events of the day. I am one of those people who can recall the dreams and fantasies of childhood in minute detail, as though they were real. Yet I strain to recall what Mother used to serve for dinner.

I left the bank and approached the bridge, making for the centre, coming to a halt on the path at the fif-teenth railing post, which was exactly halfway. I was facing east. The grassy bank was hidden from my view by a tangle of fleabane and horehound. It was easy to look upstream, at the river receding into the cleft of the mountains. The surface shimmered, the depths hidden.

There was no mermaid luring me into the river. Instead, I had a strong compulsion to turn around and an equally strong desire to remain still. Then I felt a pressure on my back, of a flat palm pressing. I couldn't make sense of it. I knew the palm belonged to no one. That it was a manifestation of some part of me, a sort of psychic paralysis. I knew, too, that I had to resist.

I drew on all my strength to force myself backwards, gripping the railings and pushing, stepping back with my left foot, crossing with my right. But I couldn't make the turn. My heart galloped in my chest. Sweat broke out on my brow. What could possibly be wrong with looking west?

There I stood, in the full light of the midday sun, at war with my innermost self and losing. I, Eva Stone, who could lie underwater for nine minutes and twenty-three seconds—surely I could beat this terror and cross the bridge to stand at the fifteenth railing post on the other side? It was only seven paces.

I must have stood there for some time. My whole body rigid. I thought I might faint with the effort. Then the pressure on my back faded away. And I was suddenly light and wobbly. I turned and found I was able to cross the bridge.

The river was different to the west. Its mystery seemed arrested beneath the bridge and all that was known of the river was known after that point. The banks were still a tangle of fleabane and horehound. Trees with tall and straight trunks and others with branches that bent this way and that shadowed the river as far as could be seen.

There was a path on the left bank, so overgrown it was almost never used, but years ago, I would see Alf with a fishing rod and a small tackle box, making his way along it, flattening the undergrowth as he went. He would head for the swathe of grass that served as a secluded spot for picnics and secret lover's trysts. Everyone in Burton favoured that spot, one way or another. It was rumoured that Hannah had been conceived there and my old school friend Sophie said that Delilah was once seen sneaking back to the bridge with her blouse unbuttoned.

Funny how one memory leads to another. Just standing on the west side of the bridge, thinking of Alf and Hannah and Delilah, and I remembered someone else who was seen, unbeknownst to her, lying on that grassy river bank.

One summer, Philip and I went down the path every warm day, and we'd lie down on the grass, throw pebbles in the water, or play hide and seek, just the two of us. We'd stay there for the larger part of the day, returning home when the sun had dipped behind the mountain and we knew Mother would start to worry.

It was the year that Aiden had measles, and neither of us cared to be anywhere near him. Mother had been distraught, for he was quite ill and covered in a flaming red rash. He was a whining child at the best of times, a demanding sniffling fat little toad of a younger brother, according to Philip, and we were pleased we had that summer to ourselves.

It was on one of our visits that we encountered Cynthia's sister, Joy. She was lying on her back on a blanket in the sun and she was naked. We crouched down behind some bushes not ten feet away and we stared. She was slender and pretty and her breasts were full with small brown buds that matched the tuft of her loins.

Oh, how I recall that body! My own breasts were little more than protruding sprouts and I had only a few straggly hairs downstairs.

Standing on the bridge overlooking the river making its westward journey, I recalled something more. Something I preferred to keep buried away. An uncomfortable memory, for all its innocence, one that would have seen both Philip and I excommunicated if we'd been discovered.

We were crouched on the riverbank, and all we seemed able to do was stare. So we stared and we stared and as we stared Philip drew closer and put an arm around my waist. Something in me froze. He'd never wanted to be that close to me before. It was all so strange, so unexpected, so furtive. He began to push himself against my thigh. I had no clear idea what he was doing. Soon he was gripping my flesh and pressing into me and breathing in my ear. I didn't stop him. I couldn't. I wanted to stop his free hand when it reached down the front of my shorts. I wanted to push him away but he made me tingle. He made me tingle as he pressed his hardness to my thigh.

We both stayed transfixed on Joy's naked form, until the tingle spread through me and Philip groaned.

We waited and watched some more before creeping away feeling cheated that our special place had been stolen from us.

ISOBEL BLACKTHORN

We never spoke of what we did, even to each other. It was our secret. Just as Mother and I shared the secret of flowers. It was then that in my heart I parted ways with the Kinsfolk. For I knew I had sinned and Philip and Mother had sinned, each of us failing to obey the strictures and none of us prepared for the punishment and the banishment that would ensue should we confess.

Looking back, I could almost miss Philip's touch. The sensitive instinctive way he had of giving me pleasure. His was like an initiation into a realm of ecstasy that no one since has surpassed. The illicit nature of our childish coupling made it all the more compelling. I confess this is a memory not lost, but one that enters my mind unexpectedly and at inopportune times, as though the stage lights in the theatre of my mind had burst onto the scene, acted out for a reluctant audience of one.

CHAPTER NINE

PHILIP

I took a draught of my beer, set it down in front of me and leaned back in my seat, discreetly wiping the condensation from my hand in a trouser pocket before letting it rest lightly on my thigh, and cursing Delilah for insisting men who drink bottled beer didn't need a glass. I was alone at my table. Delilah had taken up her sentry by the fireplace and Alf had shambled outside. I sensed Cynthia behind me, Rebekah and David in the nook. Joshua, Ed, Nathan and Hannah, they were all there with their eyes and their ears. I felt strangely oppressed.

The moment I'd entered The Cabin, I determined to maintain a casual air, which proved increasingly challenging given the company. I could do nothing but study Adam, his sculptural form, an Adonis of ostensible purity, until my earlier disillusionment returned with force. Through it I observed his precarious situation with a modicum of relish.

Already Cynthia had added to the man's poor spirits, and he'd spent much of the night so far being harangued by his other foe. It occurred to me that Eva's presence would have alleviated the situation, saving him from all that unwanted attention, sat with him and kept him safe. Instead, we'd cast him to the piranhas, Alf, Delilah and me, leaving him dangling like a minnow behind us. I might have felt a touch guilty about it when Cynthia had one of her turns, but no one took her seriously, except him.

For the duration of Nathan's set, Juan had treated Adam with the contempt I'd expected, and at that point I'd begun to wonder if Adam would cope, when I believe I heard him laugh. I had to turn an ear to be sure. They were muttering to themselves and the exchange seemed intimate. It was then that I knew I'd been used by Adam as some sort of confessional sluice.

Life had taught me yet again that those who present to the world as emotionally weak are invariably the opposite, and I wasn't altogether grateful to have had planted in my brain like a cassette on replay a number of bestial scenes, for Adam was without a doubt canine in his soul. I would rather Eva had been the one privy to his disclosures, for she would have known how to handle the knowledge, how to make use of it. She was good at that.

Instead it was I who had been left tormented by his vile habits. He shouldn't have imparted them on one as sensitive as me. I might have forgiven his thoughtlessness, for the self-centred are always thoughtless when it comes to others, but I couldn't help noticing in the act a malicious intent.

And there he stood on the overcrowded stage, guitar slung low, pose at a quarter turn to Juan at the mixing desk behind him, affecting apprehension as he adjusted the height of the music stand. Despite Juan's demeanour, all dark passion, I wasn't fooled.

Outside, the storm roiled. Every now and then lightning flashed crisp light through the windows, and thunder cracked and rumbled soon after. I thought it wouldn't be long before we lost another tree.

I find it peculiar that one event, a storm, will trigger memories of all those gone by, as if it were an anniversary. Listening to the crack and boom I remembered that Rebekah had lost her brother to a tree. And Nathan had lost his parents in the same storm. They were foolish enough to have gone to the shed to check on their horses. They were likeable folk, the Sandhursts, if horsy, and Nathan was their only offspring. I presumed their deaths impacted on him hard. He'd been seventeen at the time and left to manage the property, which he had thus far failed to do. He wasn't the practical type. A dreamer, a drifter, not a man who would repair the fences or clear the paddocks of fallen branches. The shed where his parents had been crushed along with two roan mares still stood in the field behind the house, visible from the lane. After the passing of a decade, the shed was thoroughly overgrown, sheets of rusting iron with several rotting rafters poking up on the diagonal. I saw that shed every day on my way to and from work, adding to that eyesore of a farm, situated almost directly opposite my own abode.

Alf was taking his time in the toilet again. In his wretched state he shouldn't have come to the sessions. I was sure if it had been left to him, he would have been at home, in bed. But that dominatrix Delilah always got her way. It wasn't only that Nathan needed Alf to play guitar for him as he always did. Alf was The Cabin's virtuoso, outshining every other musician in the room. Nathan pretended to know Billy

Franks, Peter Curry and Lee Reece, when in truth it was Alf who knew all those greats and many more besides. He was a legend amongst Blues guitarists of all stripes, having learned from the late master Bluesman Tommy Spinks of The Spinks Trio fame. None of which atoned for the acrid odour that emanated on his breath.

Delilah admitted to me in confidence as we'd watched Alf on stage earlier, that she'd coerced him into coming, bribing him with free drinks. The Sessions were of that much importance to her. With Benny's passing, The Cabin needed to do Benny the honour of a united front. She said she'd wanted to let him know, for he was sure to be watching, that his show would go on in his memory. Without Alf what sort of show would that be? She'd telephoned me yesterday on the pretext of a dripping tap and stated that she'd wanted Alf to run the night but he'd declined, which was when I'd mentioned Juan.

Alf, along with the rest of us, was now trapped here for the duration, and I knew Delilah's plumbing wouldn't withstand the punishing. Her septic tank had needed a pump out for some months now. I'd warned her of the consequences if she didn't attend to it straight away but she mumbled something about finding the cash first. That's no way to run a business. And of course, it would be on the foulest of nights that the system began to fail. As I'd discovered when I'd gone outside.

Joshua may have had his utility crushed by a fallen tree, and in The Cabin that had become the only point of discussion, one I had little choice but to join when I returned to the room, but I carried with me the knowledge that a far worse calamity was imminent. Sitting there watching Adam go through a sound check, I pictured raw sewerage overflowing from toilet bowls, dribbling out of cubicles, and on outside to blend with the deluge that was sure to be on its way, a fetid slurry that would seep into The Cabin under the door. Alf's malaise simply hastened the inevitable. The longer he spent out there, the more likely the men's toilet would overflow and it would be left to me to take action. Ever the hero, rescuing residents from the stenches, blockages and deluges of their own making. Only I wouldn't do it. Not this time.

I had suspected Adam wouldn't make it to the stage, prima donna that he was. After Cynthia's fit and Juan's moiling ire, I expected Adam to have a tantrum of his own. Then again, wasn't an adoration of the stage typical of the personality type? And there he stood, making three courses out of tuning his guitar. First, he picked the high E and played the B string against it. He tweaked the peg until he heard a harmony. He continued tuning down to the low E, testing the result with a full six-string G chord. All of which would have been marvellous had the high E been in tune.

Suddenly, he seemed jittery. He adjusted his guitar strap and the microphone and I began to wonder if he'd ever begin.

'I think I'll start with this,' he said at last, and strummed an E flat, shooting a nervous glance in Juan's direction. 'That's fine,' he said before going on.

Juan made pretence of nudging a slider before leaving his gargantuan sound desk, and with the gait of predetermination, walked straight over and took up Alf's chair. I resisted shunting my chair to the side.

Delilah promptly sat on the chair to my right without making a comment.

My attention I fixed on the stage. Adam's playing was light, sparse, at times almost casual. He had a small voice with a nasal timbre, but I had to admit that his delivery was good. One verse in and there was no sign of his former agitation. He engaged with everyone and no one in the room, his eyes wandering without seeing for he was seeing himself, inwardly, and with astonishing confidence. Benny had taught him well. There was an aerodynamic quality to his lyrics, and an absence of the awkward rhymes and clumsy phrasing of Nathan's songs. Adam's were simple, straight ahead, and catchy. A sideways glance and I could tell that Juan found his performance satisfactory. Beneath the table he was tapping his foot.

There was a notable sense of release in the room, Adam's music a sweet foreground of meadow flowers beneath a summer sky, a shift of focus from the dark drama playing out beyond The Cabin walls, a reprieve, the wind a background roar, like static on the radio. From time to time, the building trembled upon a sudden pounding and I noticed there'd been a directional shift, the wind badgering the door which strained and rattled its latch.

Adam had yet to come to the end of his first song when the stage light dimmed and he lost amplification. He kept on playing but looked uncertain. Juan leaned forward in his seat, poised to stand. Before he did, the light flickered back to normal and Adam could be properly heard again.

I turned to Juan, feigning concern. 'Not good for the sound gear.'

'I'm aware of that,' he said sharply.

He didn't look at me. It occurred to me he'd only sat beside me to cause trouble.

'He's come a long way, don't you think?' I said, testing my theory.

'If you say so,' he said between his teeth.

This time he looked into my face, eyes narrowed, mouth pinched, the pencil moustache curving downwards at the edges. His simmering volatility seemed to arise as if from nowhere. It was the manner of a man holding back anger with a steely will and while utterly abhorrent, I remained unmoved. For all I knew, he was putting on a show. Besides, I knew the real target of his wrath was Adam, not me, and I was determinedly indifferent to that fact.

And his misplaced jealousy was a matter I found oddly amusing.

Juan thought me capable of same sex relations. Should I have been insulted? I've never been inclined towards my own gender, and I thought it obvious to all what my sexual preference was. That I've not formally had a girlfriend should be no cause for speculation, there being a dearth of attractive females in and around Burton, available or otherwise and, despite my unfortunate liaisons with the repellent Hannah Fisher, I do have taste. It isn't a small breast large breast sort of choosiness either. The female form offers myriad possibilities to whet the appetite and while my preference errs on the petite side of womanhood, I wouldn't consider myself fussy.

The right woman has yet to enter my life. A self-contained woman, prepossessing of course, and quiet, demure, undemanding. A woman who doesn't fuss or interrogate, a woman with her own simple interests. A woman who doesn't knit.

A woman like Eva's best friend, Sophie. An unassuming young thing, compliant and uncomplicated.

It was Eva's last year of high school and I'd just finished my plumbing apprenticeship with old Frank Stubbs. Sophie lived on the other side of the river, two doors down from Alf, and the two girls would rendezvous on the bridge before taking off to the general store and then on for a walk up the track behind The Cabin.

One time I pulled up beside them in my panel van and offered to take them for a drive, hoping Sophie would get in first, which she did. They were all giggles and chatter. Sophie's naked thigh only inches from the gear stick. I took them into the mountains on Burton Road East, turning off outside of town and heading down an old logging track. It was all snaky pitted dirt with potholes and deep ruts and I drove hard into the bends, letting the van fish tail out. My adrenalin was pumping. The chatter soon stopped and the giggles and squeals became screams. The left-hand corners were the best. Sophie had nothing to hold on to and leaned into me, her thigh brushing my hand on the gear stick. While Eva was busy scrambling for her door's armrest, I opened my hand and stroked Sophie's naked thigh with the backs of my fingertips. She didn't pull away. Out of the corner of my eye I could see her hesitate. After that I decided we'd all had enough and eased off the accelerator, giving me a chance to give Sophie a winning grin.

For months I met Sophie without Eva's knowledge, sneaking off after midnight when the whole of Burton slumbered. We would steal with great care along the river path. Then I would ravage her in the grassy clearing where me and Eva used to play.

I always led Sophie to the same spot, laying her down where Cynthia's sister, Joy, had lain naked one day. Recalling as I did, how Eva and I had discovered Joy and we'd hid in the bushes and stared, fascinated, for ages, neither of us having ever before seen a naked woman.

There was something intoxicating remembering Joy's nakedness as I devoured Sophie, the two women merging into one. Sophie's breasts were Joy's breasts and when I penetrated her tight wet heat I was sliding in and out of Joy.

At summer's end, the long dry spell broke and the river path became too muddy and the clearing too wet for a midnight tryst. I'd sat behind the wheel of my panel van parked in my parents' driveway, watching the rain coat the windscreen in fat drops, wondering where else to take Sophie. I contemplated the Sandhurst's horse shed but decided against it. Before long I heard scurrying footsteps. The passenger side door opened and my lover got in.

In no time we were snuggled down in the back, Sophie writhing in my arms, the van bouncing on its springs. Then there was a sharp rap on the window and Eva's face peering in. I'd never before seen such an expression in her eyes. She yanked at the door and I thought she might start yelling and wake the whole village. So I unlocked it and let her in.

In a stifled voice she hurled insult upon insult. Not at me. At Sophie. Soon she was pulling her hair and clawing at her face and neck. I thought she was going to strangle her friend, who was so shocked she offered up no defence. It was left to me to pull Eva away. The moment I did, Eva burst into tears. I held her in my arms and she collapsed into me like a baby. I motioned with my eyes for Sophie to leave, which she did without hesitation.

I never saw Sophie again. Eva said she'd left to go to university. Her family sold up and moved out of Burton in the same year.

Those images of Sophie stirred in me a familiar sense of injustice and I resented the imposition of the memory. That confession of Adam's: Could it be that he'd been flirting with me? For all I knew he might have known Juan was hosting the night. Pretended to be fearful when all along he was trying to turn me into Juan's target. If that was the case, and I'm not often mistaken, then his plan was backfiring at an astounding pace.

Delilah led the applause with her usual enthusiastic bravos. As the room quieted, Adam launched into a tedious ode to Benny, listing all the many things he'd done for him: his generosity, his wisdom, his dedication, his charm. Adam's lips quivered. It was one of those moments when you regret the presence of the microphone, wish you could snatch it away, knowing it afforded the speaker too much power. In what I hoped were his final words, Adam said Benny had been like a father to him, Juan leaned back in his seat and scoffed beneath his breath.

Thankfully Alf returned at that point, interrupting Adam with a sudden burst of cold air. Alf had to lean hard against the door to close it, before shuffling into the room looking more haggard than ever. Spots of vomit coagulated on his shirt and there was a rivulet of mucus in the crease that ran from the corner of his mouth to his chin curtain. Seeing Juan in his seat, Alf made no attempt to reclaim it and went on past to join Cynthia at the table behind, leaving an acrid odour in his wake, one that added a brief tang to the reek in the room.

Adam resumed his speech, reiterating the patronage that Benny had bestowed upon him. The room began to stir.

I sensed a subtle shift in Juan's manner. With him seated by my side I was sensitive to his mood, and it seemed as if Adam's longwinded and teary speech that by now had descended into soliloquy, had opened a vent somewhere deep inside and I knew that soon he would not be in control of his anger. I knew, too, that he'd take time to fully erupt, that we could expect smoke and ash and seepage in advance of the inevitable cascade of molten fury.

I'd seen his process unfold on a number of occasions. I never intervened of course, not wanting to bloody a shirt. Besides, what could I have done?

One occasion sprang to mind. After a terrific Session, with Benny in top form oozing pride at having convinced Lisa Dunderdale, a jazz singer from Standlake, to make her debut. He'd given her the guest spot as a sweetener and everyone thought she was marvellous, and he in love. Juan and Adam had still been together at the time, and Eva had just gone back to the city after unexpectedly cutting short her holiday without offering an explanation. While a little disappointed at her secrecy, I didn't pursue it, being glad to be rid of her: I was keen to start renovating the bathroom.

Adam had been in fine spirits that night and we

had a running joke going about whom it might have been sneaking away from Nathan's late one night the previous week. We both knew it wasn't Hannah. We were discreet of course, not wanting to cause controversy or undue upset, whispering witticisms in each other's ear. I saw that our repartee peeved Juan but thought nothing of it.

It wasn't until the night had ended and we had all left, going off in our separate ways, that the consequences of that exchange unfolded. I was about to get into my car when I heard Juan yelling at Adam. I looked around and saw them in the vacant block next to the general store. I stood beside my car, key in the lock and watched. Adam was defensive, placating, raising his hands, palms open, but it made no difference. Juan slammed a fist into his belly and he keeled. Several more blows about his head and shoulders and he fell. Not content, Juan kicked him in the legs and back then marched off down the street towards the bridge.

Keen not to make a bad situation worse, I got in my car and drove up the hill taking a back road, and pulling over for a few minutes to give Juan enough time to get back to the church before I drove on.

It doesn't do to get involved in disputes between couples. You never know how it might backfire. Best to let them sort it out themselves. Besides, I'd decided from my observations of the movements of his body that Adam had not been grievously hurt. And I'd been right: no lasting damage done.

It was only a matter of time before something similar happened that Christmas Eve.

Why Juan insisted on reading falsehoods into innocent exchanges I couldn't fathom. Still, Adam should have known better than to flirt with the danger Juan presented. You'd think he'd have learned not to gild that lily by now.

Upon the opening bar of Adam's next song, Ed brushed past Juan on the way to the stage. Juan reared in his seat and if it hadn't been for Delilah's remonstrative hiss, that scrawny old codger with his monkey-tail tail hair may have ended up flattened as well.

I hadn't taken my eyes off Adam and can attest to the fact that he didn't once indicate to Ed with a head tilt or eye movement or gesture of any kind that he wanted his accompaniment. Who would?

Ed squashed up beside the speakers on the right of the stage, violin poised to the ready, making a show of attuning his ear. Adam shot him an uncertain glance as he broke into song, managing a few short lines before mouthing Ed the key in an interlude in the verse. No doubt regretting that directive straight away when Ed drew his bow across the strings and the violin moaned to life, cutting across Adam's melody with a discordant, low-pitched whine, drowning out the vocals and smearing our ears with its screech.

Ed ruined every one of the songs he played on. The only Sessions singer who could accommodate him was Joshua. Although as soon as the thought occurred to me I realised with a shock of annoyance that it was not my own. It was Benny who oft offered up that opinion, Benny who knew about musicianship and sound and where to play and not to play on someone else's song. Less is more he would say in one of his long rants on the travails of musical performance.

I'd have preferred to have my own thoughts on the matter.

I supposed it inevitable that Benny would leave his legacy in such intrusive ways, instilling in each of us his thoughts and opinions, implanting a little bit of himself in our minds like an infection. But the prospect that I had been infected with an identical virus to all the others in the room, that despite multiple defences I was in fact not immune, made me suddenly nauseous and I made a mental note to purge all foreign thoughts from my mind forthwith.

How long had this been going on? Was it the case that I was occupied by the thoughts of countless others? Doomed to cart around in my psyche forevermore their attitudes, beliefs and desires that had managed to find their way inside me in the course of a relentless verbal onslaught. Did I have a weakness, my guard inadequate, drawbridge left open a crack, no one watching on the battlements? Others must have endured the same invasion, unawares perhaps, or complacent, even inviting. Adam had undoubtedly invited in Benny's views, invited them in like a whore. And seated in The Cabin on the foulest of nights, we were witnessing not Adam's talent in its pure state, grown in the seclusion of a cocoon to emerge like a butterfly. He'd been groomed, musically seduced and he would always be the sort of performer Benny would have him be. Observing such a gross lack of purity I was overwhelmed, and with this new realisation I felt glad to hear Ed play all over him. I'd even begun to enjoy that winsome sound. There was something spontaneous and unique about the way he cut across Adam's music, with a counterpoint all of his own, and a new appreciation for him as a violinist grew in me.

And I was certain that this appreciation was wholly my own.

Nevertheless, the song went tediously on, and I'd begun to fancy another beer when the door flew open, slamming against the wall and scattering the chord charts that Adam had propped on the music stand. Ed stopped playing, leaving Adam to press on to the end. Joshua rushed forward to close the door.

'It was Alf,' Delilah said quickly, and all heads turned. 'Alf, you didn't close the door properly.'

Alf looked chastened and mumbled an apology but I knew Delilah had only said that to prevent Cynthia from more hysterics.

After some fumbling about for the right chord chart, Adam continued with his next song. Ed showed no sign of leaving him to it.

The storm stuck fast right above us, wedged into the narrow valley and stalling on its way east, gathering in strength as it pondered its next move. Lightning flashed sharp light with greater frequency, heavy thunder close on its heels.

The power browned out for a second time, and I could see Juan's fingers press into his thighs. Adam pulled back from the microphone, presumably in anticipation of electrocution although I had no idea what good that would do him since his guitar was running through the mixing desk as well. At least he had the temerity to keep playing. As did Ed.

I admit my oppressed state, sandwiched as I was between Juan and Delilah, grew as night wore on. Juan seemed to have made it his business to nudge my shoulder with his when he reached for his whisky. He would sniff and wipe his nose with his hand, resting it on his thigh perilously close to mine.

Delilah gripped her glass to her chest and I caught her worrying her fingernails. I steered my gaze back to the stage. I couldn't see that well in the dim light but memory completed the image of the inflamed, cracked, flaking skin of her cuticles. She'd had a fungal condition for years and done nothing to remedy it. Or nothing had worked. If she stopped playing with her fingertips, then at least the inflammation might ease. But no. There she was, absently rubbing away.

In my side vision I took in the equally repugnant Rebekah. Her knitting needles never stopped. When she came to the end of a row she flipped her knitting from one hand to the other and began the next. Every stitch of wool made on those needles passed through those podgy little hands coated in her sweat. Whoever got to wear the scarf would be choked by the fetid essence of her.

I was supposed to respect her, as I was Delilah, the two matriarchs of Burton, my aunties of a sort, yet in their company I felt only revulsion. Rebekah with her downy moustache, half man; fungal-fingered Delilah, a slattern.

Then there was Cynthia and Alf behind me. Joshua and Nathan behind them and Hannah behind the bar. I didn't need to turn around to see their faces. I'd known all my life. Christmas Eve, and I confess I wasn't feeling a skerrick of conviviality.

Midway through another song, Alf stood behind me and whispered something in Delilah's ear. I held my breath for as long as I could manage, but when I inhaled I could smell the contents of his rotting guts. I glanced across as Delilah lifted her gaze to the ceiling and during the next applause she turned to me, leaning forward and beckoning for me to do the same. She put a hand on mine and it took everything in me not to snatch it back.

'Any chance you can check on the men's toilet?'

'It's blocked?'

'Afraid so.'

'Alf.'

She nodded. I knew it! There wasn't a chance this side of the Milky Way that I was going out there to unblock her vomit-clogged toilet. I smiled in acknowledgement of her request and reached for my beer.

It's well known that plumbers get asked to do unsavoury tasks at inopportune moments. Fix the leaking gooseneck at someone's dinner party. I didn't like to ask, they say, when they asked anyway. Then they stare at you with imploring eyes. Delilah became even less likeable because of it and I made a mental note to keep my distance from her from then on to avert more liberties being nabbed from me.

Adam and Ed continued with their performance. About halfway through the next song there was a sharp snap and again the door swung open, this time slamming against the front wall. The wind blasted the stage, knocking over the music stand and Adam's chord charts. He reached down and fumbled about at his feet.

I was grateful for the fresh air.

Joshua rushed forward and tried to battle shut the door. Leaning his shoulder hard against the wood he said, addressing Delilah, 'The latch is broken.'

Much commotion ensued. Adam left the stage, visibly deflated. Ed was close behind. Juan got up to check on his sound equipment. His absence felt like liberation. Delilah called to Hannah to fetch the hammer she kept in a kitchen drawer, for all the good it would do. Behind us, Cynthia had started to fret. Rebekah, who was apparently too close to the door for comfort, inched her way out of the nook and went to the bar. David just sat there.

'What do you want me to do, Delilah?' Joshua said with a modicum of consternation in his voice.

'I haven't a clue.'

This was no time to play the helpless matriarch, manipulating her minions to sort out her negligence. That latch was rusty and bent and had needed replacing years ago.

'Put something heavy against it,' David said sagely. 'One of those speakers should do it.'

'Not on your life,' Juan growled.

'Then what do you suggest?' David sounded uncharacteristically snappy.

'That barrel.' Juan pointed to the back corner.

Everyone looked round. It was stout, its staves lacquered black and in all the years I'd been coming to The Cabin I'd never seen it in another location.

I felt no inclination to move but Delilah was already shifting the furniture to make way, ushering Cynthia and Alf from their seats and pulling their chairs to the wall. I stood and placed my seat beside theirs, helping Delilah draw back the tables and shunt guitar cases out of the way.

'Is there anything in this?' Ed said, after a fruitless tug of the barrel.

Delilah shrugged.

I thought it best to relieve Joshua at the door, leaving him to attend to the barrel. Adam, at the bar with Rebekah, appeared flustered. He wiped his brow in a pathetic display of something like angst. I was not convinced. Neither David nor Alf were capable of heavy lifting.

'Juan, come on over here,' Joshua said, realising the same.

Something must have been in the barrel for it took the full strength of those two burly men to manoeuvre it out from its tight location in the corner and walk it forward, rocking it back and forth with sharp twists.

I moved away when the barrel was close enough to catch the door and left them to wedge it in place.

Now the only exit was via the kitchen.

A silence descended on the room as Delilah and Joshua put back the furniture. The wind couldn't get in. But the sense grew in me that except through Delilah's kitchen, which she was apt to guard like a warden, we couldn't get out.

CHAPTER TEN

EVA'S DIARY – SATURDAY 20TH DECEMBER

T he mermaid hasn't returned. Which should be a
comfort but it isn't. Normally after a fish makes
its debut in my underwater world it returns, leaving
the other fish and swimming up to me, introducing
itself with a wide-eyed stare or a playful wriggle and a
flick of the tail fin. I have a chance to become familiar
with all of its special qualities—the subtle coloura-
tions of the scales, the shape of the gills, the mouth,
the fins—before it melds into the school.

The absence of the mermaid makes her single appearance all the more ominous. She was an intrusion
from another realm, one not of my making, and not
following my rules of play.

While all the creatures in my underwater world
emerge like surprises, they have come from the depths
of my imagination, summoned by a hidden will that is
in complete alignment with my conscious will, the
two locked arm in arm in a campaign to improve on
my personal best.

That my imagination brings forth a dark mass is a
signal that I am reaching the limits of my endurance.
Setting aside the inexcusable intrusion of Juan, for

which the dark mass served as harbinger. Nothing more.

The mermaid was as far from a dark mass as it's possible to be, her beauty captivating, her eyes hypnotic, her beckoning hands magnetic. When the dark mass comes, I feel afraid. When the mermaid came I was fascinated. I wanted to follow her and I might have done just that. Looking back, it was only the slow creep of dark mass dimming the sunlight up above that had caused me to resist the mermaid and with the toes of my right foot pull the plug on the bath.

The mermaid is absent from my underwater world yet present everywhere else. She's there with me in my dreams, when I brush my teeth or sit in the sun to warm my skin. She's the most pleasant sort of haunting, a companion, popping into my inner field of vision, always smiling, kind, appreciative, accommodating. She has every virtue. She is perfection and when she's with me I'm filled with the warmest glow. Her inner radiance beams through me like grace. The only time I'm not at variance with myself is when she's with me.

I've begun to crave her presence and this longing is interfering with my daily routine. Today, when I practised my craft, I couldn't sustain concentration for more than five minutes. I was not relaxed enough. And I'm becoming forgetful, neglecting the responsibilities of the day. My dreamy mood has even started to affect Philip. I have made gains with his jumper for I find knitting soothes my impatient state of mind. I prepare his favourite foods and iron his shirts but I fear I'm no longer agreeable company.

Something has changed in his behaviour towards

me. He's always been a benevolent and generous man, if somewhat restrained in his manner, concerned to treat others well and be of assistance wherever he can. Which is why, when I asked him to drive me to the general store this morning and he refused, I was taken aback. He wouldn't even look at me to explain himself.

We were at breakfast. He was tucking into the mushroom omelette with tomato coulis on rye sour dough that I'd lovingly prepared and all he did in response to my request was set down his knife and fork and gaze at his plate.

I was deflated. After some time, he said in an even voice that he'd collect whatever I needed that was heavy and that otherwise I should walk there myself.

There was no point debating the matter for I hadn't a valid reason to offer him and I didn't want to appear in any way anxious or unhinged, but I still haven't managed to cross the bridge. I'm sure he suspects this and his cool, stern, insistence is just his way of being kind. I could hardly tell him about the pressure on my back that prevents me from moving in any direction other than home.

Philip is rational. For him, reality consists of what he can see and smell and touch and taste. A practical man, applying his imagination to washers, pipes and drains, systems for fresh water in and for wastewater out. He doesn't read anything non-factual and his only hobby is practicing his guitar and writing a few songs. He isn't a lyricist, not being poetical, and it is me who assists him with all his verses and choruses.

We really are a very different species, although he isn't without his sensitivities. He's grown to have many. He dislikes conversation at breakfast. He likes the house kept exactly as he left it. Even a newspaper on the coffee table, and not in the magazine rack, makes him tut and mutter. He has a pernickety way of insisting every utensil is aligned with all its friends in the drawer; so at pains he showed me three times how I should go about it. In the bathroom it's worse. Not a hair on my head must find its way into the sink. My toothbrush, along with all my toiletries, must be kept in my room so as not to clutter the space. There's to be no spatter of anything on the mirror. I am forbidden access not only to our parents' bedroom but Philip's as well. If I must iron his shirts, I am to hang them in the laundry.

I find it easy enough to abide by the strictures, but an emerging temptation is replacing my obedience, one that grows in me daily. I've begun to experience a hot flush each time I pass my parents' bedroom door. It seems more imperative than ever that I gain access to that room. I've tried and tried but cannot locate the key.

Standing by the sink watching Philip consume his repast I thought of another way. For I know those old sash windows. A length of wood prevents the top pane from sliding down and the bottom pane is fastened to the top by a simple latch. All I needed was a screwdriver.

Philip drew his cutlery together and took his plate to the sink where he left it on the draining board. 'Make sure you rinse after washing.'

'I always do,' I said to his back as he left the room.

Before long I heard the front door close and moments later his car engine purred. I listened until the sound faded to nothing.

I cleared away the rest of the breakfast things and

left the dishes till later. I was already dressed and ready for the village so I went out and headed down the hill. I knew I wouldn't get far but grabbed my purse in case bravery took hold.

The day was breezy and warm. Fluffy clouds scudded across the narrow strip of sky. The mountains bore down, their eastern flanks in shadow, treetops swaying in the wind. I was several yards down the lane when I heard a car making its way over the rutted gravel behind me, and I turned to see Adam approaching in his white sedan.

I stood to the side to let him pass. Instead, he pulled up beside me, and leaned across to greet me through the passenger side window. 'Need a lift?' he said and I hesitated before impulse got the better of me, and I smiled and got in and thanked him.

'Where to?'

'Just the general store,' I said and he released the handbrake.

His car was new and smelled of polish and orange peel. I sat back in my seat and wished I'd said the city and not the general store, for his driving was careful and smooth and I succumbed to a sudden glow of wellbeing. I liked Adam. He was gracious and loyal and immensely attractive. He asked if I was pleased to be back and I told him, yes, certainly I was, and left it at that.

We crossed the bridge without event. I found I enjoyed the juddering sensation as the wheels bounced over the timbers. We headed east to the store and within moments we'd arrived. I was about to thank him again when he unbuckled his seat belt and grabbed his wallet from the console.

I hadn't been in the general store for years, but I

was not surprised to find that it was the same as ever. Dimly lit, with tall sparsely filled shelves lining all the walls and several wire racks and low metal shelving units arranged in a row in the centre of the floor space, along with three bargain bins filled with stock so old it belonged at the tip. There was a rancid smell of meat pies. David was behind the counter. Before him, an empty pie case on a small white plate. A dribble of tomato sauce on his pale blue shirt. It was half past eight in the morning. No time to be eating meat pies. I wonder if Rebekah knew, or cared.

Adam browsed the shelves by the counter and, keeping an eye out in case he showed signs of leaving the store, I wandered around with a wire basket, gathering milk, butter, a carton of orange juice, a packet of sliced ham, a jar of olives, washing liquid, a packet of household candles, a net of onions, a four-pound bag of potatoes and the screwdriver that was the purpose of my trip. When I reached the counter Adam, who was waiting patiently by the window, said, 'You weren't planning to carry all that back?'

'Um,' I said with a sheepish smile.

I loaded the counter with my purchases. David looked me up and down.

'So, you're back.'

I ignored him, the creepy oaf.

Adam checked his watch.

'I'm not holding you up?' I said, looking anxiously at David who was taking an age to ring everything through.

'You're fine.'

He watched on. Then he said, 'Why are you buying a screwdriver? Philip must have dozens, surely.'

'They're special. He doesn't like me to use them.'

'That one's pricey,' he said.

David looked askance.

'At least it'll be mine,' I said covetously.

Apparently satisfied with my explanation, Adam leaned back and waited.

On the way home he asked if I knew how to drive. I told him, no. A look of puzzlement appeared in his face and he said that if ever I needed a lift, just ask.

'I haven't seen you at The Sessions.'

'I'm working my way up to it,' I said, imbuing my voice with a measure of flippancy to mask the fact that I was avoiding The Cabin. I wonder if he knew, if he could see into me, even a little way.

Thankfully the trip was short and the interrogation ceased. It was a good thing I hadn't gone to the city with him for there would have been many more questions and I wouldn't have known how to answer any of them.

I thanked him again and alighted with my purchases, making my way inside without a backward glance. After putting the items in their rightful places and doing the breakfast dishes, I spent a pleasant enough day on the back veranda. Although the prize-winning rural romance I was reading proved so distasteful I had no idea why I kept turning the pages. I looked up, intermittently, at the cockatoos in the trees, shutting my ears to their infernal squawks. When they quieted, I tuned into the intermittent yet persistent knocking of the frog that must have relocated from its station outside my bedroom window and taken up a post nearby. Knock, knock, knock. Like a faulty metronome.

I settled back in my seat and reflected on how

nice it was to have spent those few minutes with Adam and that one day when I felt brave, I would head up the hill and knock on the old church door.

I must have dozed, as the next thing I knew Philip had arrived home. I heard a door slam. And another. He never slams doors. I left my book face down on the chair and went to see what was wrong.

I found him in the living room, slouched in a chair, elbows on the armrests, fingertips pressed together, his hands forming a prism. His eyes fixed on the tree fern in the garden, framed squarely by the window. I was hesitant to enter the room. Even side on, I could see the thunder in his face. I went as far as the silk rug and waited.

'I take it you're here to explain,' he said without shifting his gaze.

My mind shimmied. So it was me he was angry with? I might have felt frightened at this point and if I'd been his wife and not his sister I'm sure I would have been, but it was mirth that bubbled in my belly for I couldn't help seeing a scrawny scabby-kneed Philip livid with the entire world because Aiden had thrust a grubby little fist into his jelly.

Aiden must have been about two and Philip by then eight. He was all clenched jaw and red faced, bottom lip thrust out, his china blue eyes bulging indignation and he yelled as loud as he could for Mother. When she entered the room, he demanded justice. He demanded Aiden be punished and a fresh bowl of jelly be brought for him that instant. When Mother refused both the thrashing and the jelly, he roared and punched his fists into her thigh. I hid behind a chair.

Father, just home from work, must have heard the

commotion and he marched into the living room, already unbuckling his trouser belt.

After a brief explanation from Mother, he grabbed Philip and whipped his bare thighs with the buckle end, until Philip's yelling became screams and his screams pleas and his pleas whimpers. The thrashing seemed to take an age. When it was over, Philip lay on the silk rug, writhing, unable to touch the red welts already oozing blood.

Mother watched on. She had done nothing to stop the beating. Her face wore a blank look. She left Philip on the floor, scooped up her youngest son and left the room on the heels of her husband.

I came out from my hiding place and stared, frightened and helpless and suppressing the giggles all at once. All that over a stupid bowl of jelly. Philip didn't even like jelly that much. Even at five, I couldn't help seeing the funny side of it, for Philip had been such a sight, all pompous and defiant, and it served him right in a way, for he was the oldest. Aiden was little more than a baby and I was secretly pleased that Philip had finally been punished, albeit indirectly, for all the cruelties he meted out on me. Looking back, it was not real laughter in my belly, but that born of terror and relief.

I hid my amusement and my satisfaction and helped him up and to his room. I stayed with him while he recovered, reading the comics that normally he wouldn't let me touch. My loyalty paid dividends as he was never cruel to me again. He viewed me his ally and a new respect and closeness grew between us.

Philip was never the same. We didn't speak of that day but he knew that I had adopted his view of the situation for I refused from then on to sit on Mother's lap. At story time she would pat her knee but I always sat beside her. 'Too squashy,' I'd say.

Hovering near the doorway on the edge of the silk rug, observing Philip's steely rage, I had no idea what I could possibly have done to upset him, so I just stood and waited.

'Why were you in Adam's car?' he said, his voice controlled.

'You saw me?'

'I was fixing Alf's gutters.'

There was nothing I could say. I was stunned. I'd inadvertently betrayed him, an innocent act but one he clearly deemed inappropriate.

'Well?'

'He drove me to the general store.'

'You should have walked.'

So that was it. He only wanted me to do what was right and good and normal. Instead I'd seized a chance to avoid another inevitable hiatus on the bridge, one I seemed unable to transcend. 'I'm sorry,' I said, relieved that his anger was not the result of misplaced jealousy.

I knew Philip was fond of Adam, or that at least he felt sorry for him, lumbered with an old church he lacked the wherewithal to restore. I resolved to visit Adam at the earliest opportunity, thank him for his goodwill, perhaps return the favour with a small gift of some sort, a little produce from the garden, or better still, a bunch of herbs.

I was relieved too. Philip didn't appear to have seen Adam drive me back. For that would have resulted in another level of interrogation, one possibly

involving David's inculpatory evidence, evidence that
would have included the screwdriver.

'What did you buy?' Philip said casually, without
averting his gaze from the tree fern outside.

I hesitated. 'Now let me see,' I said, stalling.
'Mostly just butter, olives and onions.'

'Mostly just?'

'Oh, and ham and orange juice.'

'Rather a lot to carry home.'

'Not really.'

'I never thought of you a liar.'

'You must be hungry. I'll go and fix dinner.'

After that, we never spoke of the incident. By the
time his dinner was on the table he was back to his
usual cordial self. But I knew I'd need to use that
screwdriver forthwith.

CHAPTER ELEVEN

ADAM

Adam stood at the bar, trying not to focus on the barrel blocking the door, on the brown outs interrupting his performance. It was as though the elementals of air and fire had been conspiring to oust him from the stage. The solution, the barrel, trapping him inside with Juan and that hideous smell. Stargazer Stella Verne's prophesising in the morning's Gazette came flooding back, and he knew without equivocation that he'd made the wrong decision on the bridge.

He'd done his best on stage, as Benny had taught him. He'd blocked out the storm, the smell, and the audience, maintained an inward gaze, focussed on his voice and his guitar. He should be euphoric but the articulation of his songs pricked in his mind over and again, as though an irate archer were using his meninges for arrow practice.

Nathan pulled himself upright in his seat, removing his Ray-Bans to stare at Adam through hazy eyes. 'Good one.'

'Thanks,' Adam said, managing a weak smile.

'Shame about the wind.' Nathan slumped back to nurse his cider, his tight blue shirt riding up his back.

'And the barrel,' said Hannah. She was holding the stem of Adam's glass on the counter as she poured his wine.

'It does the job,' said Nathan. He belched, raising a slow hand to his mouth. 'S'cuse me.'

Hannah glowered at him. 'And if we need to get out in a hurry?'

'There's the kitchen.'

'What if that exit gets blocked.'

'It won't.'

Adam proffered a bill and Hannah waved it away. 'On the house,' she mouthed.

'What if a tree falls on the veranda,' she went on.

'What if, what if,' Nathan said to his cider.

'Yeah, well that tree came down, didn't it? And you said another tree wouldn't fall after the one last week. So what would you know.'

'Stop making a drama out of it.'

'I'm not making a drama out of it.'

'You are.'

'You did a good job Adam,' Nathan said again. It was a comment that led nowhere.

Adam took a sip of his wine and stepped away from the bar, colliding with Delilah.

'Pardon me,' he said apologetically, stepping aside.

She made the same step to the side and moved back as he did. 'Move out of my way, would you,' she said. She gave him a reproving look as she pushed past him on her way to the kitchen.

Stung, he went and took up her post by the fireplace. The storm showed no sign of relenting. Rain pummelled the roof; voices rose above the din. Adam could make out Ed's nasal treble and Rebekah's 'amens' floating over from the nook like crow's feathers. Joshua's deep and hail voice. Then, he heard Philip and Juan over by the stage.

'I'll go on after Joshua and Ed.'

'You won't!' Juan snarled. 'I'm in charge of the running list and you're on last.'

'We'll see about that.' Philip feigned calm but Adam saw that behind his back he'd clenched his fists. It was a posture reminiscent of a two-year old in the throws of a tantrum.

Quick to see that petulance which must have been evident in Philip's face, Juan laughed and retorted with 'Yeah? Go ask mummy then. See what she has to say.' And with that, he walked off to the bar.

Adam watched Philip with interest. At first Philip stood glaring at Juan. He seemed set to explode. Then, as if a switch had flicked inside, a stunned look came into his face, his china blue eyes round like a bunny's. He quickly returned to his seat.

The room fell quiet. Adam took a sip of his wine, holding the liquid in his mouth, savouring the sharp fruity flavour. Rebekah and David were looking in his direction. When Adam's eyes met with Rebekah's she quickly closed her mouth and raised her eyebrows. Puzzled, Adam looked away. He was unsure whether to remain standing by the fireplace when Joshua and Ed walked by, instruments in hand.

Joshua was first to mount the dais, guitar held out in front and side on. Once he'd positioned himself behind the microphone, occupying the bulk of the available space, scraggy old Ed squashed in behind. Juan strode back from the bar, whisky in hand, and leaned over his mixing desk, waiting.

Before Joshua had plugged in his guitar, Delilah swept in from the kitchen bearing platters of small pastries, and the room roused to life as if that was all it would take to bring about a semblance of normality to the night.

Delilah called to Joshua and Ed to come over and partake in the fare. 'A little short break is called for, don't you think?' They put down their instruments without hesitation and picked their way off stage and headed to the bar.

Delilah took much pride in her baking, offering round the platters to everyone in turn, pausing patiently as first David, then Rebekah selected several pastries each, and hovering at the front table while Alf helped himself to two. She presented Philip with a half-empty platter but he declined. She waited, pushing the platter at him, but he shrank back with a frown, before smiling gracious and forlorn, and patting his stomach. Delilah did nothing to disguise her disappointment.

She turned to Adam, her gaze flitting to his seat. Following her directive, he left the fireplace to take up his chair at Cynthia's table.

Satisfied, Delilah went and set a platter on the bar.

'You've surpassed yourself, Delilah,' said Joshua, reaching for a pastry.

'I do my best,' Delilah replied.

She placed the other platter on the table in front of Adam, and sat down beside him, leaving Rebekah and David out of reach, should they require another pastry.

Proud as a hen, Delilah watched her guests bite into the crisp, delicate crusts. Spicy, sweet, buttery, a satisfying gustatory experience, and when Adam swallowed the last mouthful of his, she offered him another. He took an apple and cinnamon scroll. She looked on, pleased.

Despite her preference for the front table, she remained seated where she was. Her motive, Adam thought, perhaps a little clearer. From there she could keep a close eye on Cynthia, who, after having settled into grim silence when Delilah censured her forebodings over the tree that fell on Joshua's vehicle, had started to display misgivings over the barrel blocking the door. 'What if we need to leave in a hurry?' she said in an agitated voice between bites of her pastry, to Rebekah, to Adam, to anyone who inadvertently caught her eye, her fears echoing Hannah's moments earlier. Delilah had taken to ignoring her but she remained watchful. Perhaps she was relieved, too, not to find herself beside Alf, now sporting trails of vomit down his shirt front. Philip had wisely shifted his seat to the side.

Whatever the cause, Adam basked in the protection Delilah afforded. Juan, who never missed a chance to offer him a moody stare, would never accost him with her in close proximity.

Adam couldn't help but be impressed that under Juan's hateful gaze he'd managed to sing through most of his set without caving in. He'd sung three new songs and two that Benny had helped him craft. True professionalism was being able to perform, no matter what. Benny would have been overjoyed to witness such progress in his protégé. Adam allowed himself a frisson of self-regard, and for a few moments he marvelled over the human capacity to find fortitude in performance, fortitude that he seemed to have packed itself away when he'd returned his guitar to its case. Adam thought back with sadness to those precious times he'd spent with his master.

After Juan had moved out Adam would spend whole afternoons in Benny's crooked old fibro cottage that leaked from its roof and half the windows, here and there buckets placed to catch the drips. The only dry room was given over to the studio. It was there that Benny showed him how to use alternative tunings, opening up the possibility for different sound patterns and variations. They examined Adam's lyrics and pondered meanings and brainstormed words, buffing until each song shone. Adam would watch them grow into little masterpieces.

He had striven to achieve a similar result with his latest works but without Benny's eye and ear for that final polish he knew they wouldn't measure up and he had hoped to showcase them tonight for Benny's critique.

It was a terrible aloneness he felt, mourning the loss of a man who had been so large in his life, the others around him, each with a lesser grief, perhaps hiding their feelings behind a veneer of strength. And then there were those with no grief at all.

He became aware of Cynthia beside him, brushing crumbs from her lap. Then she picked at those caught in the tassels of her shawl. He allowed himself a private stare, convinced she was absorbed in the task, when she leaned towards him and said, 'I'm sorry I upset you earlier. These turns, they come upon me.' She put a hand on her chest and sighed. 'There's not much I can do. But believe me. I'm not crazy.'

'I don't believe you are,' he said, wishing she'd move away.

Instead, she leaned in closer. 'There's a lot about this town you don't know. Ask Eva. She'll tell you.' She cast a suspicious eye about the room then went on. 'The people in this room, barring you, Juan and Ed, were all god-fearing believers who would have had nothing to do with the likes of me.'

'So I heard,' Adam said lightly.

'Did you really?' She paused. 'To them, I've signed a pact with the devil and just because they've relinquished that sect, doesn't mean they don't carry contempt for me in their hearts. Pure evil is God's bedfellow, not mine. Mark my words.'

He had no idea how to respond but having said her piece, she sat back in her seat without further ado.

He took another cinnamon scroll. Small comfort. His head had begun to throb again. He'd wanted to ask Delilah for some headache pills, but the moment now seemed inopportune. The smell of incense was chokingly thick and the sickly smell beneath it hit him in waves.

He reflected on the situation. One tree down and heaven knows how many to follow, the phone line dead and the power sure to die soon. The barrel blocking the exit, Juan's brooding menace. And, bizarrely, the crone seated beside him who everyone in Burton had condemned a crazed soothsayer might be turning out to be the most rational person in the room. Outside, in the hurling rain that strange figure of a man lurked by the incinerator, assuming that was where he remained.

Behind the cloud, Adam knew that the moon would be losing its shine and taking on a sanguine

163

hue. For a while it seemed to him that fear was the most sensible response to the current situation, although not the gripping, coiling sort of fear he was experiencing, fear that rose in him and contorted his guts, fear that periodically rendered him on the precipice of panic.

Adam stilled his terrified soul by attempting to make sense of the situation, even though he suspected there was not much sense to be made. Throughout his performance, Juan had sat next to Philip, a strategic choice as he was both directly in front of the stage and almost brushing shoulders with his apparent competition. Adam hardly knew Philip, and felt not a ripple of attraction for him. He wasn't drawn to petite, wiry men and Philip was too particular, too exacting in his deportment and his judgments to be anything other than an arm's length acquaintance. Besides, Philip displayed no indication he was attracted to men. They were neighbours, nothing more. Which made it all the more regrettable that he'd divulged to Philip his private life in that earlier moment of embarrassing vulnerability.

For an inexplicable reason Juan had it fixed in his mind that Adam was drawn to the man. That they were colluding towards a tryst. It was a ludicrous and baseless suspicion and Adam suspected that beneath the absence of logic lurked an irrational motive, one bent on finding justification, however spurious, for his inflammatory nature. He wanted to punish Adam, to hurt him. Even after all this time apart he seemed to carry a sense of ownership. Their separation, which one would expect might lessen his attachment, only serving to inflate his dudgeon.

Yet again Adam was desperate to get away. With

his set over, he'd fulfilled his obligation, and he could at least try to get home. He was sure to make it. Luck would be on his side, he reasoned, eclipse or no eclipse.

What was stopping him?

With Delilah's victuals consumed, Joshua and Ed made their way back to the stage and arranged themselves as best they could in amongst the sound equipment. Before Adam had a chance to get up and leave, Joshua played an open G chord and Ed drew his bow across his violin strings, and Adam knew it was rude to walk out on another performer's set. Benny had drilled it into all of them often enough. Defeated, he sat back in his seat.

'One of us is out of tune,' Joshua said aloud, but with an understanding smile.

'It'll be me.'

Ed twiddled and plucked until they both agreed that the G sound coming out of his violin was the G of Joshua's guitar.

They were about to commence the first song when there was a flash of lightning, followed closely by the boom and rumble of thunder. Rain pounded the roof. Untroubled, Joshua pressed on regardless, launching into a lively if scarcely audible shanty. Adam's gaze drifted to the barrel that barred the door. Like Hannah and Cynthia, he hoped no emergency gave cause for a rapid exit, or they'd all be scrambling to get out through the back. Before long he noticed a patch of dark on the carpet. The rain had found its way in.

He turned to Delilah and made a discreet gesture. She followed his gaze, and promptly stood and went to the bar, returning shortly after with a comment about needing to see to the gutters.

Hannah walked by with a bundle of towels, rolling them up and placing them on the floor and shoving them against the bottom of the door with her foot where she could gain access. She was as indifferent to the task as if she'd done the same many times before and had little interest in preserving the carpet.

The result, the barrel and now the towels, shut out the unfriendly weather along with any draft that might have gone some meagre way to freshening the air.

Hannah looked meaningfully at her watch on her way back to the bar.

'I wonder sometimes why I keep her on,' Delilah said when she was safely out of earshot.

'Hannah?' Adam said. 'I suppose she does seem out of sorts.'

'Her and Nathan have had a tiff,' she said, tilting her head his way. 'She's furious with him for betraying her but I can't imagine what she expects with an attitude like that.'

Adam refrained from asking with whom, or even how Delilah knew.

Alf heaved himself up off his chair and with a nod of acknowledgement to Delilah, made his way through to the kitchen.

Adam took a slug of his wine but Delilah hadn't finished. 'Hardly surprising, considering,' she said, breathing into his ear. 'You'd think with a god-abiding mother like Rebekah, she'd have developed a modicum of grace but I think she takes after her father, although you wouldn't know it to look at her.' She made a show of staring at the nook before turning back to Adam. 'David's in disgrace,' she said without lowering her voice. 'It's a wonder the general store stays in business with the likes of him at the helm. And I have to say I'm amazed he shows his face in here, as if he's as innocent as a new born.' She pulled back, drawing breath, but Adam could tell she had more to say. He waited.

'I don't suppose you know,' she went on, 'that he's been salivating over pornography. Rebekah caught him one day last week, in the shed with his fly un-done, all hot and bothered pouring over the crudest imagery Burton has ever seen. He'd been hiding the paraphernalia under some flowerpots. All whips and chains and nubile females apparently. Disgusting, don't you think?' She paused expectantly but when Adam made no comment she said, 'Although I can't blame him. Not entirely.'

'How do you know all this?'

'I popped into the store the other day and found Rebekah distraught. Must have been just after the dis-covery. Fortunately, I was able to offer her comfort. Yet she has to take responsibility for her part in all this. She's been cheating on him for years.'

'No,' Adam said. He was stunned, not only by the content of her tattle, but that she was speaking to him at all. She'd never before divulged to him gossip such as this. Not once.

'Adam, there are three in their bed: David, her, and God. It's only natural he'd turn somewhere else for satisfaction.' She paused again and studied his face. 'There, I've shocked you.' She sat back in her seat, head held imperiously high. 'There's a lot about Burton you don't know.'

Adam tried to listen to Joshua's song, but his

thoughts ran helter-skelter over Delilah's revelations. He was still assimilating the scene of a grotesquely corpulent David pouring over lewd images, with his chubby hand pulling at his member when Delilah again leaned towards him and said, 'Now I've never been that churchy, despite my father being the pastor. I followed the rules and did what I was told, but my heart was never in it. Your heart has to be, otherwise what sort of religious person are you?' She paused. 'You're not religious?'

'He shook his head.

'No? Good.' She glanced at Cynthia bobbing in her seat to the music.

'And frankly I cannot understand why anyone would wish to invest their energies in unseen entities, especially when it warps their attitudes and leads them to excessive displays of emotion. Tell me, what is the difference between Rebekah and Cynthia? Not much when it comes down to it. And you know our old church stifled our will with inhibitions and strictures of every kind. Those like Rebekah are not living their own lives at all. She's still kowtowing to an arbitrary script if you ask me.' She sniffed sharply. 'And look where it all ends up. Licentiousness: Rebekah with God, David with pornography and Nathan with heaven knows who.' She paused. 'I wonder what Hannah's been up to.' And her voice trailed off.

He couldn't be sure if her revelations were true, except that it was clear to him having heard their earlier exchange that a betrayal of some sort had occurred between Nathan and Hannah.

He never expected Delilah to hold a critical view of her former faith. He knew little about the worshippers in Burton who'd frequented his church, who'd sat in pews, gathered for Bible study, stood before the altar resplendent in a wedding gown, or lying dead in a coffin. He hadn't been inclined to give any of that traction in his imagination. Besides, he'd been too focused on the renovations and Juan's incendiary temper, spending all of his time anxious about one or the other.

Whenever he came to the Sessions all he'd seen was a bunch of local musicians of varying talent, and Benny, another outsider, carrying the night on his competent shoulders.

In The Cabin, Benny had been larger than life. He talked to everyone, laughed and joked and told his yarns, and Adam hadn't bothered forging relationships with the others much beyond casual exchanges, for there had been no need. To him, The Cabin regulars were foremost musicians. Or they were music lovers. Not religious freaks. While he had heard the odd rumour about Pastor Makepeace disgracing himself, he'd never taken it seriously.

He thought about Delilah's words some more. It seemed to make sense of a sort that Delilah would conjure a way of excusing David for his actions, in the same way she would have found a way to excuse her father. Blame god, and everyone was absolved.

He recalled an incident the other week, when Rebekah had been cleaning his house. The original layout of the building was much the same, a wide vestibule with a room to the left and the right, rooms that served as kitchen and bathroom, rooms in which Rebekah performed most of her cleaning duties. The vestibule led on through double doors to a cavernous hall with arched windows set high in the walls, and an uninspiringly plain cathedral ceiling. The vestry at the back was now his bedroom. He'd been readying to leave for work when Rebekah accosted him in the hall. In the previous weeks she'd taken it upon herself to meticulously dust the bookshelves that lined the end wall. 'So many books,' she was fond of saying whenever she passed by. He'd inherited many of them, acquired a number from second-hand book-stores and charity shops and while he had barely read a tenth of the collection, it was his pride and entirely befitted the building. Rebekah was standing squarely, hands on hips, dust cloth hanging from the pocket of her apron, her wide bulk and black-rimmed glasses reminiscent of his old school teacher. Her expression was furious.

'Far be it from me to tell you how to live your life in your own home,' she said sharply.

Inwardly he was five again, head held low in shame.

'What is it Rebekah?'

'This filth,' she growled, pointing at a section of the bottom shelf, where he kept a series of volumes on erotic art and a copy of the Kama Sutra.

'They're only...'

'This church should never have been sold. We were a devoted congregation. We could have rallied to save the building, save it from desecration. This was and still is a house of God.' Her eyes welled with tears. But the lament in her voice gave way to censori-ousness. 'And He does not allow such evil literature. You have to understand that you are a custodian. Just because you own the building doesn't mean you can turn it to ill-repute.' She took a breath and her tome changed again, this time it was almost imploring. 'God is in these very walls, Adam, in every length of timber, watching on, judging, and at times forgiving. You must repent. You must throw out that smut and start afresh.'

He offered no reply. What on earth could he have said?

He reminded himself that he was her employer. He could have dismissed her, marched her from his home, but instead of outrage, he pitied her and to some extent was amused by her, even as his skin prickled with humiliation.

He glanced over at Rebekah, seated staunchly in the nook, focused on her knitting. She'd been giving him withering stares all evening, zealot that she was, and now he pitied David, married, trapped, forced to resort to ogling illicit images to satisfy his urges. Delilah was right: There were three in that bed, David squashed to the edge to make way for her god. He'd done nothing wrong. He had caused no harm.

Yet should she be judged the cause of his actions? She didn't force him to resort to satiating himself in that way. So who was at fault? Was anyone at fault? Did it matter? David's actions hardly constituted betrayal. He wasn't molesting young girls. He hadn't even had an affair. It was difficult to imagine a man as corpulent as him having the capacity for allure. It occurred to Adam that it might not even be true. It wasn't the sort of thing Rebekah would admit and especially to Delilah. He found with distaste that he was caught up in the affairs of others, buying in to Delilah's gossip and harsh condemnations, and really, if it had happened, Rebekah was only being true to her beliefs. For her, pornography was abhorrent, and in her view even his books on erotica were pornography. Perhaps that's why she'd reacted so strongly, diverting her hurt over her husband's masturbatory inclinations to Adam's bookcase.

Yet how easily he'd fallen in sway with Delilah's analysis. There she sat in her purple gown, the matriarch of Burton, holding court over lost souls seeking companionship and a chance to play their songs. And through her censure she kept everyone in their place, at the mercy of her loose and venomous tongue.

He knew he had not escaped her gossiping mind. Perhaps she blamed him for Juan's angry outbursts. That it was his fault Juan hit him. That he'd provoked, through his anxiety, his eggshell existence, even his very being, those wild punches and kicks. Or that he'd done or said the wrong thing, inadvertently pressed the trigger of the gun Juan held pointed at his head. Is that what she thought? What others thought?

How many in the room would stand by and not defend him if Juan's umbrage filtered into his fists?

His mind sagged with the enormity. He could do nothing but pay heed to the stage.

Joshua and Ed were playing a shanty, with rolling rhythms and plenty of gusto. Ed bent and swayed and his convoluted melodies blended well with Joshua's round vocals and repetitive chord sequences. The song was indistinct, really no more than a blur of every traditional folk song he'd ever heard: hale and hearty and a touch humorous in places.

Joshua carried his songs perfectly well, his burly hairy frame the perfect complement for his shanties. There he stood, tall and proud, full of unquestioning acceptance of things as he found them, things as they should be. Except that Adam was well aware he didn't fall into Joshua's 'should be' categories. Joshua maintained his guard in his vicinity and avoided conversation, his normally garrulous good humour instantly monosyllabic.

Joshua and Ed played a short set. When Joshua thanked the audience and made to leave the stage, Cynthia left her seat and headed to the bathroom via the kitchen. Delilah watched her go, folding her arms under her bosom in a posture of disapproval, for Cynthia had not asked permission and normally no one other than her and Hannah were allowed beyond the bar.

Joshua had only just clipped shut his guitar case when Cynthia hurried back into the room in a terrible state. She clutched a side of the counter with each hand, bent low and emitted a piercing cry.

'I told you,' she gasped, pointing at Adam with a wavering finger, 'and you took no heed.'

Instantly ashamed, Adam felt compelled to apologise. But Delilah turned in her seat.

'Cynthia!'

Cynthia straightened and cast an eye about the room. The effect was dramatic, and she knew it. 'All the lights in the female bathroom are blown,' she said. Then she lowered her voice to a conspiratorial whisper, as if her previous outburst of terror had been an aberration. 'I had to fumble in the dark. I hadn't even entered a cubicle when the strip light above the mirror flickered on of its own accord.' She paused, and raised her hands to her face. Her eyes widened. 'And behind me,' she said, her voice rising in pitch and volume, 'walking out of the gloom...was the ghost...of Benny Muir,' she breathed.

There was a murmur of disbelief. Cynthia went on a ramble about how her predictions were never wrong and the greatest curse of her life was that no

ISOBEL BLACKTHORN

one believed her. And she was right, they didn't. Rebekah was knitting, Joshua and Ed were laughing at
some private joke, Nathan and Hannah were in their
own tense world at the bar, and Philip hadn't turned
round.

It was then that Alf, who'd slipped out at the start
of Delilah's malicious divulgences, emerged from the
kitchen, entering the bar behind Cynthia who was
blocking his path.

'You're using the female toilet now, I take it?'
Delilah said.

Everyone looked over at the bar and there was a
ripple of laughter and exchanges of told-you-so looks.
Adam had a private sigh of relief.

Despite the obvious cause of her ghostly sighting,
Cynthia remained inconsolable. 'It wasn't Alf,' she
said over and again.

As though sensing the growing impatience for the
night to be over, Delilah went over and coaxed Cynthia through to the kitchen.

'Come on old geezer. You look like death warmed
up,' Juan said, addressing Alf from behind the microphone and laughing at his own quip.

No one joined in his mirth.

There was a brief period of silence, then Ed
called out from the back of the room with, 'In Burton,
no one's an old geezer.'

A look of surprise flashed into Juan's face. 'Because everyone's an old geezer here. Right? Welcome
to Burton, home to old geezers.' He grinned at an un-
receptive audience. Philip glanced back and caught
Adam's eye with a knowing smile.

He didn't smile back. Instead he turned his gaze
to the bar, where Alf was taking no heed of Cyn-

thia's outburst. Hannah was nowhere in sight. Nathan, displaying none of his earlier drunkenness, sat with his back to the bar, watching on with amusement.

Juan left the stage and made his way down the room. When he reached the bar, Ed called out, 'Not a good idea to ridicule our town, mate.'

Juan froze where he stood then swung round. His eyes were sharp, his body rigid. He went and towered over Ed, so close he almost pinned him to the back wall. Then he threw out his hands, palms open as if in a defensive gesture, but the effect was anything but. 'It was a joke. Okay? Only a joke. You need to develop a sense of humour.'

'I have a sense of humour, thanks,' Ed said, holding Juan's gaze.

'I don't see any sign of one.'

'Juan,' Joshua said sharply. 'Back off.'

'It's just stage banter. And I shouldn't need to an-swer to anyone for it, least of all him,' he said, giving the air before Ed's face a finger stab.

And with that he left the room, marching off through the kitchen.

Philip turned around in his seat. 'Are you alright?' he said, his china-blue eyes searching Adam's face.

'As well as can be expected, I suppose.'

'He's a loose cannon. I really thought he was going to attack you then.'

'Me?'

'It was the way he looked at you on his way by. You didn't notice?'

'No.'

'You must have been looking back at Ed. I'll save you for later—that's how I read his face.'

Adam shifted in his seat. He didn't want to be hearing this.

'Look,' Philip said with genuine concern. He reached out and put a hand on the table as if to grab Adam's arm. Adam shot a quick look around the room. Juan had not returned. Philip went on. 'I want you to know I'm here for you. If there's anything I can do, anything at all, to keep you out of harm's way, just say the word. That man is psychotic and unpredictable, as you must know.'

'Thank you.'

'Don't mention it,' he said, leaving his arm extended, his hand on the table inches from Adam's elbow.

Adam resisted an impulse to pull away.

'After all, it's the least I can do, considering we're neighbours. I can't imagine what it must have been like living with him. I feel bad not being there for you.'

'You didn't know.'

'I know now.'

He wanted to feel relieved but the offer made him uneasy. For it was Philip who had catalysed Juan's jealousy on more than one occasion. Besides, it was easy to say and a lot harder to actualize the restraining of an incendiary Juan. He doubted Philip would even try.

The clouds parted, and the room was cast in muted red-tinged moonlight. As Philip turned back in his seat Adam saw a shadow pass across the table. He looked up at the window in time to see the back of Juan's head slide away. How long had he been there?

Adam's heart pulsed. Philip's hand on table, reaching for his. Juan right outside, looking on. The timing felt staged as if it were a conspiracy, not of two mortals, but celestial; the intersection of seemingly independent events—Philip's hand, Juan's gaze— along with the Moon glowing blood red and it seemed to Adam that he'd dithered long enough. He made up his mind to leave the moment Juan came back inside.

CHAPTER TWELVE

EVA'S DIARY – SUNDAY 21ST DECEMBER

I have to marvel at how spontaneously memory is triggered through a simple re-enactment of a task. I had it in mind to visit Adam. It was Sunday, yet Philip was at work at Alf's. The day was sunny and warm, the mist all but cleared save for the deeps of the valley where the river flowed. I wended my way about the garden, picking herbs for a bouquet, a small offering in return for Adam's generosity the other day. I chose rosemary, lavender, sage and thyme, all in flower with their exquisitely small purple petals. I placed the flowers in the large, flat-bottomed wicker basket that lived on the stoop by the back door. It was mother's basket. The one she used to collect her flowers. With the basket filled, I wandered inside. As I set the basket down on the kitchen table, those flower-gathering days came back to me in all their fullness.

After an outing we would return, basket full, and mother would set about gathering her special teapots. She was a slender woman, always garbed in a plain blue dress, her long hair pinned back at the nape of her neck and held in place with a small cotton head-scarf. To me she was sagely. She would let me pick off the flower heads and pop them in the pots until there was enough and she'd pour on boiling water and let the brew steep.

I pictured Mother reaching under the sink where she kept her bottles of alcohol and vinegar. The way she'd strew the table with little glass jars. She always let me line up the jars and cram them with flowers. She would pour on the liquid until the flowers were covered. We had to wait while they steeped. Then, reserving much of the liquid in the jars, she would pour the flowers of each jar into a mortar and ground the flowers into a mash of fine bits, before returning the mash to the jar to continue steeping. She'd let me screw the lids on tightly. Afterwards she'd brush clean the wicker basket and return it to the stoop.

It wasn't just Mother's flat-bottomed wicker basket that Philip had kept. He'd kept all of mother's things. Her knick-knacks were scattered throughout the house, many where she had placed them, a memory in every room. He must have loved her dearly, for there was a time when they'd been close. She would fuss over him always and despite it all. For Philip had been a difficult child, so the town says, and Mother had her hands full with him long before I, or our brother Aiden, had come along. She had him too young, according to the gossip, for she was barely an adult herself when he came, being just seventeen, and newly wedded to Father.

They all went to church in those days, for Burton was a god-fearing town and old Pastor Prentice would preach all manner of warnings, lest his flock fall to temptation. He imbued his sermons with vivid promises of eternity in fiery hell to those who dared sin. Pastor Prentice had been preaching for the previous fifty years, back when Burton Road West was a narrow, overgrown track fit only for horse and cart, and no one dared question his authority.

Mother must have been mortified when she fell pregnant so soon after wedlock for she couldn't be sure the moment of conception wasn't before the nuptials. Rumour had it that in fact she was convinced it had been before, Father being something of a horny stud in the weeks leading up to their wedding, privately shunning Pastor Prentice's missives about sexual morality. His interest waned soon after, as if his desire were aroused only by the illicit and forbidden nature of their couplings. She had been terrified someone would do the maths and she'd suffer the humiliation of a public confession and certain excommunication, with the added threat that most likely the child would die. If it be God's will, so be it. All this Mother took to her grave and it was at her funeral that Delilah drew me aside and confided the tale, insisting I ought to know for it may explain a lot.

Which indeed it did, for every time Philip had misbehaved it must have been further confirmation for Mother that he'd been conceived out of wedlock and was therefore illegitimate, unworthy and doomed to hell. A belief confirmed when Pastor Prentice fell down dead at the pulpit during Philip's Christening and hadn't managed the blessing. A heart attack, they say.

It was a curious union of truths. Not that I would go so far as to call my brother evil. But growing up, his deeds were nasty, especially to me: cricket balls aimed at me and not my bat, a foot stuck out to trip me up, pinches, pokes and punches, and brutal Chinese burns. That he never seemed to receive Mother's approval, that she looked at him strangely sometimes, only exacerbated his nastiness in my eyes. He needed that trait beaten out of him and while I felt sorry for him that day Father lashed him with the buckle end of his belt, all because of a dispute over a bowl of jelly, Philip needed that shock. I certainly needed him to get that shock, for he was never nasty to me again and I can't imagine any other way I might have achieved that grace.

He'd been punished before, smacked and made to stand in corners, but never belted. I don't know what possessed Father that day, but I am grateful.

And Burton was grateful when Pastor Prentice passed on, the whole town breathing a relieved sigh and for a short while the Kinsfolk relaxed.

It didn't take long for a replacement to be found.

Pastor Makepeace was a corpulent man, middle-aged and stooped, with a hooked nose and a pair of beady eyes. He came from the coast with his wife and his teenage daughter Delilah, and a raft of new ideas on how to curb savagery.

Philip and I grew close after his thrashing. For a short while we were inseparable. I forgot the jelly in-cident and all of Philip's former cruelties. I felt secure with my filial companion and even when Philip be-came a teenager, all secretive and strange, and I felt somewhat rejected and abandoned, there remained that sibling bond.

It was at Philip's twenty-first birthday party that I discovered another horrible truth about him.

Mother had baked a fine cake and invited our Kinsfolk friends. The Sandhursts came with Nathan, then a lanky teenager, the Plums along with Alf, and Rebekah and David with a precocious Hannah. My best friend Sophie Flemington was there too.

It was a cool autumn day and we were all gathered round a bonfire in the back garden. Delilah had strung bunting between some trees. Alf was umpiring a bob-the-apple competition, which Philip looked set to win. It was then that I went to the kitchen for a glass of water.

There I found Mother and Delilah making tea. I could tell I'd come in on a private conversation and fortunately they were huddled together with their backs to the door and didn't notice me. Delilah was recounting a time shortly after I was born, when Philip had stood over my pram with his hands clasped behind his back.

'Must have been three and all cute in his shorts and neat socks,' Delilah said. 'He had no idea I was there. He went away and came back soon after with a cushion and a purposeful look on his face as if he'd made up his mind to do something and was determined to carry it out.'

Mother stiffened, teapot in hand.

'I recognised the cushion as yours, Dora. The one that lives on your rocking chair. And lucky I was there for the rascal raised it up and squashed it down over poor Eva's face. That's when I raced forward. He cried out and ran back inside the house. I don't think he knew what he was doing, mind. Any more than a cat. They smother babies, you know. Maybe that's how he got the idea.'

'I knew nothing of this,' Dora said, moving away.

'Well, how could you? Although I'm surprised you didn't hear the commotion. You must have been out the back. I can tell you he was horrified, Dora. I found him howling in his room and saying it wasn't fair and that he hated that baby. I told him, Dora. I told him in words a three-year-old could understand. I told him that he didn't really hate her. That his mummy's heart was big enough for them both and I promised I wouldn't tell if he promised never to do it again.'

My mother gasped.

'It was our secret,' Delilah said with a defensive ring in her voice. 'I thought that now he's an adult you should know. I couldn't break the promise until now, Dora, could I? It's a relief to be telling you. Quite a burden to carry, I can tell you.'

'You should have told me.'

'But you do see my predicament. If I had, and he found out, then not only would I have betrayed him, I would have given him every reason to do it again. Anyway, it's all turned out fine. He obviously didn't try again,' she said, 'because she's still here, your Eva. And look how they've both turned out. They're a credit to you, Dora.'

'You're too kind.'

She sounded doubtful. By then I'd long known she regarded her first born with suspicion. She'd always been guarded and poised to remonstrate him for the smallest misdemeanour, culminating, in that one treacherous act, when she sided with Aiden when she should have sided with Philip.

I never forgave her for that and the loyalty I displayed to Philip from that day has paid dividends. I still have a true brother and ally. I hated Aiden all the more for causing the entire fiasco with that grubby little fist in Philip's jelly and I've not eaten jelly since, out of protest.

I would have been about eight when I started making flower tinctures of my own. On days when Father was working, Mother and Aiden at the shops, and Philip down by the river, fishing, I would steal one of Mother's rubber gloves and pick all the poisonous flowers I could find. I recall stealing one of Mother's empty jam jars and sneaking into the kitchen for her alcohol. I'd take a little each time, so she wouldn't notice. I pounded up the flowers as best I could and steeped them in the alcohol, over time filling the jar with a concoction of every poisonous flower in the neighbourhood. I had no idea about quantities. My theory was if I made enough and mixed all the poisons together, then one day I'd have a poison potent enough to kill. The power of it made me tingle inside, although I never planned to use it. That would have been silly. It was just a childish game. That was all.

The door to the church was open when I arrived. I climbed the wooden steps and entered the vestibule. Things were not as I recalled. Freshly plastered and painted brilliant white, the vestibule had none of the heavy dark wood panelling and drab green lining boards of old. The floorboards had been sanded and polished to reveal the grain and a decorative ceramic pot sat in each of the far corners. I called out and Adam appeared in the doorway on the right.

'This is a lovely surprise,' he said.

I entered the kitchen, neat and tidy but basic, old kitchen units placed in situ without much care and at variance with the wall tiles, the only redeeming feature a handcrafted table of finest oak with elegantly turned legs, positioned in the centre of the room.

I handed him the bouquet. He raised it to his nose and sniffed. 'Delightful,' he said, and produced a small vase.

'I wanted to thank you for the other day,' I said, feeling suddenly bashful.

'There's really no need. Tea?' He filled a kettle and set about gathering cups and saucers.

I looked around. The door to the entrance hall was painted on one side only. The back, facing into the kitchen, had been sanded back to reveal various colours of old paint. The skirting boards were partially painted, and a single coat of white paint had been smeared on the architraves and doorway reveals. A paint tin sat on the floor by the rubbish bin, a brush wrapped in cling wrap resting on top. I had no idea how Adam could stand to be, let alone cook, in such a half-done room.

The kitchen used to be where us Kinsfolk children of Burton were to varying degrees forced to have Bible study. Every Wednesday after school us Stone children would sit with Nathan and a few others in a circle on the floor, along with little Miss Fisher, while her mother, Rebekah, lectured us on the finer points of Scripture. I was an obedient child but even I had my limits and one time, when Joshua and Ed came to repair a broken windowpane, I all but lost control.

Rebekah was seated with her back to the window when in strode Joshua, toolbox in hand. With a brief acknowledgement to Rebekah, he made his way round the group. Hannah, who was seated beside her mother, turned in her chair to look behind her. When she turned back her face wore a wicked grin. She caught my eye before turning back to the window. Rebekah continued reading. I remember it was a long and tedious passage from Timothy. She was in my line of sight, so I leaned to my left to see past her, and there was Ed Smedley's visage, framed by the window.

Ed was a spritely man with an odd sense of humour, his comments sometimes strange and hard to understand. He didn't live by the social mores of Burton, not that his were amoral, just self-created and at times bizarre. He would be seen on Sundays, a day of worship, mowing the nature strips along Burton Road West, a task for which he was employed, but his choice of day was viewed as sacrilege. Apart from Joshua, he despised the Kinsfolk and seemed to take much delight in disrupting our Bible study. Glimpsing him through the window, I could tell that he was perched on a ladder. The window was in the eastern side of the building where the knoll upon which the church was built fell away to meet a flatter area. There, Rebekah had attempted to create a rockery.

While Joshua was rummaging through his toolbox, Ed pressed his face against the windowpane so that his nose went flat. Then he withdrew his face and poked out his tongue. Hannah poked out her tongue in reply. I suppressed a giggle. The exchange of tongue poking went on for some time as Rebekah read, oblivious to the goings on, until all of us were sneaking looks at Hannah and Ed.

At last Joshua found what he was looking for and at the sight of Ed's teasing, he shot a look at the group and said, 'Pack it in, Hannah.'

Upon hearing his remonstration, Rebekah stood

up and swung round, right where Adam now stood. It was in that moment that Ed's face disappeared from the window and we found out soon after that he'd fallen off the ladder and onto Rebekah's carefully arranged rocks.

'Hannah Fisher, this is your fault,' growled Joshua, much to everyone's surprise, for she was a child, precocious but no more than five, and Ed a fully-grown adult in his middle age. I never could puzzle out why Joshua was so quick to apportion blame.

They didn't do much of a repair. Looking at it now, that window, like all the other windows in Adam's kitchen, needed replacing. It was in such a bad state.

Adam must have read the expression on my face. 'The other parts of the building are in better repair,' he said apologetically. 'But I'm afraid I'm not much of a renovator and Juan left me with an awful lot still to do. I keep meaning to paint but I so quickly lose heart and soon forget about the paint and the brushes.'

'This is a lovely table,' I said, not knowing what else to say.

'You like it? Would you like me to show you around?'

I followed him thinking that a paintbrush left wrapped in cling film atop its paint tin would have driven me crazy.

He led me into the main hall, with its cathedral ceiling aspiring to godliness. The hall appeared cavernous without the seating and the altar table. In their stead, set against the brilliant white walls and polished boards, two luxurious looking sofas faced each other across an astrakhan rug. There was nothing else in the room, save for the books that filled the entire far wall.

I went over and scanned the shelves, turning my head sideways to read the spines. Adam left me, returning a short while later with a tray of tea things, to find me seated on one of the sofas, legs curled beneath me and a book on my lap. It was a volume of Egon Schiele's work and I was admiring his drawings of nudes, with their twisted body shapes, one in particular, all plump breasts and splayed legs.

Adam hesitated and seemed taken aback.

'Fabulous,' I said, raising the book and smiling up at him as he set down the tray on a small table centred on the rug.

'I was worried the whole of Burton despised such things,' he said with a nervous laugh.

'Has Rebekah discovered them?'

'She was very upset.'

'I dare say.'

I closed the book and placed it down on the cushion next to me, and set about putting him straight on the strict religious devotees of Burton old, how most had died, or moved away when the church was sold, how no one took any notice anymore except one or two diehards like Rebekah. Delilah's faith lapsed long ago. Cynthia was never a believer and Alf only went because his parents had made him. I told him my own parents were devotees right up until the day they died but neither me, nor Philip, were practitioners of any faith. 'You needn't worry,' I said. 'The church is in much better hands. What you've done here is magnificent.'

He looked relieved and genuinely pleased. I watched him pour tea from an elegant tea pot, tea strainer hovering over first one cup then the other, thinking it must be lonely for him living all the way out here amid the mountains.

'Milk?' he asked and I answered in the affirmative, adding that I required no sugar.

He passed me a cup, bone china with a delicate handle, and I took a sip of the aromatic tea and asked him how he was finding things here.

'Fine. It's a beautiful spot. Especially the river.'

He offered me a biscuit, which I declined. It was all so dainty, to be served tea and biscuits from a tray of fine bone china.

'You like the river?'

'Very much,' he said, taking his cup and settling back into the opposite sofa. 'Shame it isn't better maintained. The old river path is in shambles.'

'You've been down there?'

'Once.'

'We used to play down there,' I said.

'You and Philip?'

I didn't answer. My chest tightened. A nerve pulsed in my thigh, sending a deliciously sharp ripple through my loins. Suddenly I wanted to part my legs, reach down, enjoy a slippery moment or two beneath his uncertain gaze. But I quashed my desire. Oblivious, he sipped his tea.

'There's a grassy clearing,' I said casually, 'where the river makes a wide bend and the sun shines.'

'Alf told me about it.'

'You've not been that far?' I asked, taking another sip of my tea, enjoying its remarkable aroma.

'Hardly. Someone needs to attack that path with a brush cutter.' He laughed.

'Best leave things as they are,' I said in a tone that

was a little too serious. 'No one uses the path these days,' I added lightly.

'Perhaps that's why.'

We were silent for a while and I continued sipping my tea. He observed me with those round brown eyes and my earlier awkwardness returned. I set down my cup and fingered the corner of the book beside me. I broached the topic of his renovations, but he was vague and evasive.

The tea seemed to go right through me and I asked if I could pop to the bathroom. He told me where to find it. With much anticipation in my belly, I left him seated on his sofa, his feet nestled in his astrakhan rug.

Alas, it was not the resplendent bathroom commensurate with Adam's taste and lifestyle and my anticipation crumbled like a stale biscuit.

It was a sad room, a scruffy room, a dilapidated room, entirely out of keeping with all that Adam was. Bare floorboards, scrunched newspaper rammed in cracks around the window frames, a lavatory of green porcelain chipped about the rim, a pedestal basin with a dripping tap, a brown stain fanning out from where the drip hit the basin, all the way to the plughole. The shower was over the bath, screened by a bland curtain spotted with mould, and the bath itself was narrow and coloured the same dismal green.

When I returned to the hall I hid my dismay, but I was no longer in the mood for Adam's company.

I made small talk for another five minutes, then I said, 'I better go.'

'So soon?'

'Things to do,' I said apologetically, keen to squeeze in a bath before Philip returned.

'Take the book,' he offered.

'I better not.'

He seemed disappointed. 'Do visit again soon if you like.'

'I'd like that,' I lied.

He saw me to the door.

CHAPTER THIRTEEN

PHILIP

I studied my bottle of beer. Condensation had softened the label and I worried a corner, rubbing away the description of the contents, before setting the bottle back on the table. Why was it always my fault? That was the question I contended with. Always blamed for things that have nothing to do with me. Seems to be a narrative theme of my life.

All I'd done was rest my hand on Adam's table, inches from his, and I'd leaned forward for the sake of discretion, as I hadn't wanted to embarrass the man. I'd offered him my support, upon what I suppose was a stab of conscience, an impulse I regretted even as I followed through, it being remiss of me, or so I thought, to neglect his welfare. He was clearly a strong and nimble man, perhaps capable of taking care of himself, although lacking Eva's wiles and strength of character, and definitely weak of will. What was it in the strong that they should seek to protect the weak? An instinct as basic as life itself. Juan was an animal. Of that I was sure, and it takes more than one person to stand up to something like him. I'd paid heed to a primal call and on reflection felt proud to have done so.

I kept returning to the fact that I had to show concern for Adam. It appeared to me at the time the right thing to do. Cynthia might be as nutty as a fruitcake but in this case, she was right: Adam was in mortal danger. Juan's rage might latch on to whoever was his momentary target but it was Adam he had in his sights. After Juan's outburst at Ed I had been quite prepared to set aside my abhorrence of Adam's sexual appetite and offer him support. For Ed was just the entrée. More like a nibble on a peanut to stave off the hunger of a bear, whetting the appetite for the feast to follow. Odd how fickle the mind is in the face of perversion.

I hadn't planned to frighten Adam with my remarks. Only to offer protection, but his reaction was strange, looking down at the floor then glancing around, as if he didn't value or wish for my support, and I found that impossible to understand. He ought to have been grateful and relieved to find a true ally in the midst, for who else would stand up to Juan? Rebekah, David and Alf were incapable, Hannah too limp and feeble although I dare say she could fight like a cat if she had to, Cynthia wasn't even a consideration, which left Ed, Joshua and Delilah. Joshua could be formidable when roused but he's a staunch homophobe and would more likely have shrugged his shoulders and left Juan to it. Ed might have defended Adam but his loyalty was to Joshua and he wouldn't wish to be seen to be disloyal: A leech needs its host. Delilah was capable of the most imperious control yet in the face of physical violence, she would most likely retreat to a safe place. Which left me.

Given the circumstances, if I were in Adam's shoes I would have made a point of demonstrating my gratitude to secure my protection, thence my life. Instead, throughout our exchange, he avoided my gaze. I began to wonder if I would bother to assist him should Juan finally explode. What was the point in putting myself in Juan's way to save a victim who shunned so flagrantly my humble offer of assistance? It was counter-intuitive. I'd be making his situation worse, adding to his pain chagrin that I'd gone against his wishes. Surely it was better to grant him autonomy to choose his own fate than to interfere? What right did I have to override his will, do what I thought best over what he knew was best for him? It would have been wrong, I decided, and I settled in my seat comfortable in the knowledge that when the moment came I would do the right thing, which was nothing.

It was a decision sealed when I recalled how he'd glanced at the window, and a look of alarm had appeared in his face. I'd followed his gaze but saw nothing. A dim red glow of moonlight disappeared behind the clouds and beyond the window was black. Whatever he'd seen was gone, or perhaps it was the hue of the moon that startled him. After that, Adam had stood up abruptly, downed his wine and gone to the bar. I was stung. It was a blatant rebuff of my offer and I wish I'd never made it.

And there I was, instantly back to thinking he was becoming more like Cynthia by the minute and I half expected him to have a weird turn and rant that the beetles were out to get him.

The storm was much the same. A nagging wind and heavy rain and the occasional bolt of lightning. The Cabin still had power, which was remarkable with at least two trees down. We were trapped and maybe there was no harm in that, but to avert my tendency to claustrophobia, I had to keep reminding myself of the exit through the kitchen. The Cabin was a sturdy structure, I reasoned. Better to be here than in many places in Burton. The fug of incense couldn't mask the smell of rotting corpse but I was used to stenches. It seemed all in the room that night, except for Adam, were used to stenches as well. And Delilah's Christmas fare had certainly lightened the mood. A little buttery for my taste, and I wouldn't partake of victuals mauled by those fungus-infested fingers, but the others didn't notice or mind her offerings.

Not even Cynthia's latest outburst had shaken the determination of everyone here to get on with the night. Juan's altercation with Ed left no residue, for the tension had dissipated once the exchange had ceased, neither Joshua or Ed having the insight that they were witnessing a slight release of an explosive pressure building inside their host.

With Alf on stage and Delilah tending to Cynthia in the kitchen after Alf had frightened her half to death, I was alone at my table as was Adam at his. It would be of interest to see where Juan situated himself once Alf commenced his set.

It was remarkable that he'd made it to the stage. His face was shiny with sweat, his eyes heavy, and there was a suffering downturn to his mouth. His guitar failed to mask the dollops of vomit staining his shirtfront and I noticed, glistening in the stage light, several globules attached to the plaits of his beard. From then on I was determined not to watch him.

There was the usual tribute to Benny, how he'd

been a loyal customer in his guitar shop, never bought his guitar strings from anyone else, apparently. How they'd chewed over musical days gone by, complained about the lack of well-paid concerts, and the prevalence of open stages in the region.

Someone coughed and I saw that Delilah had returned to the room with Cynthia. They hovered by the bar while Hannah fixed them both a drink.

Alf went on to voice his thoughts. He was well aware of the importance of grace behind the microphone, everyone duly thanked and acknowledged, yet on that Christmas Eve, probably due to his exceptionally poor health, he had done away with false gratitude in favour of a more controversial, almost acerbic stance when it came to musicians' remittances. It was to no avail. Delilah would pay no heed. Nothing was about to change and certainly not in Burton.

When he stopped speaking David said, 'Just get on with it.' He smirked to himself and looked around, adding, 'Daft toad.'

Someone gasped.

'Do you have to be so insulting?'

I allowed myself a private smile. Alf's retort, spoken with force through the microphone, had surely put that lump of blubber in its place.

No one spoke. Alf filled the silence with a few random chords, then he said, 'Some of us have no grace,' and he opened his set with his old-school Blues, his slide guitar releasing its twangy whine. I pitied his harmonica, receiving a good dose of his fetid breath and acrid spittle.

Cynthia and Delilah resumed their seats, bookending Adam. Juan had chosen to stand by the fireplace, arms folded across his chest and one ankle

crossed over the other in a posture that was at once
contrived and deceptive. For he was as far from relaxed as it was possible to be and while I could see
him in my side vision, I refrained from turning my
head, reluctant to goad him with so much as a glance
after my failed negotiation over the running order. It
was the worst slot and he knew it. The final act always performed to the stragglers and the grossly inebriated. He'd remained immutable and I, one of the
more talented acts in the room, had been relegated to
the last slot. Although on this occasion I would have a
captive audience.

Fortunately, Alf's playing was entertaining. He
was by far the best musician in Burton and all of the
surrounds. He had a knack of capturing the essence of
the river, although I was almost certain he sung of a
different river somewhere far away: The source, the
meandering journey, the speed as it raced through
channels carved in a narrow valley, the unexpected
deep downs where secrets lurked, the deceptively
strong current, the eddies, the cold that took away
your breath, then the widening, the slowing, the lazy
way it made its way to the coast.

Alf was a river man to his core, which was why I
didn't mind him. He was perceptive, yet discreet. He
kept his own counsel. Not someone I would confide
in, but then, I'm not the sort to confide. I've never felt
the impulse, never having carried anything I've
wanted to offload.

Alf had integrity. He lived a musical truth which
had to be admired, and it was a pity for him that his
family had come to Burton to live out their days, for
he belonged in one of the world's Blues capitals, rubbing shoulders with the greats, where he was sure to

have been a great himself. And Nathan would have announced his apologies for Alf's absence from behind the microphone, and asked someone else to play guitar in his stead. But here he was, Alf Plum, an undervalued master bluesman so ill he could barely stand, his shirt front blotted with vomit, a man at the end of his days, his insides rotting away, yet still he played.

Impressive.

His songs were short and he wasted no more time with banter. Without doubt his set was the high-water mark. When he sang his last chorus the night was set on a rapid descent: Hannah; Rebekah and David, who called themselves As Best Us Can, which wasn't much; then Delilah with her awful folk tales—that was the running order. Elevated once more by the final act: me.

During the applause, Juan slipped through to the kitchen and on outside to charge himself up again. I drained my glass and went to the bar. Hannah handed me a light beer before making her way to the stage in a hurry, presumably before anyone else came to order a drink. She seemed eager to be done with the night. Although I couldn't imagine why. Here was far superior to that cruddy little caravan she squatted in, parked up at the back of the general store.

I scanned the room, observed Adam seated like a dumb duckling between two mother ducks, then faced the bar and acknowledged Nathan with a weak smile.

I thought better than to portray hostility so I filled the palpable awkwardness rapidly building between us with, 'You two had a falling out?'

He looked at me strangely. I wondered if he knew about me and Hannah.

'I saw you arguing earlier,' I said lightly. 'Things not good between you?'

'You know the answer to that,' he said under his breath.

So he knew.

'I didn't mean it to happen. Honestly mate,' I said, suddenly relieved of the burden, finally able to convey the truth, for no doubt Hannah had embell-ished the couplings with all manner of twists.

'Is that right,' he stated flatly.

'She was upset. I offered her comfort.'

'So that's what you call comfort.'

I took offence. He ought to be believing me over that trollop of a girlfriend.

'If you must know,' I said with blunt honesty, '*she* took advantage of *me*. I'm the victim here.'

Nathan swung round, wrenching off his sun-glasses and baring his face. 'You saying she raped you, then.'

That rattled me. What right had he to apportion blame onto me for what happened? I had to set him straight. I replied to his vile accusation with, 'Look buddy. Your whore of a girlfriend uses her distress to coerce me into sex. Happy now?'

He leaned forward and hissed, 'And you know why she did it?'

It? Then he only knew about yesterday. A number of reasons sprang to mind but I was unpre-pared for his next remark.

'To get back at me for screwing your sister.' He released his words between gritted teeth.

And with that he stood and went straight to my

chair, sitting down jerkily, the questions that crowded my mind left to hang like carcasses on a butcher's hook, dead and ready for dissection.

When? That was my initial question. Could have been any time in the last decade. At first I thought it would have to be the last time she was here. Two years before, that time when she suddenly cut short her visit without explanation. So here was the explanation. She couldn't face me finding out. Perhaps she was scared of what I might do, but I'm a reasonable man and after the initial shock of discovering my sister, my own flesh and blood, had been defiling herself with that Sandhurst creature—a wastrel with little talent and an excessive dollop of delusional ego—I would have regained a semblance of equanimity, especially once she was dispatched back to the city, and that would have been the end of the matter. But Hannah wouldn't have waited years for a chance at revenge. It had to be recent, in these last ten days since Eva had been back. Yet she hadn't even left the house, save for a few walks to the bridge and that time I caught her in Adam's car. Except for the day before yesterday. When I'd done with Alf's and gone to Standlake for plumbing supplies. They must have done it then. Which meant Hannah's defilement of my good grace took place not forty-eight hours after Eva had coupled with Nathan.

My mind reeled. It was no longer possible to seek redress.

Contributing heavily to my chagrin was the knowledge that through Hannah's base trickery I was bound, sexually, to my own sister. Nathan had slid his member into my territory and I, in turn, had slid mine into his. I felt unclean. There may even be traces of

Eva in my genital folds. The situation was not far removed from incest. I was aghast to have unwittingly completed that sordid chain.

It wasn't like me to hate but I found myself hating. A festering growth lodged in my heart. Its pus seeped and seeped through my whole being, distorting all my thoughts. In their newly twisted forms these thoughts in turn fertilised a malevolence I couldn't recognise. But it grew in me like a revelation. Enabling me to see with clarity sharp as ice.

Juan strode back into the room, wiping his nose on his cuff. Nathan stood and headed unsteadily to the kitchen.

I resumed my seat, and looked at everyone in turn through my new lens of awareness. I remained calm. I accommodated myself to my newfound perception confident that the night would resolve itself favourably without much effort on my part.

For a dark mist was masquerading as morality in that room. A mist through which truth cannot be seen.

I was bathing in the foul mizzle of others' lies and deception. Hannah the slut, Nathan with his absurd delusions. Alf in the grip of a malaise he seemed determined to deny. Fat-bellied Rebekah and David imposing their pestilent faith and their prejudices. Fungal-fingered Delilah playing charades with the lives of others. The deranged Cynthia. Adam with his pathetic babe-in-the-woods veneer that was as conniving as Cynthia's turns. And Juan, the only honest person in the room, other than me, a man who would kill as soon as breathe if it suited him. It was a wonder I was still able to; the air was suddenly so thick.

CHAPTER FOURTEEN

A bath is like a dam: water pours in from a tap and the plug prevents its flow. Today I lay in my dammed reality, at one with the little fishes of my imagining, content in the splendour of Philip's bathroom, at peace. I was sure the mermaid would not reappear, having not done so since that one occasion. I was so at ease I felt sure to surpass my personal best, yet it was not to be. My concentration wavered for no reason that was apparent, a dark mass pooling on the horizon of my vision, and I had no choice but to lift my head and pull the plug and hit the stopwatch.

Eight minutes and seventeen seconds.

I was disappointed and euphoric all at once. I wondered what had interrupted my focus when I heard a sound that was at first unfamiliar. I sharpened my hearing and there it was again, a high-pitched whine. I puzzled over the sound for a few moments and upon hearing it a third time, I recognised it as a lyrebird on the forest floor, mimicking Alf's slide guitar.

The river is the opposite of a dam. Free flowing from source to sea, always on the move, sometimes ponderous, others agitated, the water sighted at any given moment never the same as that of before or after, the river keeping its appearance of continuity, its contents always in flux. Alf loves the river. When I was small I would see him standing on the bridge, gazing downstream. He was young then, although to me he was grown up and therefore old. A slim and handsome man with a spritely gait, always nicely turned out in trousers with upturned hems and a fitted shirt. He didn't have a beard back then. His skin was honey brown, and his eyes, shaped like almonds, were perfectly clear. He always wore a smile. He wasn't one for conversation but he would greet me and ask me if I was keeping out of mischief.

These last years it's been so sad to see him grown old and hunched over that great paunch of his, always coughing or wheezing though he'd never smoked. No one knew what was wrong with him. Once when I inquired, Delilah told me he had everything wrong with him, which seemed an unpleasant thing to say and hardly fair. He was a sad man, a man who'd never found a suitor, whose great love of music was requited in the limited way that Burton could provide. Somewhere in the woods outside, the lyrebird mimics the winsome cries of his slide guitar, testament to the loneliest man that ever lived.

There's a dearth of suitors out here. And few leave to find a mate. It seems that in Burton people either wed young and for life, or they're doomed to solitude, like Alf and Cynthia and Delilah and Ed.

Philip hasn't found anyone and I worry that he, too, never will. I don't know that he's had a woman since my best friend, Sophie Flemington.

It's been twelve years since Sophie left never to

return and neither of us has heard from her since. A pity, for I loved her dearly. But she betrayed that love along with my trust. Back then things for me were black and white and everyone I loved I kept in a box in my heart. Sophie was in a box. Philip a different box. To discover them in the same box was simply too much.

It was a squeak that alerted me to the goings on. A rhythmic squeak that interrupted my reading of *The Crucible* for school. I put the book face up on my bed and went to the window. I couldn't see into the night through the rain. The squeaks were persistent and ever more frequent. Curious, I went outside.

The noise was coming from Philip's panel van parked in the driveway. I saw the suspension bouncing. Ignoring the rain, I sneaked over and took a peek through the front window, careful not to be seen. I saw Philip's bare buttocks pounding away and Sophie's head thrown back in ecstasy. Instantly betrayed, I didn't find the sight in the least titillating. And I didn't remain in the rain. I stole away back to my room and cried myself to sleep.

I couldn't speak to Sophie again. She tried, but I wouldn't even look at her in class or in the corridors of school. She even wrote me long letters of apology, but I burnt them without reply.

It was over between Philip and me too. I no longer let him touch me.

I might have hammered on the van window, or confronted Philip later with his illicit trysts, threatened to tell all and secured his banishment, and I was building up to do just that, when miraculously I no longer needed to, for Sophie was gone.

The lyrebird stopped calling Alf's slide. I left the bathroom and scuttled down the hall to my bedroom.

The day was sunny and hot. On impulse I put on a fine cotton dress, sleeveless with a plunging neckline that revealed the plump flesh of my breasts, tailored about bust and waist, moulded round the hips, tapering down the thigh to end at the knee. A dress that accentuated every curve of me.

For I, too, am alone.

And thirty is no age to be a virgin.

I have been feeling ashamed of this stark reality for some time, only I have never encountered an available man that didn't either terrify or repulse me. Even as I dressed to provoke, I felt certain I wouldn't meet a suitor in Burton. Only a deluded woman would return to Burton to find her match and I'm not deluded.

Sitting on the end of my bed I began to wonder why I did come back, when I remembered the unfinished business. Something nagging at me from deep in my psyche, even though I still had no clear idea what it was. But I sensed I was getting closer. The memories were guiding me back.

When I was working at the post office, shunting letters into boxes, blocking out Ruth Cartwright's droning voice complaining to first one customer then another that the sea fog was keeping people from collecting their parcels, parcels that were cluttering the floor and creating trip hazards, I knew only that I needed a long holiday. I had to return to Burton. I had a niggle at the back of my mind, telling me there was something important that had to be attended to, a niggle that grew into an annoying persistent itch. I had to find something, I was sure of it, or reclaim something. Or maybe clarify something. I couldn't be sure, for back then my mind was a fuzz.

When I first saw Philip's bathroom I was momentarily convinced that was what I had come back for. To me, the renovation was a symbol of atonement for all the cruelties of the past, although he would never have seen it that way.

I note there's been a marked change in my brother. I hadn't expected Philip to behave this way, as the last time I was here he was welcoming. I can't fathom what, if anything, has precipitated the change. After giving my all to make him feel welcome in his home in my presence, and receiving little except cool hostility and censure in return, I've taken to retaliation. And my desire to gain access to our parents' bedroom grows stronger by the minute. That has become my unfinished business; he has no right to lock me out of my past. What at first had been genuine affection on my part and a willingness to be of assistance has become an act.

It's transparent to me that I can't remain in my brother's house for much longer. I've decided I shall make plans to relocate to another place to practise my breath craft after Christmas.

For I believe I have found the ideal bathroom.

Meeting Nathan was not the unfinished business I had in mind when I came here and never in any of my dreams would I have found him attractive. Three years my junior, he'd always seemed immature, a lad with grandiose pretentions and a rock star swagger.

Perhaps it was the way he emerged out of the silvery mist that settles thickly each night above the river. I'd wandered outside and I was hanging around by the front gate in my figure-hugging shift, pretending to tip prune a camellia, as if to watch the world that was Burton go by. And there he was, framed in grey, suddenly immensely attractive, with his trendy haircut and his Ray-Bans, and as he neared I could see that the innocence of his youth was rent from his gaze. Despite the ironic twist to his lips, the assertive tilt of his head, he seemed lost and troubled and my heart pinged a note of sympathy.

I hadn't seen Nathan for years and was still adjusting to the sight of him when Adam drove by and I raised my arm in a friendly wave.

'Eva,' Nathan said in a surprisingly soft voice, stopping by the gate.

'Hello Nathan,' I replied brightly.

'I heard you were back.'

'Couldn't keep away.' I laughed.

He lingered, worrying a small stone lodged in the straggly grass of the verge.

'Is everything alright?' I asked.

He looked up then down the street, before leaning forward to speak. 'Lee Reece has offered to play guitar on one of my songs,' he said quietly.

'You should be ecstatic,' I enthused, not wanting him to know I couldn't abide Lee Reece.

'I am. But keep it to yourself. No one round here believes I even know him.'

'Let's celebrate,' I said with girlish delight.

His mood lightened immediately. 'My place?' he said, at last taking notice of my dress. 'I'll show you my studio.'

I glanced back at the mist thick in the valley. I never imagined I would find myself walking with Nathan to his place. Philip had no time for him at all.

Nathan was Aiden's age, and when we were

growing up, the two boys played together all the time. For years, mother would instruct me to go and get Aiden from the Sandhurst's, or take Nathan back and make sure he got there safely before returning. When tragedy took Aiden from us, Nathan was inconsolable and many in Burton believe he never fully recovered from the loss. In typical muckraking style, Delilah insinuated that his affection was somewhat exaggerated and represented something other than ordinary friendship. Perhaps it was true for he's a baleful young man. Then again, he's also lost both his parents to a terrible storm, which must have compounded the earlier loss, and the poor lad's been bereft ever since.

The Sandhurst's house was across the street and up the hill a short distance. The gate had scant purchase on its hinges and was in dire need of paint. The front garden an overgrown frenzy of foliage: an out of control oleander crawling with tendrils of ivy; a carpet of wolfsbane struggling for breath in a tangle of buttercups; horehound fighting it out with angel's trumpets; and Virginia creeper choking the life out of a silver birch.

The old weatherboards that clad the house were in a worse condition than the gate and the window frames were rotting at their corners.

I followed Nathan down a cluttered breezeway, passing a number of closed doors before reaching an enclosed veranda.

Entering the narrow and long room I was transported to a different world, one that spoke not of decadence but of a richly vibrant realm of innovation. It was a music studio with a vast assortment of equipment. Everywhere I looked there were dials, knobs and sliders and snaky black leads. Entirely esoteric to me and I felt uncommonly heady at the sight of all the matt black and the shiny chrome. It was an emporium that had so taken me by surprise I looked around, searching for somewhere to sit down. Seeing me all but swoon, Nathan reached behind me and shoved a scattering of song books to one side of a petite sofa, upholstered in black fabric, that I had failed to notice on entry.

'You like my studio?' he asked, once I was seated.

'It's magnificent,' I said, gazing at the row of guitars hanging on a rack on the end wall, some plainly hewn, others lacquered bright red or blue.

'I've been collecting bits and pieces from Alf for years.'

'Has he seen what you've achieved here?'

'Not yet. I'll invite him up when it's finished.'

'It isn't finished?'

'I've been saving up for a twelve-channel mixing desk.' He pointed to a piece of equipment on a desk. 'You're the first to see it.'

'Then I'm honoured.'

He offered me coffee and I sat alone in his studio while he made it.

When he returned, carrying a percolator and two cups, he asked me if I could sing.

I said I had no idea.

'I need a female singer to do some backing vocals. It's for the Lee Reece track.'

'I doubt I'd be any good.'

'Give it a try?'

He handed me a cup of steaming black coffee. I had to hold the cup by its handle and the tips of my other hand at the rim to keep the contents from spilling as I looked around for somewhere to set it down.

'Come over here,' he said and I stood up, still with the cup barely steady in my two hands, and I went to where he'd set up a microphone stand. He took the cup from me and gave me a pair of head-phones. 'Before you put on those, have a listen to this,' and he pushed the play button on a cassette player.

The bones of a song, on guitar and vocals, filled the room. It was a plaintive song, sung in the staccato voice of someone on the verge of tears, and when it came to the chorus he indicated for me to pay close attention.

'*I didn't intentionally break the banister*
That caused you to tumble down those seventy-seven steps
Like a half full canister...'
He pressed the 'stop' button.

'What I want you to do is sing those words in harmony.'

I must have looked nonplussed because he imme-diately scrawled out the chorus on a notepad and in-vited me to sing the melody along with him. Five attempts later and I had the gist of it. 'Now,' he said, 'I want you to sing something like this,' and he sang a different melody that seemed as if by magic to blend well with the first. I sang the new melody through with him many times before he slipped back into the original tune, leaving me to concentrate on the har-mony on my own.

We practised until my coffee was stone cold.

'Now, can you modulate your voice so that it's breathy and soft?'

I did as instructed and he clapped his hands together and grinned.

'Let's do a take,' he said, indicating for me to put on my headphones.

Several takes later, he seemed pleased with my contribution. We sat down together on the little black sofa and listened back to his song. It was thrilling despite my acute self-criticism that had me convinced every second note was flat or pitchy.

He had his arm straddling the backrest and as I sank down he let it slip round my shoulders. I turned my face to his and held his gaze and it suddenly seemed an obvious conclusion to the morning that we kiss.

The touch of his mouth on mine was delicious and I felt no compulsion to pull away. Neither did he and we sat there wrapped up in each other's arms kissing and canoodling for a while. I felt a rise of warmth as desire opened up in me and before long we were pulling at each other's clothes.

Down there I was so plump and wet beneath his touch. After a while he spread my legs and pressed himself into me. I let out a soft moan.

There was nothing but me, him, the studio full of black and chrome, the smell of coffee and sweet sweat. I was climbing to a peak, ready to soar, so full of heat and eager for release, when something inside me flicked a switch and I was instantly numb.

A dense and heavy screen of nothing had placed itself between me and all those warm and fuzzy feelings. I sensed they were still there, they had to be there, down there in the plump wetness of me. Yet so completely out of my reach. All I could do was hide from Nathan my disappointment and maintain a pretence until he had attained the pinnacle of his own pleasure and released his grip. Everything faded and I was left with the strong sense that I had done something wrong.

I wanted the bathroom, wanted to wash away the sticky evidence of his pleasure and my disappointment. He told me where to go. Down the cluttered breezeway. Second on the left. And when I opened the door my eyes widened.

So much red!

The floor tiles and wall tiles the freshest and purest red I'd ever seen. The basin and bath a sanguine hue. Curtains, towels, everything was some sort of red, and the whole effect enhanced by a touch of gold or cream: taps, a vase, a towel rail. It was like entering a womb and I felt reborn just standing there.

My eyes lingered on the bath. Claw-footed, deep and wide, and positioned away from the window.

Perfection.

And it was then that I knew that I would be crossing the lane, making the switch from blue to red, foregoing one sort of watery paradise for one even better. And I no longer cared, or even remembered, my recent disappointment. This, this was all that mattered.

CHAPTER FIFTEEN

ADAM

The flash white lighted The Cabin. The crack came in an instant. The boom so close The Cabin shuddered with the force of it. There was to be no break in this weather, Adam was certain of it. The storm had settled into the valley as though it had signed a lease and taken possession of the key.

Cynthia seized the moment to recount to him in hurried sentences the other times storms had lodged in the valley. Each time, Burton had been flooded, she said. The great flood, the devastating flood, the killer flood, there seemed no end to it, and she leaned in closer towards him, breathing her halitosis-laced recollections, imprisoning him in a ghastly intimacy.

Of the time Alf's house was flooded to its ceiling. The time a weatherboard house nearby had been lifted clean off its stumps, the floodwaters carrying it off some twenty metres downstream before losing interest.

The deluge would cascade down the mountain, she said, and the river would swell and swell and swell, bursting its banks, surging down Burton Road East with the force of a tidal wave, ripping at everything, pushing and dragging. That's how the town lost Rebekah's older brother, Gabe. Silly fool tried to cross the bridge—Cynthia's eyes narrowed as she said it— and when he reached halfway he lost his footing.

'Doesn't take long for the waters to rise,' she said. 'Minutes. You could be walking along, feet dry and snug, and before you get from the general store to the bridge you'd be waist deep in it and clinging for your life to a tree trunk, hoping as you do that the damn thing won't fall.' She made a show of looking around before fixing him with her gaze. 'You'll have to stay here, Adam,' she said urgently gripping his hand. 'Tell me you'll stay.'

His breath caught in his throat. Forced to stare into her withered face, he felt drained and nauseous and terrified. It felt as though his brain was pounding in his skull, not helped by the muscles tensing in his shoulders. Panic gripped his belly. He needed to inhale air free of the stench, free of Cynthia, but he couldn't move.

He heard snatches of conversation from the others in the room but didn't take them in.

Searching for relief, his mind wandered. He was back at home, seated on a sofa in his living room, feet snuggled in the soft pile of his Astrakhan rug. But there was no comfort in the imagining. For Eva was opposite him. They were making polite conversation and sipping tea. They spoke of the river, the overgrown path. He detected something reticent in her manner, almost evasive, as if she'd wanted to deter him from walking down the river path. Why? Perhaps she knew something. Knew about the necklace. Had she been there that day when Joy was murdered? If so, what had she seen? A sudden brilliance lit his mind, his thoughts charged with the potency of day bursting on the horizon of his awareness. If she had been there, had witnessed foul play, had seen the necklace fall, then why had she left it there?

Doubt was quick to cloud his questioning. He felt like a startled frog leaping from assumption to assumption. He told himself he'd succumbed to a false dawn, a dawn born of fear, a fear so strong he could taste it. He could no longer trust his thoughts. He'd become unreliable to himself and he dismissed as idle speculation the entirety of his reflections as tantamount to the twisted assumptions of that warmonger Delilah Makepeace.

The storm intensified. Wind tore through the trees. Rain bucketed down. Lightning flashed. The booming bass that rumbled soon after shook the floor. It was astonishing that The Cabin still had power. What little good cheer there may have been at these Sessions had long since vanished, replaced with a pervasive anxiety that at any moment the situation would worsen even more.

If only Benny were here, but Adam was all but done with 'if only.' He knew he shouldn't feel betrayed by Benny, but he did. Betrayed by his passing, as though Benny's death were the root cause of the blows and the kicks sure to follow. Caught in the jaws of his mounting anxiety, Adam could see by the set of Juan's face, the cold in his eyes as he leaned against the barrel with those sodden towels at his feet, that the punches would be unrelenting. It was all Adam could do to reassure himself that at least for the time being he was safe. Delilah had taken up her position as guardian of the table, and Cynthia had sat back in her seat, content to fiddle with the tassels of her shawl.

He needed to stop thinking about Juan, told himself he was obsessing.

He let his eyes fall on Philip's back, the square of his shoulders, the cropped hair trimmed in a straight line at the nape of his neck. As he took in his form and his posture, misgivings coalesced like a murmuration, starlings thick in his awareness, a vast swooping shape-shifting mass. He wanted to grasp at the flock, but it flew out of reach, at last coming to rest when Philip reached for his beer. Philip took a slow sip then returned the bottle to the table, nudging it, making sure the label was facing away and the bottle aligned to his liking with the curve of the table. Adam told himself those were the actions of someone exacting and particular, just a foible, and he was most likely bored and impatient at having to wait so long for his turn to perform.

But there was something else; Adam was sure of it.

He tried to think. But his mind fogged. The murmuration a thin black trace swirling high above. He concentrated, tried to see into the grey. It wasn't anything Philip had said, or anything he had done. It was something to do with his cool, detached manner that was so puzzling when put beside the empathy he occasionally expressed. Somehow his shows of support had ignited Juan's ire, but that did not demonstrate complicity. For one thing, Philip couldn't have known Juan planned to watch from the window. It was a coincidence, another among the many that had taken place that night.

He told himself Philip was a respected local and

neighbour. A regular sort of tradesman. Nothing more. He was letting paranoia eclipse rationality, which immediately brought to mind Stella Verne's warnings.

He would do better to remain on guard against Juan and not lose focus by pontificating the flaws of his own allies.

Hannah slouched to the stage and stood behind the microphone, facing away from Juan, pointing her guitar neck at the audience. She was left-handed. She wore her guitar slung low and bent her head so she could see where to press her fingertips. Realising she was nowhere near the microphone she reached for the stand, pulled down the arm and angled the clip. Juan watched on closely.

Satisfied, Hannah strummed an open chord. 'Yeah, this is Sadly,' she said without looking up. The opening chord sequence was simple. The fingernails of her right hand made additional clicks. Then she took a breath.

Hannah didn't sing. She emitted a soft nasal moan, periodically swallowing her voice, pretending to hold a melody by bending every utterance so that somewhere in amongst it all she hit the notes. She imbued her lyrics with no emotion, and her indifference left Adam wondering why she bothered. Her chord sequences were unimaginative and repetitive. In all she was difficult to listen to. Adam surmised she used her position behind the bar to stand in the limelight, which she manifestly enjoyed, for when she did look up her eyes showed a deep satisfaction and she issued a gloating smile upon her parents' energetic applause between songs.

David, who had yawned openly during the other

acts, sat up in his seat with his hands flat on the table, agog. Adam caught Rebekah shooting her husband disapproving looks between rows of her knitting.

During Hannah's third song, David eased himself free of the nook and lumbered to the stage, placing the music stand that Juan had set to one side, back near the microphone. Then he went to the bar and squeezed past Nathan seated on his stool. Nathan was forced to press himself against the counter to let him by.

David heaved the other bar stool out of the corner and made for the stage. On his way by, one of the legs hooked on a tassel of Cynthia's shawl and she emitted a yelp as the stool leg yanked the shawl from her shoulders.

'David!' Delilah said. 'Keep still.'

David stopped in his tracks, stool in hand, and turned. Cynthia, clutching her shawl, was forced to stand.

It was left to Adam to disentangle the shawl, something he did without hesitation.

'Thank you,' Cynthia said as she sat back down.

David headed on, managing to ram the stool into Alf on his way by.

'Can't you lean?' David said.

'No, I cannot.'

'You're in the way of my stool.' David made a show of heaving the stool on.

'Do you have to be so oafish?' Alf said, roused.

David ignored him. He was about to mount the stage between the speaker and the mixing desk when Juan, leaning against the barrel, shot forward and, with a censorious hand, told him to hold off.

Visibly rattled, David plonked the bar stool directly in front of the mixing desk and gave Juan a withering stare, before returning to the nook. He hadn't yet managed to ease himself into his seat when above Hannah's apathetic moan came a violent roar.

In seconds the roar was overhead. Lightning struck the ground nearby, momentarily strobe lighting The Cabin. The thunder that followed felt like a bomb blast. The lights dimmed before extinguishing altogether, a second later flickering on again.

Cynthia gasped. Adam braced himself for more but the roar passed and before Cynthia had a chance to wail there was a rustle of soot. Whatever it was that had been lodged in the chimney all evening, fell into the grate with a dull thwack.

Cynthia was the first to react. With a piercing shriek, she leapt from her chair and edged back towards the bar.

Everyone spoke at once.

Hannah held a hand to her mouth and tried to rush from the stage, entangling herself in the lead caught in her guitar strap. She yanked at the lead, resting the jack from Juan's mixing desk and hurried through to the kitchen with the lead trailing behind her.

'You dumb whore!' Juan bellowed, making a dash for her.

Alf stood up and blocked Juan's path.

Towering head and shoulders over Alf, Juan strained forward, eyes bulging, teeth bared. He stood back and made as if to lunge, repeating the backward and forward motion. Adam watched with alarm. A trigger, could be a switch or a slider or a jack plug, even a guitar string, and the violence in the man came barrelling out.

Joshua rushed to assist. Juan looked set to barge past them both when Delilah hurried her seat back against the wall and yelled, 'Joshua!'

She was gazing with disgust at the black and bloated body of a possum lying in the grate.

The room choked with its odour. Adam had to quash an impulse to follow Hannah to the kitchen.

'Joshua,' Delilah said again. 'You better see to this.'

And she went to take his place, facing Juan.

'Isn't it about time you showed my regulars some respect,' she said. She stood before him, hands on hips, bosom to the fore, her voice loud and indignant.

The room held its breath. Alf took his chance to steal away to the bar.

'She's breaking my equipment,' Juan yelled.

'You sound like a child.' Adam wondered if she was about to slap his face. But she didn't. 'Hannah's had a shock,' she said. 'Where's your concern for her welfare?' She didn't wait for an answer. Leaving him standing there, she swung round, went to the bar and poured herself a brandy, gulping it back in one.

Juan remained where he was, jaw clenched, the muscles in his neck twitching. Adam couldn't bear to look at him.

Without Alf to block Adam's line of sight, Rebekah and David came into view. They both stared at Juan, sharing a frozen demeanour, blank with disbelief but little else. As if they were slow to take in what had happened, slow to react to Juan's menace, slow to defend their daughter. Watching Rebekah take up her knitting, Adam was reminded of his grandmother, and the dismissive way she had of dealing with playground spats that had left Adam

220

bruised and sore. 'It's your own fault for getting in the way.'

There was a brief lull in the room. Adam sat still and lowered his gaze, not wanting to draw Juan's attention.

Another second and Juan turned with a private scowl to check on the damage to his mixing desk. Satisfied that no harm had been done, he

leaned against the barrel, wedged against the door.

It was then, with half the room crowded around the bar, that Adam's attention was drawn to Philip. Throughout the entire altercation, from the wind, the possum in the grate and Cynthia's curdling scream, to Hannah's frantic stage exit and Juan's volcanic reaction, Philip hadn't flinched or even so much as fractionally turned his head. He was, as his surname suggested, a stone. As if sensing Adam's eyes on his back, he turned in his seat and fixed his blue-eyed gaze on Adam, a slow smile appearing at the corner of his lips.

'The night just keeps getting better,' he said, standing.

Not wanting to be left alone in the centre of the room, Adam stood as well, wondering where best to put himself. Before he'd made up his mind, Joshua rushed through from the kitchen with a shovel. Hannah followed him into the room, stopping at the bar.

Adam stepped aside as Joshua scooped up the dead, rotten-to-black beast. Maggots fell into the grate. Maggots that fell like live raindrops, wriggling off every which way, sprinkling the floor behind him as he took the possum outside.

Cynthia covered her face in her hands and groaned. Rebekah bent her head down, and knitted furiously. Alf looked queasier than ever.

No one showed any sign of dealing with the maggots.

After a long pause, Ed moved forward and began stamping his foot, grinding the plump creamy wrigglers into the carpet. Delilah stopped him and told him to get a dustpan and brush.

'You have to be joking,' he said and returned to stand against the back wall.

Delilah looked around, and suddenly everyone stared into laps. A maggot inched its way towards Adam's foot. He stepped backwards and looked up. His eyes met Delilah's and a flicker of satisfaction lit her face. She said his name and waited.

He didn't respond.

'Adam,' she said again.

It was her tone that left him no choice. Defeated, he asked where she kept the dustpan. Hannah went to retrieve it, returning moments later and thrusting it at him. 'Here,' she said and disappeared into the kitchen.

The maggots were moving off on the carpet in all directions. He crouched down and with brush and pan in hand flicked in one after another. One. Two. Three. The fourth overshot the pan and fell against his wrist. He blenched. And he brushed in the others we greater care, keeping a watchful eye on the dustpan where the maggots were inching their way up to towards the handle.

When he had a substantial collection, he stood and rushed through the kitchen to the back door and on outside to the garden where, facing into the wind and the rain, he shook the dustpan and swept off the wriggling fiends before returning to gather their mates.

The room was agog. Nathan had given up his stool to Cynthia, who gaped with her hands pressed to her face, her skirt bunched up tightly about her knees. Alf stood beside her, offering what little reassurance he could muster in his feeble state. Joshua and Delilah went about shunting the furniture, leaving Adam to scramble on his haunches on the sweep. The maggots in the grate were disappearing back up the chimney where the stench of rotting flesh was so intense he began to wonder if that dead possum had left behind a mate, or worse, its young.

He tried to hold his breath, only taking in short gulps of air. He tried not to think. Tried not to look at Juan who seemed to be relishing in watching him scrambling about flicking maggots into a dustpan. He felt like tossing the pan in Juan's face but thought better of it. Instead, he made a final trip outside.

He tossed the dustpan's contents as far into the garden as the weather would allow. Beyond the veranda's reach was a curtain of rain: a scintillating cascade in the patch of light filtering outside through the kitchen windows. Bogans slapped against the fly wire door. The incinerator couldn't be seen. No one would be out there, at least no one in their right mind. Branches flailed, trunks strained and here and there Delilah's carefully sculpted shrubs lay broken at the base.

He was about to head around the corner to the toilets when he saw Hannah, huddled on an old church pew. She was sitting sideways hugging her knees to her chest. She'd been crying. There were streaks of black on her cheeks. She didn't look at Adam as he approached.

'Hannah, that's the last of them. I promise.'

'She let that possum rot in the chimney for weeks,' she said between shivers.

'Surely not that long.'

'I heard it. I heard its cries. And she wouldn't listen. What's wrong with her? What makes someone that cruel?'

'I don't think she's cruel, Hannah. Thoughtless maybe.'

'There's a difference?' she asked. 'Anyway, she is. You don't know her like I do. She never does anything unless she wants to or has to. You should see the men's toilets.'

He was suddenly in no hurry to do that after the punishing Alf had been giving them. If he found himself desperate, he'd use the Ladies.

'It's over now Hannah,' he said, trying to sound encouraging. 'Let's go inside. It isn't safe out here.'

'Safer than in there.'

'The maggots have gone.'

'Not the maggots.'

'I don't follow.'

'There are two men in there who haven't a clue what's in here,' she said, pointing at her belly with sudden honesty. 'And I don't want anyone guessing.'

'You're pregnant?'

'And it isn't Nathan's.'

He quickly ran through the men in the room, with the exception of her father. Alf was clearly incapable and far too old. Joshua and Ed were unlikely too, both much more than twice her age and she didn't seem to care for either of them. Juan was hardly a candidate. Which left Philip.

He recalled months earlier when she used to blush in his presence, give him wistful sidelong glances when she was sure he wasn't looking, how her gaze would linger on him as he walked away.

'And Nathan knows,' he said aloud, his thoughts culminating in that stark fact.

'I told you, he hasn't a clue.'

'About Philip.'

'How did you...?' Her voice trailed off.

'You have to tell him.'

'Nathan?'

'Philip.'

'I can't.'

'You must. He has a right to know. It's his child too.'

She hesitated as if this obvious consideration had never occurred to her. 'Maybe you're right,' she said with a smile.

He couldn't read the expression that came into her face beneath the black smudges, but if he had to give it a name he would have called it triumph.

CHAPTER SIXTEEN

EVA'S DIARY – TUESDAY 23RD DECEMBER

I t was seven eleven when I threw open the curtains on the day, after another dreamless night. The frog was quiet. Mist hung thickly down by the river, thinning on the upper flank of the saddle. The sun shone through low thin cloud a brilliant silvery light. Patches of Philip's zigzag path gleamed, fallen leaves dazzling like stars on the pavers. The pencil pines to either side of the gate cast long fingers of shadow. I opened the window to a sough of wind. It was uncommonly warm.

Philip had risen before dawn to clear a backlog of small jobs before Christmas. I revelled in the solitude. With the whole day ahead of me, I had ample time to find a way into our parents' bedroom. For today I determined I would do it. Eight years was a long time to keep a room shut up and it was time to brush free the cobwebs, liberate the chattels, clear out wardrobes and chests of drawers for future use, whatever that may be. It was time to give the room air. Time to purge the ghosts and move on.

And move on I shall, just as soon as the business is done. I have a new vision in my heart, the source the man across the lane. Nathan Sandhurst with his talent and his splendid bathroom. Red is my colour. I thought it was blue, but I was wrong.

Just thinking about our entwined bodies on the sofa in his studio the other day brought me all aflutter, like a butterfly dancing above a pond. I couldn't wait to visit him again.

I pulled away from the window and hovered out of sight as two figures walked up the lane, emerging out of the mist like strangers. Before long I heard voices and knew Hannah was accompanying Nathan back to his house. I couldn't suppress the quick churn of jealousy in my belly. They walked slowly and were suddenly in the path of the sun. Hannah paused and tilted her face, as if relishing in its unexpected warmth, although her expression was not one of joy but of preoccupation. Two figures in black, just two locals walking together, consumed in innocence, only they were much more than that and the jealousy that had me in its tight clasp became so fierce I fled to the kitchen and splashed my face with cold water.

I wanted her gone, wanted her out of his life, leaving clear my passage to him. I wanted him. And I wanted him with unanticipated desperation. He'd awakened in me a craving that had lurked unsated for as long as I can remember. Joy in another's embrace, that glorious sense of belonging to another person. It was something I hadn't felt since Philip's earlier betrayal. And it occurred to me that this was my unfinished business: the reclamation of joy.

As the sun cut away the mists of night, I stood in the sharp silvery light, caught in the tendrils of jealousy, feeling a little hackneyed as if my character had been carved from a trashy romance, when I experienced a memory sharp as a blade. A memory I had shunned from my mind, rejected and rejected so often it had stopped bothering to tread the long passage to my awareness, not even penetrating my dreams.

I couldn't even be sure it was true. The mind is an unreliable witness, grabbing recollections of this and that like so many photographs from a vast montage, splicing separate images together and presenting them to the mind, a collage of snapshots that may or may not be illusions, may or may not be arranged in the correct order.

Philip's lust had brought me joy of a sort. I enjoyed four years of his loyalty. He'd watched me grow and change through puberty. At the end of those four years when I'd reached a comely fourteen, I was fully aware that our union would not be looked upon kindly by the inhabitants of Burton, for Father Makepeace would often make references to impure carnal acts that would secure the sinner's place in Hell, although I no more believed, if I had ever believed, in the mores of the Church.

All I knew was that I'd been replaced, long before the Flemingtons moved to Burton and Philip bested Sophie, although he still sought my filial favours.

I'd been stalking Philip since I was about eleven and over the years, I'd become a well-practised sleuth. I found it wasn't hard to do. By the time he was seventeen, Philip thought he was a grown man at his own beck and call and no one else's. By then I'd grown acutely aware of his habits, his every movement.

He had no idea he had a stalker.

It began when his voice broke, and he no longer welcomed my company except when he wished to sate his urges. Rejected and still a child despite my little breasts and the hairs down below, I had no desire to play with sulky and bad-tempered Aiden, a boy only happy when with his playmate, Nathan. Which he so often was since Mother and Mrs Sandhurst were both delighted and relieved their little boys had each other for company, the one an only child, the other openly rejected by his older siblings. So I invented a secret game of my own.

Philip's movements were easy to monitor. He was punctual, habitual and orderly, always attending to this before that. He never brushed his teeth before breakfast, always wiped his shoes and left them side by side by the front door, and he always went to the bathroom before he went out, spending a minute or two attending to his hair. Through the adjoining wall of the living room, if I stood close and held my breath, I could hear the order of his ablutions and then I'd tiptoe to my bedroom, ready to climb out my window and creep round the side of the house, poised for when he exited the front door.

At first it had not been much more than a bit of furtive fun, the additional thrill of not being seen intoxicating. Then there was the long period after Aiden's death when Philip scarcely left the house and by the time he resumed his outings I'd almost lost interest. Stalking had become merely a compulsion. I'd begun to consider giving up the game due to Philip's rather tedious adventures, taking a walk along the river path or to the general store and up the track past The Cabin to the redwood forest. All he did was walk and stand around, settling somewhere secluded to read a book or comic. He never met anyone or did anything untoward or titillating or otherwise devilish. I'm not sure I would have had the strength of will to break the habit, but looking back I wished I had.

One warm sunny day, I followed him along the river path, a safe distance behind, careful as ever not to make a rustle or snap, locating as I went the nooks and crannies and deep recesses ahead that afforded me obscurity. As he neared the clearing at the river's wide curve where he would sit and read, he stopped and crouched behind a clump of bushes. I hid from him further back, unexpectedly breathless. He glanced back up the path, his eyes searching, pausing to stare straight in my direction, and for a moment I was convinced he'd seen me, but he hadn't for he turned back to peer at the clearing and I reassured myself that my obscurity was intact. After all, dressed as I was in khaki green with a matching canvas hat, I was well camouflaged if a little hot in attire better suited to the winter months.

I stayed huddled in my hiding spot, puzzling over what had so attracted his attention and rendered him as furtive as me, causing him to hide in the very spot where we had both hidden that day four years earlier, the day Philip had reached for my most hidden places and given to me such pleasure. Making it that I belonged to him. Only he'd always overlooked the fact that since I belonged to him, he belonged to me. He was under the illusion that he was free, I thought, yet in that one illicit act he was bound to me by twine that would never be cut.

I was shaken from my musings when he stood and entered the clearing. I waited a few moments and when he didn't reappear, I counted to ten then took a chance and crept forward, inhabiting the spot where

Philip had been only moments earlier, the air still warm with his breath.

I peered through the bushes to see Philip standing over Joy, who was buttoning up her blouse. They talked in low voices. She pointed behind her and stood and they walked over to the far side of the clearing where they remained, in close proximity to each other. Before long he drew close and she pulled away. He pulled her back. She laughed lightly and he reached and held her. They kissed and he led her back to her blanket on the ground.

There, in a frenzy of scrambling hands, they both disrobed and he lay her down and straddled her, his hands reaching for those rounds of flesh, kneading, pulling, teasing. She threw back her head.

Spreading her legs with his own, pinning her hands above her head with one of his, he took her. I could hardly believe it. My face burned and I wanted to rush forward, yelling, and force them apart. But another burning held me fast and I decided to attend first to releasing that sensation between my thighs.

As they both moaned and writhed and gasped so did I, privately, my hand repeating Philip's soft strokes on my slippery folds.

Once I'd zipped up my fly I stole away down the path, leaving them alone to their coupling.

After that, Philip's bathroom ablutions extended an extra minute every day for the rest of that summer and his ritual had become so regular, always leaving at the same time each day, that I was ready, in wait by the side of the house, my loins warm in anticipation. I was in a voyeuristic paradise, the sight of Philip and Joy's couplings never failing to arouse in me the most intense of passions, and my hand would do its own glorious work. It was for this reason that my natural jealousy was kept at bay.

Towards summer's end everything changed.

I'd followed Philip along the river path and, as usual, enjoyed their tryst to the full. I was zipping up my trousers when I noticed that something was wrong. Joy had sat up. She looked upset. Philip hurriedly dressed and stood over her. I couldn't see his face.

Anticipating a swift departure, I left my hiding place and hid further back, my clothes snagging in some brambles. In moments, Joy rushed down the path, followed closely by Philip. Once they'd passed my hiding place, I followed on a safe distance behind.

I had to stop abruptly and steal into more brambles when he caught her arm and swung her round. I could tell by the tense way he held his body and the jerky stilted movements he made with his arms and legs that he was angry. She was sobbing and trying to pull away.

All this I remember with clarity. I have always remembered watching them make love, how could I forget that, I even recalled the moment when they raced passed me. In the remembering, I'd left the kitchen in favour of my bedroom. Lying on my belly on my bed, writing as if a confession of my own sexual pleasures, enjoying once more the afterglow of a heat now sated, I couldn't be sure of what I saw next, not absolutely, for it might be that my mind had reconstructed, re-ordered or worse, invented the fragments.

The first fragment was of Philip's fist landing squarely on Joy's jaw. She reeled, stumbled, fell back and landed in a bramble bush. And she screamed. It was the lyrebird scream. I knew that fragment of memory must be true for I had heard the lyrebird make that exact scream only days ago. It must have been there as well, lurking in the bushes that day, listening and upon hearing Joy's shrill scream, emulated it perfectly, perhaps relishing in the release of such a raucous sound, over and again for all these years. Do lyrebirds live that long?

I recalled Philip helping to pull Joy free of the brambles and I thought that might have been the point at which they resolved their differences and kissed and made up but it wasn't to be. He yanked her hard and she tumbled forward and fell flat on her face.

Without hesitating he bent on his haunches and, using the strength of two arms, rolled her down the bank and into the ice-cold water of the river. I am sure I saw all that. I am as sure as I can be that I also saw him climb down to the river's edge and, steadying himself by clasping a willow branch, put one foot out above the water as if pressing down. My imagination completed the only picture possible, of Joy's body in the water, held submerged by Philip's foot.

About half a minute later he crouched down and shoved. Then he made to turn and I hunkered, scoring my skin on more brambles.

I waited until I was sure he had gone before emerging from my prickly hiding place. Cautious, I went to where the tragedy took place. Signs of the scuffle were everywhere: footmarks, broken twigs, crushed weeds. I set about making good, masking much with rocks and sand, when I saw something glinting in a clump of weeds.

It was Joy's necklace. It must have come off when she fell. I thought about taking it, but that would have implicated me. I thought about tossing it in the river to complete the masking of evidence, and then I thought I'd leave it where it was, tucked away well out of sight, for some wanderer in years to come to stumble upon and puzzle over. It was as if I had left a thread, just a filament of a trace back to Philip.

I closed my journal, rolled on my back and stared at the ceiling, going over the fragments of that scene.

It was time to set matters straight.

With a renewed sense of purpose, I retrieved from the bottom of my wardrobe the screwdriver I'd bought in the general store. I went outside, and after checking that no one was around, not even a mouse, I approached my parents' bedroom window, two along from my own.

I needed to stand on something to reach.

I went round the back and returned with a rickety wooden chair. It was all I could find. I hoped it would hold. I'm not heavy. I wouldn't fall from a great height onto a pile of rocks like Ed, but I didn't want to fall at all because I had a thorny rose bush to my left and a blooming hydrangea to my right, the one a prickly hell, the other a mass of soft stems and crushable leaves, evidence of where I'd been.

I needn't have worried. The chair held me fast, its legs sinking a little in the soft ground. I pushed the screwdriver into the thin crack between the top and bottom windows, and drove it against the catch, hoping to flip it open.

The catch was stiff. It didn't seem to want to go anywhere. I tried, again and again, thinking maybe it had rusted shut.

Then I took a rest and looked around, my hearing

acute. Parrots chattered in a nearby tree. The lyrebird made its winsome whine like Alf's guitar.

A blackbird flew down on the lawn to watch with his sharply observant eye. I hesitated, thinking Philip had sent a spy.

My arms were sore but I returned to the task. I was about to give up when finally the latch gave way. I let out a sigh. I put the screwdriver on the window ledge and with two palms pressing the frame of the bottom window I pushed up. Nothing happened. I pushed again and kept pushing until my palms felt raw and my arms ached even more.

Then I saw the two large nails that had been hammered into the window casing, hard up against the top edge of the bottom window.

I was livid.

I stood down, grabbed the screwdriver and the chair and went round the back.

I deposited the chair with the others gathered beneath the old maple tree father had planted decades ago, making sure I left it exactly as I found it. I returned to the side of the house and stopped at the sealed window. The chair legs had left cylindrical holes in the soil. I strew debris and arranged tendrils of convolvulus to mask the evidence.

Then I went back inside and down the hall and when I reached my parents' bedroom I took out my rage on their door with a hard kick. The door rattled.

I kicked again and again, furious with Philip for locking it for all these years. Then I stepped back and ran at the door with my shoulder proud. It slammed against the door, sending a stab of pain along my collarbone and down my arm. The door didn't budge.

I thought for the briefest moment. Then I stood

squarely, raised my leg and kicked the door aiming for somewhere near the lock. I heard a soft crack of splintering wood.

Three hard kicks, each one sending arrows up my shins. And the door gave way.

CHAPTER SEVENTEEN

ADAM

A dam left Hannah whimpering on the veranda and went inside, dustpan and brush in hand. He stopped in the kitchen and made himself focus on his surroundings to steady his nerves. Applying a technique a work colleague at Chattergull's had shown him, to help calm him down after an irate caller had made death threats, he paid attention to things he could see, one at a time. The kitchen was lit by a single opaque globe hanging in the centre of the ceiling beneath a lacquered metal shade in the shape of a dinner plate. He noted the plainness and the square dimensions of a room that spoke nothing of Delilah's aesthetic. The exits to the bar and veranda created an invisible passageway. In the far wall, another door led to Delilah's quarters. It was closed. The rest of the wall space was taken up by cupboards, painted off-white, above and below a red Formica bench edged with a shiny black strip. The sink and the cooker were spaced several feet apart in the only windowed wall. On the opposite wall, a large fridge stood behind the door to the bar. A table, too small for the room, was laden with Delilah's empty platters. Altogether the room spoke of drab.

The technique had limited success. Adam leaned with his back to the bench beside the fridge. The storm raged on, relentlessly, the thundercloud overhead sending lightning onto the mountaintops and into the valley indiscriminately, as though lashing out at the residents of Burton in a fit of vengeance.

Somewhere beyond the thundercloud was the Blood Moon. Did it matter that it could not be seen? Surely that wouldn't reduce its potency? Stella Verne had said nothing about that. An alignment was an alignment, regardless of local weather. The ancients must have known this, but Adam thought it no accident that the philosophers of old who'd gazed at the skies lived in deserts. On clear nights they looked into the firmament ablaze with a million stars, and studied fate.

He couldn't shake the sense that everything was too late. Too late for Benny. Too late for Joy. Too late for Hannah. And, he thought grimly, too late for him.

Doom must have overshadowed Benny and Joy as they neared the end of their lives, the one at the mercy of an internal pestilence, the other a pestilence at large. As for Hannah, what chance did she have carrying Philip's child, living in a caravan at the back of her zealot parents'? That triumphant expression on her face—he couldn't make sense of it. What gains did she hope to make telling Philip she was carrying his child? Financial? There'd been no love in her eyes, no care or regard. Adam wondered what seed he had inadvertently planted in her mind, a seed quickly germinating in fetid soil, turning Hannah from a teary-eyed wretch to a cauldron of cunning in an instant.

And suddenly he felt responsible. He'd given her an idea, handed it to her like a pastry on one of Delilah's platters, and he wished he could undo time and never have taken it on himself to care.

He roused himself, recalling his colleague's advice, and steered himself back into the visual now, the table, the sink, the cooker, the doors.

Another flash of lightning, followed close behind by a crack and a boom and a protracted rumble. He braced himself and rounded the fridge, readying his nostrils, wondering with trepidation what he was about to walk into.

The smell hit him on the way in.

Unable to repress a strong urge to wash away the previous half hour, he joined Nathan at the bar.

The room had been returned to its usual arrangement. Alf and Philip sat together at the front table. Behind them, Delilah sat with Cynthia. Joshua and Ed stood by the back wall. Rebekah and David were making their way to the stage. Juan leaned against the barrel, hands in pockets, wearing a look of strained patience. Adam lowered his gaze to the floor, scanning about, hoping he wouldn't see any straggler maggots. There were none. The grate was empty save for a discarded matchbox.

The incense sticks, smouldering in bunches of five on the mantelpiece, only added yet more fug to the stench filled air. It was all Adam could do not to retch. His headache returned with overwhelming force and he winced. It occurred to him he should have followed through on his earlier decision to leave.

Not wanting to reveal to Nathan that Hannah was outside crying, and needing to make light of his own absence, he said, 'Soon be over.'

'What will?'

'The night.'

Nathan slurped the dregs of his cider and gestured at the stage. 'The worst is ahead of us.'

Adam let out a short laugh.

They were silent for a while. Adam idly scanned the bottles on the back-bar shelves. In his side vision he caught Nathan bringing his hand to his mouth almost in time to catch his belch. 'I could do with another drink,' he said.

'Same.'

'Where's that Hannah when you need her? Stupid cow.'

'She's sitting outside.'

'She should be in here.'

'The possum got to her.'

'Yeah, funny how she can't stomach a few maggots.'

'Don't remind me,' he said with an upward glance.

'You did a good job,' Nathan said. He lifted his glass to his lips to drain the last few drops of his cider. 'Damn that girl.' He thumped down his glass. 'Hannah!' he yelled.

Ed came over and stood beside Adam. 'What's up?' he said to Nathan.

'I need a drink.'

Ed ignored him. 'We owe you one, mate,' Ed said, addressing Adam. 'What'll you have?'

'Forget it, Ed,' Nathan said. 'Unless you wanna serve yourselves.'

'She'll be right back, I'm sure,' said Adam.

'Yeah, you relax,' Ed said. 'You look like you've had enough.'

Nathan sat up in his seat. 'Gotta wash away the maggots, man.'

'Got them all then?' Joshua said, joining the others, ale in hand.

The last thing Adam wanted was to be talking about maggots.

Ed surveyed the floor. 'Looks like it.'

'Been testing God, have we?' Joshua said, slapping Adam on the back.

Adam jolted forward. He thought it must have been the first time Joshua had addressed him in conversation. 'I don't follow,' he said warily.

'He's talking about Job,' said Nathan.

'Job's faith in God to be precise. The devil struck him down with boils and other pestilences and his faith never wavered. How's your faith, Adam?' he said accusingly.

'I don't know about Job,' Ed said, 'or his god. But we're sure having a devil of a night.'

There was a brief spell of awkward laughter.

'On the eve of Jesus' birthday, no less,' Joshua said, suddenly sounding grim. Adam felt diminutive beside his hefty hairy presence.

'Oh, come on! You don't still believe in all that crap?' Nathan said. 'Next you'll be telling us Moses parted the Red Sea.'

'He did.'

'Bullshit.'

'He did. Only it wasn't the Red Sea. Someone wrote it down wrong. Moses parted the reeds in the sea. Easy enough for a man with a strong pair of arms.'

'An understandable mistake, I suppose,' Ed said reflectively. 'Red and reed.'

'I guess it must have gone from 'reeds in the sea' to

'red in the sea' to 'Red Sea,' in that sequence,' Joshua said sagely.

'Hang on a minute,' Nathan said, raising himself up on his stool. 'Since when did Moses speak English?'

Joshua laughed. 'Thought I'd lighten the mood. It's one of my favourites. Pastor Makepeace told it better.'

'The lolly man, you mean,' said Nathan with a scowl.

'Lolly man?' Adam said.

'We called him the lolly man behind his back. Because he always had a lolly in his pocket ready for any kid passing by.'

'Well, I don't know about that,' said Joshua, 'but I do know he didn't take to me.'

'Why not?' said Adam.

'He didn't appreciate my sense of humour. Do you remember, Nathan? Or maybe you were too young. Anyway, before he was hounded out of town, the Kinsfolk were complaining about the length of his sermons.'

'Yeah, he did go on and on.'

'And on. So, I went up to him one day and suggested that he could cut down on communion by mixing the bread and wine together to make a trifle.'

'What did he say?'

'He didn't take kindly to my wit, I can tell you.'

'You were lucky not to get excommunicated,' said Ed.

'For a joke?' Adam said.

'Actually, the Kinsfolk were no joke,' said Nathan. He rested his elbows on the bar, face in hands.

'He could have done, But he didn't dare. The Elders didn't like him and were waiting for a chance to pounce.' Joshua looked thoughtful.

They were quiet for a moment, then Ed said, 'You're much better off without all that in your life, Joshua.' And he went on to recount the day he fell off a ladder and damaged his back. Adam listened with interest, picturing Rebekah leading the Bible study, Hannah being precocious, Ed teasing. 'And I fell on her goddamn rockery.'

'No need to blaspheme.'

'Of all the places I could have fallen,' Ed continued. 'And all because she startled me, turning so suddenly. It was a conspiracy.' He went on to describe the details of his injury, the time he spent lying on the ground, the ambulance, the hospital, and Adam's attention waned and shifted to the stage.

David was tuning his guitar. Juan leaned against the barrel, arms folded, watching.

Cynthia's voice rose above the storm, and Adam diverted his attention to the centre of the room. She was addressing Delilah, who refused to look at her. 'How could you have forgotten? You, Delilah Makepeace. It's you! You put that possum up the chimney. Tell me I'm wrong. You put it there to torment me.'

'You're being ridiculous.'

'Am I? Am I? What about that day I lost my Joy— How could you forget the smell in here? And you, you just sat there, denying it all, until that crow fell into the grate.'

'It was a raven.'

'You'd put it there. I know you did. And you sat there defending Philip. He must have been—What?— Seventeen? And you believed him. You sided with him. And all the while you were conspiring...'

'How dare you insinuate I'm a liar!' Philip swung round, his face ablaze, his china blue eyes wide as cups.

Delilah raised her hand in a censorious gesture to Philip as she at last looked Cynthia in the eye. 'Indeed, how dare you! Joy caught the bus and left town. Heaven knows why but she did. Now shut up, you silly old fool.'

'Oh, oh, it's a conspiracy!'

'Cynthia!' Alf said, turning in his seat. 'Calm down.'

'Get her a drink.'

'Brandy?'

'Where's Hannah?'

'Oh, I'll get it.'

Delilah bustled to the bar, head high, breath shallow, rolling her eyes at Adam as she returned to her seat with Cynthia's drink in hand.

On the stage, David tried to wedge his music stand between the foldback monitors and the speaker beside the wall, allowing enough space to raise it to the required height. Rebekah stood behind him, pinned to the back wall by her music stand and her husband's stool. David stood for a while, hands on hips, surveying the situation at his feet. His vast bulk took up half the width of the dais. Then he shifted his microphone stand to one side and bent down, pulling the monitors towards him and angling them into a vee to create a small space at the front edge of the dais. Satisfied, he placed his microphone stand in the space, adjusting the arm so that it extended over the monitors. He reached for his guitar and drew up his stool.

At last Hannah slumped in, her face drawn, but

she'd fixed the black smudges beneath her eyes. She stood behind the bar fiddling with her fingernails.

'Where have you been?' Nathan said.

'Outside.'

'We're parched.'

She ignored him. 'What can I get you?' she said, eyeing Adam cautiously.

'Something strong I think.'

'Go on, Hannah,' Nathan said with a snigger and a downward point of his finger.

She reached below the counter and extracted what appeared to be a bottle of vodka. With a furtive glance in Delilah's direction she set down a tumbler and filled it half full, secreting the bottle away the moment she was done.

'Careful,' she said as Adam raised the tumbler to his lips.

He took a large gulp and nearly choked. The liquid scalded his throat and his ears burned like lamps.

'Whoa,' he gasped.

'It's hooch,' said Nathan.

'Delilah's?'

'Joshua's home brew. He's got a still.'

'Devil's blood, Delilah calls it,' Hannah said.

It was the first time Adam had seen either of them grin that night.

He was about to take his drink back to his table when Hannah leaned forward, reaching out a hand to stop him. 'Better have that here.'

He settled back against the bar, raised his glass and sipped some more. It didn't burn quite so much the second time. His headache began to recede.

Rebekah and David were still dithering about in

search of the most comfortable arrangement of their personages. With David's stool centred in the available space, Rebekah hadn't room for her music stand. David shunted forward to allow her more. He twisted round to see if he had succeeded, inadvertently nudging his microphone stand with his foot. He was too slow, too encumbered by the lack of space and the guitar on his lap to reach for the stand before it toppled to the floor.

Juan rounded the stage to retrieve it. He picked up the stand, extracted the microphone and waved it at David. 'You any idea what this cost? It's my best microphone. Bloody idiot.'

'Juan,' Delilah said sharply.

Juan took no notice of her. Upon inspecting the damage, he roared with all the force of a hurricane. He raised his hand, still gripping the microphone like a weapon, and yelled, 'You stupid fat fuck!'

'Juan Diaz,' Delilah said. 'I'm warning you.'

He swung round, pop-eyed, and pointed the microphone at her.

'See this,' he said, tapping the end, 'See this here. That douchebag has put a dent in the head. You know how much this cost me? A fuck ton of dollars and that prick has destroyed it.'

'I won't have you talking to my guests like that,' Delilah said, standing up. Her bosom heaved and the hair in her bun trembled. She looked like a teacher telling off a schoolboy. 'Juan Diaz, you've a mouth like sewer.'

That was all it took to set Juan off again. With microphone in palm, he made a fist and raised it to her face, grabbing her arm with his free hand.

'Get off me! You drunkard!'

'He isn't drunk,' Philip said.

Alf went and stood between them, holding out his hand for the microphone.

'Give it to me, please.'

Juan waved it at him and pointed. 'See. See there.'

'I said give it to me, please.'

Juan looked around the room. Alf's remark had taken him by surprise and he wavered. Then he handed Alf the microphone and stood over him, waiting.

'It's just a dent,' Alf said.

'A dent. A dent. Is that what you call it? A dent. For all I know, that dent is death.'

'We'll see, shall we?' Alf's tone was remarkably controlled. In the wake of his words, Juan calmed enough to put the microphone to his lips.

There was a high-pitched screech and Juan's voice bellowed through The Cabin.

'Seems perfectly fine to me,' Alf said and went back to his seat.

'There now,' Delilah said, softening her tone. 'There's nothing wrong with it. Now let Rebekah and David play their set.'

Juan relented, albeit sulkily, as if he'd been censured by his parents.

Adam had never before seen the child in Juan. He'd always been too close to his anger to examine the source. Watching Delilah and Alf manage his volatility was revelatory, as if for the first time Adam understood. His angst untangled enough to form a single long strand in an instant. And there was Juan, a beanpole of a man despite his ex-army strength, all swagger and sparkling white teeth, a little-loved boy, thrashed to within an inch of his life by an alcoholic father. Not that his past excused his violence. Explanations were never excuses. It didn't matter what happened in a childhood, there was always the chance to divest from that past and put the psychic energies to work on being nice. Adam considered himself nice. Hadn't he, too, suffered abandonment, rejection, neglect and the harsh cold parenting of his grandmother? Each of itself a justification for the perpetuation of revenge. Yet that was the path of avoidance. A lifetime spent blind to the self, a refusal to look inside and find what's there and oust it in a quest to change. Juan still blamed. For him, the world was not onside. So he pitted himself against it.

In Alf, Juan had found a good father. It occurred to Adam that if only he'd been more like Alf and less himself, Juan would never have hit him. Instead he'd been the perfect target, placating, beseeching, pleading. He vowed never again to let himself fall foul of a violent man. Adam craved whatever it was in Alf that gave him authority. And he realised that even with Benny, he'd been a child.

David, who had sat throughout Juan's episode bemused and unapologetic, pushed back his glasses that had slipped from the bridge of his nose and watched as Juan returned the stand, with microphone intact, to its former location.

Behind him, Rebekah wore a look of disappointment. No doubt she'd been hoping the microphone was damaged. Adam reflected on that time she'd found his erotic art books and later, in a hurry to find an explanation, he'd told her they were Juan's. She'd gone on to ask him why he didn't simply throw them in the bin, but he gave her a look that left her under no illusion that to do so would be to put his life at risk.

Even as apprehension stirred inside, Adam turned to face the bar, unable to help the smile spreading across his face at the sight of Juan strutting about beside his mixing desk. It was a smile that quickly left his face when he noticed Juan's gaze fixed on the back-bar mirror, staring straight at his reflection. Fear snapped in his belly. His mouth went dry, yet he swallowed. He'd never be commanding like Alf or Delilah. He wanted to scream at Juan to leave him alone. But when Juan was spoiling for a fight nothing would stand in his way.

He slugged the remaining contents of his tumbler and joined Cynthia's table, taking up the seat between the two women, the alcohol in his belly providing him slight respite.

David readjusted the microphone and said, 'We're called As Best Us Can, here to keep you entertained on this wild Christmas night.' And without further comment, he began the first song. It was an uplifting song about a man who had lost then found his gal. David delivered it in a flat steady voice, singing with the front of his mouth, out of key. He didn't have much of a vocal range and his guitar playing was basic. When he reached the chorus, he looked down at his guitar and abruptly stopped playing. He foraged in his pocket and extracted a capo. Once in place halfway down the fret board he began the song again, singing out of key and making chords and strumming on, but there was little variation of note emanating from his guitar. Then Adam noticed he was making his chords on the wrong side of his capo.

David looked confused then stopped playing. He removed the capo and carried on, this time picking up at the chorus. He was still out of key but seemed oblivious to it. Then Rebekah joined in, attempting to keep time with her tambourine, and she provided accompanying harmonies in a rasping nasal voice that had an affected whoop in it. Adam found it better for his state of mind to block out the entirety.

He felt no compulsion to converse with Cynthia so he turned to Delilah.

'Your hair looks good tonight,' he said, contriving to make incidental conversation.

'I'm glad you think so,' she said, giving her bun a pat. 'Rebekah's creation.'

She returned her attention to the stage. There was a murmur of applause and David began his next number on the back of it.

'I hate to tell you, but your garden's in a bit of a state,' he blurted on impulse, the alcohol in his blood finally lending him the courage to seek clarification of an event that had been disturbing him all evening.

Delilah didn't take kindly to his remark. 'It's been through worse,' she said abruptly.

'I dare say.'

She showed no inclination to talk but he persisted. 'Have you been having work done out there?'

She looked surprised. 'I have no idea what you mean.'

'There was a workman out there earlier, loading what looked like sawn limbs into the incinerator.'

'That was Philip.'

He paused. 'I thought he was fixing your sink,' he said slowly.

'He was. He asked me if he could put some garden waste in my incinerator in lieu of payment.'

'A strange request,' he murmured.

'If you say so.' She pulled back, clearly not wishing to hear any sort of criticism of Philip.

He let it go and sat for a while, Joshua's hooch dulling his senses, enabling him to tune back into Rebekah and David's song.

Then every cell of his being came to a sudden halt. The phantasmagorical face was Philip's. That much he could just about handle. But why would he be putting garden waste in her incinerator when he could just as well have disposed of it on his own property? His garden was huge. Many times Adam had seen him piling limbs, fern fronds and pruned branches onto a heap in a clearing in the bottom corner of his land. He would wait until the pile was high then, on a still day in spring, he would set light to it and the smoke would billow up the hill and Adam would be forced to close all his windows. It didn't make sense that Philip would wish to use Delilah's incinerator, at least not for garden waste.

He must have been disposing of something else, something he didn't want left on a pyre in his garden. Something domestic? Papers? Some sort of evidence? And why that face? Why that look of horror?

A cautionary voice burst through the morass of his suspicion, his grandmother's voice. 'Stop making a song and dance out of nothing,' she always said whenever he was upset about something that was huge to him and trivial to her.

He wasn't reassured by it, but he calmed enough to regain an awareness of the room. As Best Us Can had launched into their third song. To his left, Cynthia was nodding and swaying in a show of appreciation that could not have been sincere. Delilah was just as attentive, without the swaying. He avoided looking in the direction of Philip's back, and beyond, to Juan leaning against the barrel.

The wind outside rampaged about, now and then sending a blast down the chimney. The smell emanating from there was as rank as ever.

In a break in the song, just before the bridge, there was a clatter behind the bar. Adam jumped. It took him a few moments to settle, and he only achieved it by focusing on Rebekah and David. Dreadful as they were by every musical criterion, they gave him something to pin himself to, something to curb the fluctuations that flapped about inside him like startled rodents.

David droned on in his lazy voice and Rebekah followed him with her abrasive discordant harmonies, one song meandering into another and it was probably a relief to everyone, when their set came to an end. Except to Adam.

Delilah stepped in with her usual vigour and cheers. Behind the bar, Hannah's applause was astonishingly rigorous as well, and it left Adam thinking she was surreptitiously seeking to needle her parents.

Juan came forward to protect his gear as Rebekah and David made their way off the stage. Delilah stood immediately.

Not wanting to be left alone with Cynthia, Adam left his seat and went to the bar. Hannah poured him his wine, although he wasn't sure he needed it, and when he went to pay she glanced up and raised a dismissive hand.

'Thank you,' he said.

'Not a problem.'

He hovered and thought he might join Joshua and Ed, take up the space left by the barrel, when Rebekah, who had managed to get away from the stage area with surprising speed, grabbed his arm. 'I've been trying to attract your attention all night,' she hissed, glaring at him through her black-framed glasses.

'What is it?' he said, rescuing his wine, his senses suddenly sharp.

She took a forward step, the vast, undulations of her torso squashed into her navy and fawn striped dress, brushing up against him. He could taste the whisky on her breath.

'What are you doing with Joy's necklace?' she said in his ear.

'Excuse me?' he said, inwardly recoiling at the closeness, the sheer weight of her bearing down.

'I found it when I was cleaning your room.'

'I told you never to clean my room.'

'Now I know why.' She moved back a fraction, the better to glare at him.

'That necklace was hidden away in a box in the bottom of my wardrobe,' he said, keeping his voice low. 'I hardly call your ferreting through my things cleaning. It's spying and you've no right.'

'I have every right. It's my church, not yours. And now I demand to know how you came to be in the possession of that necklace.'

'I found it.'

'Where?'

'On the riverbank.'

'I see.'

'What do you see?'

'That was Joy's favourite necklace. In the end, she only wore it for one man.'

She took a quick look behind her. David approached with his bar stool and pushed past them both.

'And that could hardly have been me, could it?' Adam said, trying hard not to sneer. He had no idea what she was trying to insinuate.

'Of course it wasn't you,' she said. 'It was Philip.'

'Philip.'

He looked around. Philip was still in his seat.

'Are you sure?'

'Of course, I'm sure.'

'We should be having this conversation outside.'

'I'm not going outside.'

'Then...' And he made to move away, narrowly colliding with David making his way back to the nook. They both waited for him to pass.

'There's more.'

'Really, Rebekah, I...'

'Philip's a liar. He didn't see her get on a bus. Joy was pregnant and she'd gone to tell him that day.'

Something in Rebekah's manner made him certain she was telling the truth. He knew she had been close to Joy. She would mention her from time to time when he went to collect his mail. Always with a wistful look in her eyes.

It was as if dawn had stalled on its rise.

Uppermost in his mind, eclipsing his own danger, was the stark thought that if Philip had been having an illicit relationship with Joy, and had somehow been the cause of her death, what now of Rebekah's daughter? He regretted urging her to tell Philip about the baby. For all he knew that might have been the motive to kill, although it baffled him how any man would wish to harm the mother of his unborn child.

He needed to talk to Hannah again, retract his

earlier statement, warn her that she was better off keeping quiet. But rationality weighed in again sounding like his grandmother, and told him it was none of his business. Philip was no more a murderer than anyone else in this room. He wasn't capable of it. Just an ordinary guy, a nice guy, a little reserved and particular but those were not the traits of a killer. He thought with quick dread that the traits of a killer lay in the heart of only one person in the room: Juan's.

He stood fast beside the bar and watched Rebekah return to her seat.

CHAPTER EIGHTEEN

EVA'S DIARY – WEDNESDAY 24TH DECEMBER

I didn't have a good night's rest. I awoke in the wee hours hot and clammy. I threw off the covers, but my past shrouded me in its skin. The knocking frog that had dug in right below my window was unrelenting. Knock, knock, knock. A microsecond pause. Then off it went again.

Sleep wouldn't come. All I could do was lie on my back with my memories compressing me like overly tight bandages. My chest felt heavy and my heart thrummed.

By way of distraction, I recalled the fragments of Joy's last moments. How easy it had been, Philip's foot on her submerged head. But I couldn't be sure. I was leaping to an ill-founded conclusion, quick to find my brother, my own flesh, guilty of murder. He may just as well have been trying to reach her, hook his foot in a sleeve to raise her up perhaps, and pull her back to the riverbank. He would have been immobilised by distress. Stricken, seeing her body sink below the surface, carried downstream by that cold persistent current: his love. He was prone, my poor dear brother, to finding himself in the wrong set of circumstances, privy to, not perpetrator of, some heinous event. My memory was an unreliable witness. Fancy creating a collage of fragments and calling that truth! Reconstructing any old how, and damning my darling brother in the process. I held on to that thought, satisfied that I'd done my best to explain away what I'd seen.

If only that were all I had to contend with.

I could hear Philip pacing back and forth from one room to another, his feet stomping down the hallway. He was still livid with me for breaking into our parents' bedroom.

I didn't discover much, ferreting about through our parents' things. Their bed was neatly made, the sheet folded down, pillows plumped and precisely placed at the bed head, the quilted coverlet of blue satin, smooth and straight. It was nothing like the bed in my dream, and of course my parents were not there, lying down, although I pictured them there, deathly still, eyes closed, their arms outside the covers by their sides.

In the wardrobe their clothes hung in a well-arranged row, starting on the left with Father's suits of black twill, and ending on the right with Mother's summer dresses. Two in all, both calf length and waisted, with long sleeves and high collars. Her blouses began where his shirts ended and it was hard to choose between them. Everything was clean and pressed but the wardrobe smelled musty. In the tall boy Mother's undergarments formed the neatest pile of lingerie I have ever seen. Father's the same. A chill swept through me and I glanced at the bed a few times to make sure their dead bodies hadn't jumped from my imaginings into real life.

There was not a speck of dust on the dressing table. An empty vase sitting on a white lace doily took up the centre of the shiny polished surface. I opened the drawers to find the same neat arrangement, this time of cardigans and jumpers.

I had begun to tire of the search when I found in Father's carved wooden chest my old nativity set and a sack of Christmas decorations. It was providence, a glorious treasure at the end of a quest, and I gathered it all up into my arms like booty.

Laden, I left the room, pulling the door to with a spare finger, unable to close its shattered lock. Consumed with childish delight, I thought nothing of it.

I laid out my finds on the kitchen table and proceeded to make a festive arrangement on the bench of the kitchenette. I was at pains to arrange all the little people and animals of my nativity set, placing baby Jesus in the centre. I sensed I was following a ritual of old but I couldn't recall it. I found I had no recollection of setting up those figures in the past and thought perhaps some other member of my family had done it instead. Aiden?

I enjoyed pulling out lengths of golden tinsel from the small canvas sack and creating a golden frieze around the nativity scene. At the bottom of the sack was the little angel that had sat atop the Christmas tree Father would erect in the living room each year. I sat her down in pride of place on the tinsel, her gaze fixed on baby Jesus. Altogether it was a fine arrangement that brought much cheer to the room. Satisfied, I wasted no time in running a bath.

I sat in my wicker chair, and stared into the greenery outside, the jubilance I felt in my brief interlude of festive adorning sliding quickly into a state of perfect calm.

Before long I found myself taking several deep breaths. And I slid into the bath and closed my eyes.

My underwater world filled with frisky little fish and fascinating coral and intricate sea horses. It was Christmas there too, of a sort, all sparkling colours and gaiety. And the dark mass stayed away, leaving me to enjoy the splendour of my imaginings for a whole nine minutes and twenty-four seconds.

Nine minutes and twenty-four seconds!

I had a new personal best! The euphoria I felt afterwards stayed with me for hours.

Then Philip came home and ruined it all.

I had thought he would be pleased. It was the first time I had been here for Christmas since our parents had passed. It was only natural I would want to have our past share it with us. All part of the cleansing that we both needed, for to lock away a dead person's things, keep their room like a mausoleum, only locks away grief, a grief that cobwebs all that was once theirs and now belongs to no one.

Instead, when Philip returned home and saw the decorations, he told me between gritted teeth to clear them away. I refused. Then he threatened to put them all in the bin. He paced a small circle he'd made for himself in the kitchen, muttering to himself and gesticulating as if pushing away the air around him. I hadn't seen him that agitated in a long, long time.

I stood with my back to the kitchenette, arms spread wide.

It seemed to slowly dawn on him where the decorations had come from. He stopped in his tracks and bolted from the room and down the hall. I heard our parents' door creak open. Then his heavy treads on the floorboards as he marched back to the kitchen. I remained guarding the dresser and he stood in front of me, pinning me with his china blue eyes.

'How dare you!'

'I had every right,' I said defensively.

'You had no right.'

'They are my parents too.'

'I think you forfeited any right to mourn their loss long ago,' he said with low menace.

His remark blasted me into pieces, memories, so many fragments, littering the ground of my mind, ground swamped by a deluge of guilt as if Philip's accusatory remark had cracked a dam wall.

I gathered enough of me back together to say, 'You had no qualms turning Aiden's bedroom into a bathroom,' deciding it was better to deflect his remark.

'That was different.'

'One rule for you and another for me then,' I snapped.

'This is my house,' he said coldly. 'I make the rules.'

There was nothing I could say.

His fury was punishing. He carried on pacing the floor, taking long strides back and forth and clenching his fists. He didn't seem to know what to do. I knew I couldn't placate him. So I just stood there. Eventually he left the house muttering to himself that he needed a walk.

I couldn't steady myself. I realised I was still guarding the kitchenette. I pulled my arms away and sat at the table. I couldn't look at my nativity nestling in waves of gold tinsel. Christmas had been eclipsed. I rued my own wilful nature. I should never have opened that door. Whatever had possessed me? I'd left the post office and come back home with a compelling sense I had unfinished business. It had been a spell, one that rendered me as single-minded as a Zombie. It's a wretched thing to be possessed by a single idea. Especially when I didn't even know the nature of that idea. It was barely formed, yet held within itself Titanic power. Consumed with that power I'd forced open our parents' bedroom door, forced it open with strength I never knew I had. And my world had changed in an instant.

Leave well alone. Leave the door locked. The dead are better left undisturbed. Memories are better left undisturbed as well. Their business is finished. And I had no business resurrecting them. Unfinished business indeed! Now I had to face the past all over again, before I could return it to its grave.

My parents didn't die old and they didn't die young. They died of grief, and that was the soil I would have to shovel on the coffin of their memory.

It was Easter. I was twenty-two and I'd come back from the post office for the long weekend. I set my small suitcase at my feet, knocked on the door, and waited.

Mother and father were both at the door when it opened, with Philip behind them. Father was in his mourning suit and mother was wearing her long black dress, full-skirted, with pin-tucked bodice, high collar and full-length sleeves. Her long brown hair was pinned back behind her ears by a plain white head-scarf tied at the nape of her neck. Philip was in a suit as well, of dark blue. The tenth anniversary of Aiden's death and my family were determined to make a deal of it.

I recall feeling nonplussed. I had been looking forward to unwinding over the Easter break, after a deluge of Easter cards and letters from abroad had glutted the post office. The Cartwrights had overseen my every move, determined as ever to meet the sorting deadline. I hadn't a chance to savour a single stamp. Facing my parents across the threshold, I saw immediately that there would be no chance to relax. Theirs was a solemnity I hadn't seen since the funeral. They'd even managed to coerce Philip into mourning. Although I was sure his was pretence, for I doubted very much his sincerity. Staring at those three dour relatives dressed in their funereal apparel, my anticipation of a convivial and restful holiday was thoroughly dashed.

Aiden was nine when he passed away. I was twelve and Philip a secretive and belligerent fifteen. It happened a year into my stalking adventures and I had yet to develop the recognition of Philip's ritualistic behaviour whenever he planned to leave the house. So I lay in wait in the oleander bush for half the morning after he mentioned he was going fishing.

It was lunchtime when he set off. As he gathered his things I was called inside and had to wolf down a chicken and salad sandwich while striving to come across all polite and innocent, asking to be excused upon the last mouthful. I walked slowly down the hallway and out to the front porch, before running through the front yard to see him cornering the bottom of the lane. I was about to creep out the gate when Aiden shot out from nowhere and bolted down the hill yelling, 'Hey Philip, you're in dead trouble.'

I knew Philip would ignore him. Aiden loved it when Philip had done something wrong and he would invent situations to see if Philip would squirm. Philip was only fooled the once. After Aiden's claim had proven false, Philip disregarded all of Aiden's shenanigans.

I followed Aiden, a safe distance behind and when he too cornered the lane by the old sycamore tree I broke into a sprint.

At the corner, I saw them both on the bridge facing away from me, so I scurried across the lane and into a thicket of horehound and lay low. It was hard to hear above the river—I was a bit too far away—yet the wind blew in gusts from the west, carrying snatches of conversation.

'Show me how you do it, Philip. Pleeease.'

'You put the bait on the hook, see.'

I peered through the horehound. Philip rested the rod against the railings and bent down.

Then I heard, 'Don't stand so close.'

Aiden shunted aside as Philip stood up and cast the rod out over the river. They both stood there until the shade I was in had turned to sun. I was considering heading home when there was a yell of excitement. I raised myself up on my elbows.

Philip was reeling in a fish. Aiden bobbing on his toes. Then Philip stopped reeling and the little fish thrashed about on its hook, straining the rod. I stood up and crept forward to a nearby tree for a better view. Philip told Aiden to do something but the wind had dropped and I couldn't hear. He pointed at the fish and turned to Aiden, grinning.

Aiden reached over as if to grab the fish and Philip moved the rod, jerking the fish out of reach.

Aiden started to whine. Philip leaned over, dangling the rod further out. 'Go on! What are you? Chicken?' Aiden stepped on the bottom bar of the railings and leaned over, yelling and giggling all at once. He leaned out further and further still, grabbing at the fish that Philip kept pulling away at the last moment.

Then Aiden lost his footing and tumbled over the railings.

Philip was quick to set down his rod. He left the fish thrashing on the bridge, and raced round to the riverbank downstream.

But the banks by the bridge were a dense tangle of brambles and thistles and it was impossible to get to the river's edge.

Philip rushed back across the bridge and sprinted past me, cornering the sycamore tree and on up the lane. When he was about halfway home, I went to the bridge and looked at the river but Aiden was nowhere.

Hearing a commotion, I hid again, this time a little downstream of the bridge, on the bank beside the lane. Mother cornered the lane in a panic, with Philip close on her heels. Behind them sprinted Father. When he reached the river, he dove straight in over the brambles, still in his shirtsleeves and trousers. Philip and Mother went and stood on the bridge. Mother was wailing. Before long Alf was there, and Delilah and the Sandhursts. They all watched the river with hands to their throats and their faces.

Seeing the huddle of stricken Kinsfolk on the bridge, Joshua pulled up in his old utility.

A much better swimmer than Father, he ripped off his shirt and dove in, and the others watched his head emerge, mouth taking in as much air as his lungs would manage. Off he went, making his way further and further downstream, bobbing up for air and diving down for as long as his breath would hold. Until one time, still in sight of the bridge, he was a longer time underwater and when he emerged like a great whale, opening his mouth wide and gasping for air, he had Aiden in a headlock and swam with him upstream and back to the bridge to a patch of river-bank that was somewhat free of weeds.

Mother was beside herself. Delilah tried to console her but it had no effect. Mother turned to Philip and yelled, 'You did this! You!'

Philip stood there on the bridge, mouth open, face ashen. I couldn't bear to stay in hiding a second longer. I came forward, calling out several times. 'What's happened?' As if I didn't know.

'Where were you?' Mother shrieked, but before I could answer, Philip grabbed my hand and pulled me away. We headed back up the lane.

We hadn't got far when we passed Pastor Make-peace under the sycamore tree, ostensibly on his way to the bridge. A stout, balding man in a shabby suit, he peered at us over his brow-line glasses propped halfway down his nose. He fished about in his trouser pocket and extracted two boiled sweets.

'Thank you for running for help, Philip,' he said proffering his special gifts to each of us in turn. 'You're a good boy.'

He reached out to pat Philip's head. Philip shrank back. A look of umbrage flashed into Pastor Make-peace's face but he said nothing.

'Thank you, Pastor Makepeace,' we both said in unison and quickly walked on.

'It wasn't my fault,' Philip said between his teeth,

once we were out of earshot. 'I didn't make him follow me to the bridge. I didn't want him there. Mother knew that. She should have stopped him.'

'She didn't know. He just took off, bolting after you.'

'Don't be fooled. She knew all right. She probably sent him off after me. She knows I like peace and quiet. She knows Aiden torments me. All I wanted to do was fish. Alf gets peace and quiet to fish. Everyone gets peace and quiet to fish. Why can't I?' He paused as if to think about what he had said. When he went on his voice had a slightly defensive ring to it, beneath his righteous anger. 'He pestered and pestered. You know what he's like. I didn't make him like that. I didn't turn him into a spoilt brat. If anyone's to blame, it's Mother. And Father. They should have taught him to swim better. Instead of babying him.' His pace quickened. 'And I tried to save him. Really, I did. They weren't there. No one was there. No one saw me race to the riverbank and try and drag him out. And no one has any idea how fast I ran up the lane for help.'

I said nothing. Walking along beside him back up the lane, I knew I would never divulge to him that I had seen everything. That I was, in fact, his only witness. For I would have had to reveal to him my habit of spying, and that was not something I was prepared to do. Besides, his narrative omitted the little game he'd got Aiden to play.

Unable to compete with Philip's arrogant stride, my pace slowed and I lagged behind. We were each caught in our own retelling. The ugly reality was that we'd both lost a brother, and neither of us cared.

As we neared the house, Philip turned and waited

for me to catch up. 'He leant over too far,' he said emphatically. 'The greedy little bugger. He was so damn keen to get his hands on my fish. He would have been fine but his foot slipped on the railing. He lost his balance. It wasn't my fault. I was the one who ran for help. How can Mother say it was my fault when I was the one who ran for help?'

He ushered me into his bedroom and in the ensuing hour his thoughts looped round and round until I was dizzy just listening to him. In his crafting and embellishing he'd erased all memory of his taunting and held fast to a new, much rehearsed version of events.

But no one adopted his view.

He was locked in his room for three days and three nights and fed his meals through a swiftly opened and swiftly closed door. I wasn't allowed even to pause in the hallway outside. The house fell into the quietude of grief.

After his incarceration, in which he was required to fester in his shame, he was made to wear a black suit and tie and attend the church for a public confession.

He had to stand in front of the altar before a packed congregation. And there he was, head bowed, hands clasped behind his back, as Pastor Makepeace ranted on the ways of irresponsible boys and their ungodly acts. I sat with Mother and Father, gazing at the pattern of my dress.

When Philip spoke, absent from his speech were all of his former accusations. I looked up, fascinated. His manner was that of utter contrition. He apologised. He wept. He pleaded. He hadn't meant for Aiden to fall in. He tried to get him to stand on the bridge. He could see that by standing on the railing he might topple. But he had hold of his rod. He was trying to reel in a fish. He was distracted. He tried to reach out and grab Aiden but he was too late. Sitting there listening to his pleading voice ringing out in the hushed silence of the room, I was the only one present able to note the lies, the omissions, the fabrications.

The Kinsfolk were attentive. When Philip finished speaking the hall was silent. Not a murmur, a breath or a shuffle. Then Pastor Makepeace launched into a long and tiresome speech on the reasons for excommunication. Everyone in the church expected the worst. Then Pastor Makepeace told the congregation that Philip had not contravened first one stricture, then another. That in fact he hadn't contravened any of the strictures. Pastor Makepeace acquitted him there and then of all sin in the eyes of God.

There was a collective sigh of relief.

I swallowed a gasp.

All was to be forgiven.

But Mother never forgave. She forced upon our household a long-lasting and dour mourning. There would be no more laughter. No more conviviality. No more flower gathering. Father shared her attitude of blame. For months Philip was ostracised by them both.

He bore his fate with steadfast diligence beneath which I saw in him a smouldering resentment. Privately, he held fast to his first version of who was to blame that day: Mother.

Only I knew the truth. I knew that our parents were right in their blame, if not their analysis of the tragedy, for they were not privy to what I saw. Yet I never spoke a word to anyone. I didn't want to lose my brother. Instead, I started to hold my breath.

When I stood on the doorstep that Easter weekend facing the three of them in mourning attire, Pastor Makepeace was still ruling the town and Philip continued to live in a cloud of shame. For our pastor never let Philip forget Aiden's demise. In his sermons he made insinuations, singling Philip out for one of his accusatory glares. His decision not to have Philip excommunicated motivated by his vile desire to exact a different and far crueller punishment, and in the hearts of the Kinsfolk of Burton grew a wary mistrust of my brother.

It was another two years before Pastor Makepeace was caught in the vestry with his pants round his ankles, holding the member of Rebekah's cousin's son, Simon. Somehow, that moment of disgrace exonerated Philip entirely. A new and terrible shame had eclipsed the tragedy of the Stone family, and Burton lost its pastor and its church in one swoop.

Despite his newly acquired grace, Mother and Father treated Philip much the same. I could never understand why Philip didn't leave Burton, like me, but he was a Burton boy through and through. He gained a plumber's apprenticeship and was soon to qualify and he knew he looked forward to years and decades of modest prosperity in a town at the mercy of appalling water and sewerage infrastructure. Yet, standing between Mother and Father in his dark blue suit, eyes lowered, greeting me with a soft hello, he wasn't the Philip I knew. He was a lifeless Philip, an automaton, as if drugged into compliance with his parents' wish for him to be who he could never be: a good son.

Even so, I was baffled as to how they'd managed to make him wear that suit. He never wore a suit. He was always neat and scrupulously clean, but for him a suit represented stricture and he didn't much care to be restrained.

'Lunch is at one,' Mother said with a sweeping eye over my casual attire. 'You'll be wanting to change.'

'Hello Mother, Father,' I said, pushing through the door with my suitcase. I went straight to my room, which remained exactly as I had left it: the bed with its pink quilted bedspread, and my dolls lined up on a high shelf, their legs dangling above the white painted dressing table with its winged mirror. Arranged on a coat hanger hooked on the wardrobe door, was the black dress I was to put on. It looked homemade, a replica of the one my mother was wearing.

I stood in that room, clutching my suitcase, and wondered how I would survive an hour in the house, let alone a whole weekend, traipsing about in that ridiculous dress.

There was no bus out of town for the rest of the day. My resistance quickly became fear, fear of my ability to comply. It was an asphyxiating sort of fear. I repeated a saying Philip had told me once, when I wouldn't step beyond the middle of the bridge. 'The easiest way to deal with fear is to become that which you're afraid of.' It seemed to make sense. I was afraid of not complying. So I wouldn't comply. And the fear was extinguished by a brilliant awareness.

I reached up to the high shelf where my dolls looked pretty in their frocks, all wide-eyed innocence.

I hadn't forgotten that hidden in the bowels of the plump rag doll in the middle, carefully wrapped and stitched in place, was the little jam jar in which I had stored my poisonous potion all those years before. As I undid the stitching I doubted the liquid would do more than upset a tummy or two, perhaps cause diarrhoea, nothing worse. But with the jam jar on my bed, I found the resolve to disrobe and take the mourning dress from the hanger. I slipped the little jar into the pocket of the full skirt before brushing my hair and pinning on the white headscarf that my mother had so painstakingly pressed. In the mirror, I was just another Kinsfolk girl, indistinguishable from every Kinsfolk girl who had ever lived: obedient, chaste, devout. And a deep cynicism fizzled and sparked in my core, in unison with the cynicism in Philip. Retribution for all of the misplaced reprobation he had suffered would today be his.

They were seated at the table when I walked in. Father had his Bible open before him. He was reading from Isaiah. *Surely he has borne our griefs and carried our sorrows; yet we esteemed him stricken, smitten by God, and afflicted. But he was pierced for our transgressions; he was crushed for our iniquities...* [53: 4-6] And I felt sorry for Jesus, for I was to cause Him more pain.

Philip's head was bowed. When Father came to the end of the reading, Mother stood, and I followed her to the kitchen.

The crockery and cutlery was on the bench. Mother removed a shepherd's pie from the oven— Aiden's favourite— along with a serving dish of vegetables. I took the cutlery and went back to the dining room. After laying out the knives and forks, I glanced at Philip remained staring at the table. I quickly left to fetch the plates, passing Mother in the hallway.

I hurried but she was behind me too soon. 'What are we to have to drink, Mother?' I said.

'Father has said we are to have whisky.'

'We normally just have tea.'

'Do not question Father, Eva. He wishes to make a toast to Aiden's memory.'

She had her oven-gloved hands wrapped around the shepherd's pie.

'Shall I pour?' I asked submissively.

'If you wish.'

She left the room and I extracted the jar. I tried to unscrew the lid but it was too tight. I ran the lid under the hot tap and tried again. It gave way but just as I went to pour the potion into Mother and Father's special tumblers, all ready and receptive on a silver tray along with the whisky bottle, Mother re-entered the room. I screwed on the lid and turned around, arranging my face in a pleasant smile.

'Father will pour,' she said in a change of heart. Which left me no choice. As she left the room with a tray of condiments atop the plates I'd failed to carry, I poured the potion, all of it, into the whisky bottle. I pocketed the jar and carried in the tray.

Father was surprisingly generous with the whisky.

'Before we eat,' he said, 'I would like to make a toast.'

I took a tumbler. So did Philip. I passed one down to Mother. Then Father said grace. With Philip's head bowed I couldn't attract his attention. I slid my bottom to the edge of my chair and reached out with my foot. The table was wide and his legs hard to find.

I leaned further, hoping not to attract attention, at last feeling the cloth of his trouser leg. I kicked. Philip looked up. I shifted my gaze to his glass, and made a face that was meant to convey a warning. Philip stared at me for a short while before looking back down.

'Now,' Father said. 'A toast.'

'To Aiden.'

'To Aiden.' And Father and Mother both took a long slow sip.

I held my glass to my lips, tightly closed, keeping my eye on Philip. He seemed puzzled, hesitating with his glass pressed to his lips. I set down my glass and he followed suit.

There followed some moments for private prayer.

Mother had only just begun to serve when Father started to convulse. His breathing became tight and he clawed at his throat. Sweat broke out on his brow. Mother dropped his plate, the pie portion spattering the tablecloth. Then she sat back in her seat and caught her breath. She started convulsing too, and fell to the floor, clutching at her throat.

Philip and I had no time to react. Not that we could have done a thing. It was over in less than a minute.

Now that it had happened I had no idea how I would get away with it.

'Weed killer,' Philip said firmly, as if reading my thoughts.

'Weed killer? But...'

'No buts. Mother infused the whisky with a few drops of her herbal tincture, the one she uses to kill weeds.'

'But...'

'I told you. She made a mistake. She wanted to flavour the whisky with a few drops of her aromatic tincture, the one she puts in cakes. But she muddled the jars.'

'She didn't.'

'She did.'

He grabbed the whisky bottle and I followed him to the kitchen. He took the jar of weed killer from under the sink, poured the contents into the whisky, then wiped the jar clean before putting it on the shelf beside the flour.

'Why didn't we drink the whisky?' I said.

'Bring me our glasses.'

I did as instructed and he washed them thoroughly, dried them and put them back in the cupboard. 'Here,' he said, handing me two glasses of water. 'Put them on the table and call an ambulance.'

'Not the police?'

'Why would you do that?'

And so it was that a suicide verdict was declared at the inquest. I knew that Philip's version of events was a fabrication and that I'd gotten away with murder. Yet over time I'd adopted his story as my own, made it truth and sealed away in some dark chamber all memory of what I had done. Only now, I remember. Lying on my back, my eyes closed against the dark, the covers bunched at my feet, I felt a sudden rush of gratitude towards my brother for keeping locked our parents' bedroom door. He'd been trying to protect me all along, protect us both from our own misdeeds.

The frog went knock, knock, knock as if it concurred.

In his bedroom, next to mine, Philip had stopped his pacing.

Yesterday, after I'd found the Christmas decorations, compulsion made me go back into that ghastly tomb of the past. I'd wanted to find Mother's mourning dress. I hadn't seen it hanging in the wardrobe. I'd checked and it wasn't there. I looked around. I was sure I'd searched in all the cupboards and drawers and even in Father's chest. Then I remembered that I'd overlooked searching in the bottom of the chest when I'd found the Christmas decorations. I knelt down and opened the lid, extracting with care a small collection of ornaments, a framed painting of Jesus, some candleholders and Mother's tableware. There, right at the bottom, hidden from view by a stiff black cloth, was a small suitcase, the sort that little boys take to school. I lifted it out and pushed open the catches and there it was, Mother's dress.

I laid the dress on the bed, straightening the collar and the sleeves and smoothing out the fabric of the skirt. It was then that I felt something in the pocket. I delved in my hand and extracted a note of buff writing paper, folded neatly in half and half again.

I opened the note and when I read the first words of my Mother's hand, my mind lurched sideways. 'To whom it may concern. It is with much regret that we must inform you in this way, but please know that it was with great consideration...'

It was a suicide note.

All those years I'd buried misplaced guilt and it had been a suicide pact all along. The mourning dress, the special lunch, whisky instead of water—the coroner's verdict had been right. Worse, they had planned to take their children with them. That was why Mother had insisted Philip dress in his suit. Why they had greeted me at the door and insisted that I too, wear the garb of the aggrieved.

I sat down on the bed and shoved the dress aside. I felt stunned. In trying to poison our parents, I'd saved our lives.

And there was Philip covering up for me when he needn't have bothered. I felt an enormous sympathy for him and berated myself for my thoughtless will. I wanted to make it up to him. I wanted to give him Christmas.

I tidied away the dress along with the contents of Father's chest, taking the suicide note and tucking it into my journal. I resolved to explain and beg forgiveness when Philip returned home.

No, I didn't have a good night's rest. Dawn is breaking and I've switched off the light. Philip has resumed his pacing. And I'm still confused, I thought that writing down my recollections would help me make sense of all that had happened, but it hasn't. It hasn't helped at all. I can't settle my mind. Some part of me wants to run away but I've been doing that all my adult life. I'll stay. I won't go to Nathan's. I'll stay here and make amends. I need a chance to explain. Once Philip understands that I didn't kill our parents, and that in fact I'd saved his life, he'll adjust and we'll be friends again, closer than ever before. I'm sure of it.

CHAPTER NINETEEN

PHILIP

It was painful to watch. Without a backward glance, Rebekah waddled off the stage with her music stand gripped in a podgy hand and, leaving the stand on the floor beside her husband's guitar case right in the way of anyone needing to get by, she went and joined Adam at the bar. David was left to contend with his guitar and music stand, and the bar stool. He leaned the guitar against the back wall and carried the stool to the edge of the stage. Using Juan's mixing desk to steady his descent, he stepped off the stage, grabbed the stool and set it down on the floor. He retrieved his music stand in similar fashion.

Juan, who'd been leaning against the barrel with obvious impatience, moved forward.

'Are you done?' he said and barged past David onto the stage. He grabbed his microphone stand, removed it from David's vee and straightened the monitors. Then he spent some time inspecting the microphone.

David deposited his music stand next to his wife's and returned the stool to the bar, before easing himself back into his seat, having evidently forgotten to collect his guitar.

I could scarcely contain my contempt for them both. It was only the presence of Alf beside me that kept me from rearing in my seat. It wasn't like me to be so riled. I pride myself on being a calm, self-assured man, but that Christmas Eve my equanimity had been trampled, and finally pulverised by Nathan's disclosure that he'd had relations with my sister. Taken alone, the news would shake a saint, but it was made all the worse when coupled with the fact that I'd been abused by Hannah Fisher, used for the purposes of her revenge.

I had to cleanse myself, restore myself. Anyone would have done the same.

So great was my chagrin that all concern for Adam's welfare had vanished from my thoughts. I no longer cared if Juan's wrath erupted. No longer cared who he lashed out at. They all deserved it, one way or the other. No one in that room was redeemable. And so emerged in my mind a strange alliance, for I would never before have aligned myself with the likes of Juan.

Every human is flawed. I know that. No matter how hard we strive for perfection, we'll never achieve it. The Kinsfolk would harken back to original sin, to the fall of Adam, to the stain of evil innate in us all. And the need to envelope oneself in God and seek redemption. Yet the Kinsfolk, for all their godliness, were the biggest sinners of all. Examples were not hard to find. Rebekah's affair with God came immediately to mind, something Delilah was apt to go on and on about, to me, to anyone who'd listen. The ultimate adultery she'd said, one that had drawn David to slather himself in pubescent flesh, if only in his imaginings. Delilah was right to assert that there were three in the Fishers' matrimonial bed.

Little wonder when those two coupled they produced a creature as base as Hannah. She was a trollop with the sexual mores of a guttersnipe. No amount of scrubbing would erase her juices from my loins. Juices that had penetrated my skin, entering my blood stream to be pumped through my system forevermore. For I doubted they could ever be expunged, or that my kidneys had the capacity to filter and flush away those alien juices coursing through my body. Hannah's juices, imbued with the cells of my own sister. I all but gagged.

And I'd never be free of her.

I knew I should have loved Eva but I didn't. I rued how she'd coiled her way back into my life, occupied my home as if it belonged to her, breached every code I had in a pathetic attempt to claim supremacy over my domain. Then, in a final act of disregard for my needs, she broke into our parents' bedroom and had a free-for-all rumble through their things.

And she'd been thorough too. She must have been, to have located the Christmas decorations buried deep in Father's chest, in a sack obscured by a crowd of boxes and religious knickknacks.

And yesterday morning there she'd stood, proud as a child before the display she'd made of her finds on the kitchenette. I couldn't contain my outrage. And she just stood there, blabbing about how it was time to move on. Move on! When I was the one left with the house, haunted by memories of our parents. Memories I had painstakingly stored in their honour.

She'd been punished long enough, she'd said.

Eight years she'd waited. Eight years to let go. I told her I understood her distress, really, I did, but she had to realise how hard it had been for me too. I was still grieving. Surely, she could see that?

I begged her, I implored her to put back the decorations, but she refused. I was incredulous. I couldn't escape the fact that she'd flouted my needs in an act that could only be thought disrespectful, if not sacrilegious.

I couldn't stay there. I was frightened of what I might do. I left her to her shrine, left the house, and took myself off for a long walk.

Down the lane I strode, rounding the sycamore tree and over the bridge. Then I headed east. I walked on by the general store and up the track past The Cabin. There was no one about. I trudged up the rise and entered the redwood forest following the path I had taken many times before, when I was young.

The day was unnaturally warm and I found I was sweating. I slowed my pace. The familiarity of the redwood forest, the cathedral of trees, their sturdy trunks of thick fibrous bark, the soft litter of needles carpeting the ground, the still, scented air, all of it did nothing to calm my nerves. Eventually I arrived at the clearing where I used to sit and read my book. Sometimes my comic. It was the same book and the same comic but she never figured that out. Perhaps she never got that close.

I sat down, leaned back in the crook at the base of the tree.

She'd always been clingy and furtive. Back then when she followed me everywhere I couldn't have known there was anything wrong with her. It had taken many years of speculation and observation to reach the conclusion that she suffered from some form of psychosis. There could be no other explanation for her peculiar behaviour. I'd accommodated her foibles, been the benevolent other, her brother and guardian, protective yet vigilant. I suppose I always knew that one day she would overstep the mark.

I sat in the shade and the stillness, deciding on the best course of action. She had to move back to the city. I couldn't cope with her in the house a day, or even another hour more. I was reluctant to confront her in her manic state. I must have sat there and waited for hours, going over and over the events in my mind with my anxiety mounting. Eventually, when the sun had set and only the moon lit my way, I made my return.

The house was quiet. I hesitated before opening the front door. Then I thought it best to wait until morning before confronting her, although I didn't sleep.

When the new day began, I left my lair and went in search of her.

I found her in the living room, sunk back in my sofa with her feet curled beneath her. Upon my approach she sat up.

'I found something else in that room,' she said. 'Something that changes everything.' Her tone was accusatory.

'I haven't a clue what you're talking about,' I said, annoyed by her diversionary tactic, for she must have known I was about to exact the only punishment I could conceive: banishment.

'That's why you kept the room locked, isn't it?' she said, waving a piece of paper at me. 'To keep the truth from me.'

I told her again that I had no idea what she was talking about.

'I found the note, Philip,' she said, still waving the paper.

'What note?'

'The suicide note.'

I took the note from her and read it. The writing appeared to be that of Mother. But the tone was wrong and the wording not typical of Mother, or of Father, who I supposed might have dictated it.

'Face it, Philip,' Eva said with a note of triumph. 'You owe me, big time. I saved your life.'

'Don't be ridiculous.'

'Then who was it that stopped you from drinking that whisky?'

'Saved my life?!'

I had to think fast. I re-read the note to stall for time. I couldn't have her believing she hadn't murdered our parents. I knew she hadn't. Of course she hadn't. No amount of her silly potion could have done the deed. She hadn't been the only one livid with our parents that day. The deception was warranted and had to be upheld. It meant we'd been equals all these years. It was my insurance: We'd both caused death, albeit in my case inadvertently. Both covered it up. And wasn't it I who helped her cover up that vile act? She'd never have managed on her own. Where was her gratitude?

'You murdered our parents!' I said convincingly. 'All these years I've been covering up for you, and you have the audacity to contrive this.'

I threw the note back at her. I told her no. No, no, no. I said it couldn't be. She had to be lying.

'You're the one who's lying,' she said. 'You're a

cruel, heartless, scheming man riddled with lies. I know better than anyone and you'd better be nice to me or I'll tell.'

'Tell what?' I said.

'All. I will tell all.'

She was threatening me. My little sister. My poor deranged little sister.

No one threatens me.

'You don't know anything,' I said calmly and left her perched on the sofa to stew over her note.

It didn't take long to make the atmosphere in the house intolerable. I crashed a few doors, slammed about in the kitchen, threw one of Mother's vases at the wall. When I came back down the hallway she scurried out the front door. Then, I went to her room.

It was a shock to smell her presence in there, musky and stale like yesterday's sex. Not pleasant, and neither was the sight of the unkempt bed, the clothes strewn about.

Despite her appalling personal hygiene, I had no qualms sifting through her belongings. She'd forfeited her privacy. In fact, she'd forfeited much more than that.

Her diary wasn't well hidden. I found it under her pillow. Unable to stay in her room, I took it with me into mine, closing the door behind me.

The paragraphs were filled with confessions, fabrications and childish justifications. I might have dismissed as ravings her hurried sentences, but I was fascinated by her habit of holding her breath in the bath. Did she really do that? It was an activity that if true, served to confirm my diagnosis that my sister was mad.

I found her thoughts about me intriguing. She

seemed determined to care for me, yet I needed no care. I read on.

Several pages in and I was shocked by the evident sickness of her soul. That she would conjure incestuous perversions she clearly found sexually arousing and then scribe them in such pornographic detail. No doubt in order to arouse herself some more, there for her to read over and again whenever she felt like it. And she'd used me to augment her masturbatory inclinations! She'd defiled not just me, but Joy. My pure and beautiful Joy! This sordid addiction she indulged beneath my roof, our parents' roof, as if she'd returned to sully us both with her twisted fantasies. It was repulsive, to think that this is what she'd been doing all these weeks. It was all I could do not to retch.

Despite my disgust I kept reading. It was all more or less the same, a string of invented stories masquerading as memories and I skipped past the bulk of it, losing interest. It wasn't until I neared the last entries, that my blood stopped flowing as if it had turned to stone in my veins. Aiden. She actually believed I had murdered our brother. She was a liar. Worse, she believed her own lies. She never saw me and Aiden on the bridge. She couldn't have done. I heard Mother tell her that after lunch she had to go and clean her room.

She was insane. Sick and insane. A delusional paranoid. Only, her recollections were much more than pure make believe. They were dangerous. Leafing through the pages knowing Eva was somewhere outside, I was beginning to feel at risk of my life.

I realised later, much later, when the day had passed into night and the hot still weather had been cast aside by a violent storm, when time had released into my mind fragments of truth like rain, it wasn't until then, when I was seated in The Cabin awaiting my turn on stage, that I realised Eva was little more than Cynthia in young skin.

All evening Cynthia had sat behind me in The Cabin that Christmas Eve, nursing a brandy and lemonade, teasing the tassels of her shawl, periodically squawking like a currawong, and every so often bursting forth with a tirade of nonsense upon pretence of intuition. She was no more clairvoyant than any other old maid. The way she'd fixed her gaze on me when she sang that ode to her sister was ridiculous.

I had no part in Joy's death and every part in trying to save her life. I had done my best to catch her before she fell; attempted to grab her, and all I managed was to inadvertently rip her necklace from her neck. I must have dropped it and wherever it landed— did the chain break? The clasp? —there it would be unless a bowerbird had chanced by and carried it off.

Thank goodness the path was so overgrown no one ventured down it. The grassy clearing all but forgotten, for it was surely a dangerous path to take and Burton could not afford to lose another life to tragedy.

How I missed my Joy! How I loved her!

What is love? It's so hard to comprehend but if I were to describe how I felt for Joy I would have to name it love. Pure love. From the very first moment I saw her naked on the grassy knoll by the river.

I must have been seventeen and half her age. Yet I was a mature seventeen-year old, dare I say worldly, and she was a youthful woman, a primary school teacher full of optimism and a wondrous appreciation of life. She yearned to escape Burton and the oppressive clutches of her sister and the river represented access to the open plains beyond. She would dream of building a small raft. She had a gathering of fallen branches and assorted lengths of discarded timber she'd foraged, hidden in the brambles on the far side of the clearing, well away from prying eyes. She showed me once. I'd gone down to the river to clear my mind after Father had yelled at Mother for allowing me to drive the car without his permission. Apparently, hers alone was not enough. I'd marched along the riverbank in an indignant fury, to find Joy seated on a small blanket, buttoning up her blouse.

I tucked behind some bushes and watched her for a short while. The sun shone down and her hair gleamed. When she stood, I could no longer resist revealing myself and I stepped forward into the clearing. She gave me a coy smile and said with an almost coquettish giggle that she was glad I'd arrived then and not five minutes before.

We talked. I shared my recent slight and she empathized with stories of her own, of Cynthia's cruelty, and then of her plans for escape.

After marvelling, as I was meant to, over her collection of branches and timber, I was at once relieved that, with my untrained yet shrewd eye, she would never make a raft out of that pile. She lacked the wherewithal and the materials she'd gathered were unsuitable. It was relief born of desire, a desire that came upon me unawares and consumed my every cell.

Sensing her heightened state as well, I took my opportunity and drew her close and nuzzled my face in her hair. She giggled like a schoolgirl and whispered for me to stop. I went on to tell her how I wished I had been five minutes earlier for I would have partaken in a rare feast. She giggled again.

She offered no resistance as I unbuttoned her blouse and stroked the smooth warm flesh within. My mouth reached for hers and I kissed her hard, parting her lips and pressing in my tongue, my fingers pinching her tiny hardening buds, making her moan.

After a short while she tried to pull away but I gripped her by the waist, hushing her will, and I walked her across the grass. Then I pulled her down to the blanket on the ground.

One hand slid inside her panties.

She was hot and wet and at the touch of those luscious folds I couldn't hold back and I yanked free of my shorts a hard and dripping member. She was on her back, her eyes closed, nervous, and I had to part those milky white thighs to gain purchase.

It was over too soon, the excitement too much, and I knew I had to offer her satisfaction as well so I pinned her arms above her head and stayed on top of her, still inside her, raising myself up a little on my elbows and knees so as not to crush her. I waited.

Such is the manhood of a seventeen-year-old that it felt like only seconds and I was grinding into her loins, slowly this time, holding back, measured and attentive, urging her on with kisses on her neck and her ears, until her mouth reached for mine and her back arched a little and her body succumbed to a few short spasms. And then my own desire again consumed me and my pace increased. A few hard thrusts and I was done.

Somehow, I knew, even before I saw my flaccid member streaked with blood, that she was a virgin.

Her blood congealed and hardened on the skin and hair of my groin.

She was embarrassed and mortified all at once. The blanket was sodden with it. The back of her skirt, crumpled up about her waist, sported a few smears.

I had to think fast. There was nothing around to clean up the mess except the river. The river would rid the worst of it.

Without hesitation, I pulled off my shirt and shorts and dived in, the force of the cold taking my breath away the moment I hit the water. A quick rub around the loins and I was out. I stood dripping and shivering. Joy looked up at me. I didn't expect her to follow suit, but when she said she couldn't swim, a wave of frustration lurched through me. I kept standing there, staring down at her in her bloodied state. Then I came up with an idea.

I explained how I'd hold her and never let her fall in. She could press her feet against the bank and lower in her buttocks, and I'd have a hold of her. I promised.

In my imagination it seemed a plausible manoeuvre, although it proved much harder to actualise. Joy at first opposed the plan, slowly acquiescing as I explained the fine details, eventually squatting at the edge of the bank, holding my hands. I was in position, seated facing her, my legs astride, knees bent, feet pressing hard against two large and half-buried boulders. Even if she slipped she couldn't fall in as long as she held on.

I admit I was proud of the plan until she lowered in her nether region, gasping from the cold, and I knew that with her two hands gripping mine she hadn't any means by which to attend to the mess between her thighs. I asked her to let go of one hand and give herself a bit of a wipe but she refused. I waited and waited, when at last she screamed for me to pull her up, which I promptly did, admonishing her with a hiss to keep quiet. Watching as rivulets of translucent red coated her inner thighs.

Back on the knoll I found a clean handkerchief in my shorts' pocket and I wiped her down and spent some time rinsing off the blood on our clothes and the blanket.

There'd be a lot of explaining to do at both houses. So I told her we had to cut ourselves to account for the stains. She was by now behaving sensibly and agreed that something of the sort had to be done. There were brambles all around. I soon found a long woody stem snapped off from its mother and thick with spines that were rigid and sharp.

She recoiled at the sight of it and I had to coax her, talking her through it, asking her to help me choose the right spot.

She identified her outer mid right thigh.

I told her to kneel and I knelt behind her with my arm wrapped around her shoulders, hand covering her mouth. I pulled her skirt up a little higher and stroked the tender flesh before lashing down the spiny stem, making sure to execute a horizontal pull when the stem met the flesh. It was an intoxicating moment. Her body tensed and she emitted a muffled scream. Blood rose quickly, oozing from shallow gouges surrounded by several long grazes, rapidly plumping.

I released my grip and kissed her mouth then crouched down beside her leg and gently licked her wounds. Her blood was warm and sharp with a musky undertow. It was an act of loving kindness and

I wanted to demonstrate that love to her, make her realise how much I cared, that I would do anything for her, and go to any lengths to protect her. And her reputation.

Thankfully there was no requirement to graze my own legs. After I'd given her that lashing I found that the stains on my shorts had all but disappeared.

The shadows were lengthening and the air began to bite so we decided to part ways. She left first and I followed a good ten minutes later, making sure as I emerged at the bridge that there was no one about.

I saw her often after that. All through summer we would find time to be together.

The last time I saw her was the worst day of my life. We'd met in our usual spot on the riverbank as arranged. Then, after an hour of glorious lovemaking, after I'd consumed that soft moist gash, after we'd sighed and moaned and gasped, after we'd shared our most intimate juices, only then did she come out with it.

We were preparing to head back, we were saying our farewells, each of us with a heart filled with longing.

And she told me she was pregnant.

I've never felt horror like it. My mind boomed with revulsion. I couldn't understand how she could let it happen. If the truth came out, I'd be excommunicated. The baby doomed to a certain death. For it was God's will, Pastor Makepeace had always said, just as Pastor Prentice had said before him, that the son always paid for the sins of the father with his life. Or the sins of the mother. Who was I to say otherwise?

Joy, heathen Joy, she wouldn't understand, wouldn't know she was carrying death.

My faith had never been strong but I wasn't able to argue against the will of God. And I wasn't able to face excommunication. It would have been unbearable. All connection with Burton gone. Yet with me still a child, and her a grown woman, a teacher no less, the consequences of the accusations would have been for her certain ruin. She'd have lost her job, her reputation, everything. When it was I who had seduced her. No, there would have been no way back from that.

I was only seventeen. I could have had no idea Pastor Makepeace would soon shame the whole town with his bare backside and the Kinsfolk of Burton would be no more. I'd already suffered his relentless persecution over the death of dear Aiden. All I knew was that I wouldn't be treated so kindly a second time, not for a sin I could not deny, even if it had been her fault for letting me seduce her.

Joy wasn't a Kinswoman. She didn't face the trauma of excommunication. And as my reaction set in, I became livid with her. And I was livid with her for another reason too—for not telling me sooner. I'd been innocently thrusting into her, releasing my very essence deep inside her, and there lurked, just membranes away, another life.

Irrationality took hold. Right there on the riverbank I wanted to suck back my juices. Joy's was a betrayal of such magnitude it was a wonder I didn't strangle her. I had loved her and that love changed to hate an instant.

She saw in my eyes my reaction, and she skittered away up the path.

I followed.

About halfway back to the bridge I caught her arm and swung her round to face me. She was crying. But she had no right to be distressed. I went to draw her closer, thinking for a fleeting moment that I wanted to make amends, when she lost her footing.

It all happened too fast. I made to grab her and instead my hand caught her necklace. It broke in my grasp. I reached out, suddenly desperate to save her, but I was too late. She toppled backwards into the river and was gone.

Poor Joy. It was a tragic conclusion to a terribly hard life.

The alarm was raised the following day. Cynthia, of course, became instantly hysterical. The whole town was worried that Joy had met with foul play and there was talk of dredging the river. That was when I told the police I had seen her alight the bus the day of the tragedy. For I loved her, and I didn't want Burton to know that she'd been devoured by an unforgiving river. And in saving her from the awful shame of her pregnancy, there was not a chance that anyone would say it was my fault. A harmless lie to save face, that was all I was guilty of.

That Christmas Eve morning, alone in my bedroom, I flicked back through Eva's diary and found her version of the tragedy. Or rather, her cauldron of lies. Written out in hurried scrawl that slid down an imaginary slope, the length of the lines shortening as I progressed to the bottom. The last three lines reduced to a single word.

Philip.

The.

Killer.

I snapped shut the diary knowing I had no alternative. Her punishment would be more severe that I'd first conceived. Banishment—yes—she would be banished.

My mind sallied forth a thousand justifications. Self-preservation was uppermost in my mind. I suppose I panicked. In my heightened state, I knew I'd been walking on egg shells since Eva's return. She'd been suffocating me slowly with her domestic niceties, always cooking for me and ironing my shirts, in the process curtailing my freedom, knitting me up in her ghastly jumper, until my image emerged imprisoned in the pattern. And all along, her oppressive smothering domesticity had been a ruse. She wasn't there for me. Despite her claims in her diary, I didn't need her. Then why had she come back? It was suddenly so sickeningly obvious. To plant evidence in our parents' bedroom. To exonerate herself and implicate me all at once. For, thinking about it again, she must have poisoned my parents with that potion of hers. She must have. Just as she'd written a suicide note to exonerate herself. And now I had a killer on the loose in my house.

Eva knew not to meddle and meddled she had. I struggled to remain rational. I had to think things through. An old affection rippled through me. I was almost swayed by it. I admit that during our childhood I had developed a fondness for her. She had been my ally, prepared to stand by me or offer me comfort. In payment, I'd taught her many tricks and games. Yet she'd grown into a tiresome woman, excessive in her attentions. Her mithering unbearable.

Worse, I was sure she'd been going through my things in my absence.

A few days earlier I thought I might start to reciprocate, take advantage of a brief time when I found myself alone in the house. She'd gone to pay Adam a visit. Slipped out, she'd called it. 'I'm just slipping out for a bit to visit a neighbour,' the note on the kitchen table had read.

Yes, she'd started leaving notes. It was a level of control I couldn't bear. And she used those little scribblings to goad me. 'Slipping out.' She would have known what that phrase implied. An illicit encounter. She'd become secretive. When it was only me and her who had secrets. Yet there she was, sneaking off to Adam's, or so I had thought at the time, to share secrets with him.

I had to take responsibility for the past. Had to take back control. Had to reclaim my sense of self, my authority. Somehow, I'd lost my centre to her.

You have to be an eldest child to know what it's like. You're the object of attention, nurtured at the breast, bounced on the knee, then mother's belly swells and along comes the competition, only there is no competition, you've been replaced. Some other creature has pride of place on breast and knee and suddenly you're alone, told to go away, to stop doing this and that, and when you try to show how you feel you're slapped. Everything has become your fault. Your innocence, your joy, both wrenched away and you must share what is rightfully yours. But what's mine is hers and what's hers is always hers, the thieving little sister.

The situation worsened when mother's belly swelled again, shooting from her loins a little brother this time: Aiden. By then I was six and Eva three. Aiden was a sniffling, whining, sickly wretch of a creation and I loathed him from the first. He was so molly coddled he grew into a perfect brat and my tribulations as the eldest child intensified by the day.

My childhood was a relentless grind of punishments for misdeeds I'd never committed, but I bade my time knowing one day Aiden would get his comeuppance. I had to wait a long time. That day didn't arrive until I was fifteen, the day my fate changed for the better and the worse all at once, destiny sweeping to my rescue, the river ridding me of my saboteur. Of course, I was thoroughly shaken at the time. I'd rushed home to relate the news to distraught parents. Mother cried and Father became frantic, both sprinting down to the river, but there was nothing anyone could have done to save young Aiden, who was an atrocious swimmer.

Yes, I was involved. I was right there beside him. But I didn't kill him. He fell. I didn't make him fall. Eva implied I made him fall. Joy fell too. And I didn't make her fall either.

So many justifications when only one might have been needed. Any sensible, law-abiding man would have to agree by now that it would be a blessing for the house to be rid of the infestation.

Eva couldn't swim, I was certain of that, but she could hold her breath, or so she said in her diary. Unless that too, was a lie. I flicked back through the pages in search of the minutes and seconds recorded: Nine minutes and twenty-three seconds, seven minutes and eleven seconds, three and twelve, nine and fifteen, eight and seventeen, and her record, her personal best, nine minutes and twenty-four seconds. Impressive, or it would be if it were not implausible.

But I didn't doubt the ritual. She'd turned my bathroom into her shrine. A shrine for her black art.

Then it came to me in a flash. She'd been in training—but for what? Revenge? Was that it? Both Joy and Aiden had drowned. She'd come back to wear me down and when I was supplicant, she would have taken me to the river, dragged me to the water, held me down.

There really was only one solution to the matter of Eva. One she would understand. Didn't Arthur hammer a stake through the heart of his Lucy? Wasn't that the only way to rid the world of evil?

Demons take many forms. Each required its own unique version of death.

I pushed open the bathroom door, stepped up onto the dais, put the plug in, and ran her bath.

If I was wrong, if she was innocent, then she'd be able to hold her breath for the full nine minutes and twenty-four seconds.

I went back to her room and found her toilet bag in the cupboard beside her bed. The stopwatch was tucked in a side pocket. I took it with me and went to find her.

My reverie was interrupted when Delilah finally took up the stage after placating an irate David, who'd no doubt come up with a tirade of excuses as to how the microphone stand fell off the stage, except of course the obvious—his size.

She began thanking everyone for coming to celebrate Christmas Eve on such a tempestuous night.

She stood tall in her purple gown, surveying the room, her ukulele hanging from its strap, her pride. A baritone ukulele no less, with its black hearted sassafras body, replete with rope binding, an instrument she'd decided best suited to her voice. Not that she sang. Instead she put her poetry to music. With her fungus-infested fingers she would strum a single chord in a deliberate bring, and issuing a - to her - meaningful phrase, she would lose herself to her own words.

'There was a man,
So grand was he,
One day long past,
On bended knee,
He pledged fidelity...'

It was excruciating to listen to and I made every effort to shut it out, averting my eyes from that cavernous mouth, those plump red-painted lips stretching wide as she enunciated in elongated syllables every second word.

She was a quarter of the way in when I saw stirrings in the nook and David sidled along in his seat, easing out a leg and heaving himself up holding onto the edge of the counter and the table, which Rebekah judiciously leant on. Once upright he went to the stage.

Delilah's gaze darted his way. But she chose to ignore him.

One hefty stride and he made it onto the dais behind her, whereupon he retrieved the guitar that he'd left leaning against the back wall.

With one hand on the mixing desk to steady his descent, he stepped down to the floor.

Juan hadn't moved. A muscle in his neck

twitched. He looked ready to mouth his fury but David refused to look in his direction.

A murmur of laughter came from behind. It was Ed, who seemed determined to goad. I suspected he was still annoyed after his previous altercation with Juan, and didn't seem to know when to let a thing go.

Juan ignored him. For whatever reason, Juan was holding back. It seemed he was unwilling to interrupt Delilah's set. Perhaps his professionalism held sway; although I was sure he was well past any level of self-control.

The wind had changed direction and was belting The Cabin from the south. Hannah had closed the door to the kitchen, presumably to block out the draught, for the kitchen was a later addition to the original structure, with a low skillion roof, and thinly clad walls, one replete with louvre windows. It was astonishing that Delilah chose to use the space as a functioning kitchen but she said she liked its aspect, overlooking her garden.

Her rooms, as she called them, were accessed through a door cut into the eastern wall, and down a short interconnecting corridor. The small weather-board dwelling sat on a sleeve of level ground cut into the hillside, its southern and eastern flanks sheltering behind steep batters. The northern wall obscured from the road by a Cyprus hedge. Passers-by from any direction would be hard pressed to see the Make-peace residence and few had been inside. Delilah kept visitors corralled in her garden.

I had the dubious honour of finding myself summoned to her bathroom last year to attend to a dripping tap. A windowless *ensuite*, no more than a cupboard, and fortunately the tap had been quickly reparable with a new washer and I was free to leave, for I had to focus solely on the matter at hand. All the while Delilah stood over me, blocking my exit, and if I should have chanced to lift my gaze, it would have landed in the deep cleft of her bosom. She had an arm raised high against the doorjamb and the other on her hip and her chatter was all breathy and modulated and I was convinced she would orgasm with one deft stroke of my Stillson. But I resisted, preferring to leave her unsated than open the hatch on her irrepressible lust.

With the door to the kitchen now closed, the sickly smell of rotting carcass intensified. There had to be another beast in the chimney. It was a smell no amount of incense would obscure. While not normally affected by the stench, accustomed as I was to blocked drains and sewers, I was beginning to feel inordinately claustrophobic. The events of the day weighed down on me like an edifice, floor upon floor of betrayal. I couldn't take any more. The whole structure was set to collapse on me. I'd be crushed beneath the rubble. Even now I could feel it tremble.

In a break between songs I went to the bar for another beer. Hannah was bending down, replenishing the shelves, her flat buttocks and the crease in between caused a flashback to yesterday afternoon on Delilah's veranda and I was once again appalled I had allowed that slut to have her way with me.

A feeling reinforced when Nathan piped up with, 'Hannah, lover boy is here.'

Hannah stood up and looked around, catching sight of me. Instead of the hostile glare I'd anticipated, there was a look of expectancy in her eyes. She grabbed a low-carb beer from one of the shelves and opened it, placing it on the bar and indicating for me to follow her into the kitchen. Leaving the beer on the counter, I happily obliged, for no other reason than that I was keen for some fresh air.

Delilah had begun her next song and I knew she'd be watching but I didn't turn round. No doubt running through her mind would have been all manner of false assumptions, a new scandal in the making, shaping into her version of headline news replete with all the sensationalised embellishments of a daily rag. Heaven forbid Burton should ever be privy to the truth.

Hannah wasted no time telling me.

She went over to the far side of the room and stood before the gas cooker. She was suddenly all vulnerable, arms outstretched, a hand clutching the bench to either side. I admit I felt a pulse of animal desire at the sight of her, until she leaned against the cooker knobs, and there was a short hiss before she moved away to the sink.

'I'm pregnant,' she said to the floor.

'So?'

'It's yours.' She shot me a wilful stare with those bush baby eyes.

'You can't know that,' I said with certainty.

'I can and I do,' she said in a tone that was unequivocal. 'It's yours.'

The shock was so great I couldn't speak. I couldn't move but inside I was swaying back and forth. My mind was abuzz with sharp thoughts. A swarm of vespers, disturbed from their nest, determined to attack the cause of their disturbance.

Christmas Eve, when the world abounded in good cheer, I'd suffered a deluge of licentious revelations.

Eva, Adam, and now Hannah, all had committed prurient sins that brought into question their right to mortality. But the world was just. It had to be just. And God should, he would smite them each in turn.

Everyone has limits and I'd reached mine. Nothing occupied my mind except the horrific knowledge that my seed had united with Hannah's ovum, to form a foetus growing in that degenerate belly, feeding off that lubricious blood, doomed to spring from filthy loins to be nursed at the breast of a woman with the mores of Mammon.

I couldn't let it happen. I would have thrust a hand up inside her and ripped the damn thing out, thwacked it hard and tossed it in the incinerator where all unwanted dead things belonged, but that was fanciful and I'd never commit such a brutal act, not even on Hannah.

'Will you keep it?' I said, suddenly aware of a similar conversation sixteen years before.

'I have to.' She made it sound as though her beliefs prohibited abortion, although I couldn't quite believe her.

'See Cynthia,' I suggested, scrambling for a way out. Rumour had it she'd helped a few women terminate unwanted pregnancies.

'She's not coming anywhere near me!'

'Don't I have a say?' I felt the anger rise; welcomed its power.

'You?' She looked me up and down with contempt. 'Why? It's my body.'

And in an instant there was Joy, running from me, pulling away, slipping, falling in the river, sacrificing herself, freeing us both from scandal. And here I was again, seeding a child, only this time not with a woman I loved, a woman I cherished, a woman I respected, but with Hannah.

Disgusted, I turned from her and left the kitchen, quickly arranging my face into a bland expression. I paused at the bar and conjured a private smile. I pointed my gaze at the stage to meet Delilah's. Then I took a long draught of my beer and went and sat with Alf.

I maintained a causal demeanour while I tried to think through the situation and decide on a sensible solution, one that would be most beneficial to all concerned. It seemed to me that everyone in the room was implicated; blame spread thickly upon each and every person there. It was hard to isolate an ultimate cause.

But there had to be one.

Delilah's voice penetrated my thoughts. If she had told Hannah to go home yesterday, instead of imprisoning her in a job she despised, then the sordid event would never have taken place. Rebekah and David had produced the vessel, and were therefore inseparable from it in the final analysis, although theirs was a distant culpability. Nathan's infidelity had much to contribute. Then there was Cynthia, who had made Joy seek solace in my arms. Alf, Joshua, Ed, all had played their part, however small and incidental. Even Juan.

I don't recall how I settled on Adam. He was certainly on the other side of luck. Perhaps through his own fall from grace he symbolized a collective fall and therefore he owed Burton an ultimate sacrifice, to purge the town of a pestilence. Besides, he was an outsider, and a bestial one at that.

The pressure I'd endured all evening, worrying

over his vulnerability with Juan in the room, built up in me. When all along Adam had been trying to insinuate that I had something to do with Joy's death, casting into doubt my explanation and even going so far as to suggest the case be re-opened. What had Eva told him? All I knew for certain was Adam had become a risk to my reputation.

Burton is a small town. In small towns, everyone knows everyone's business. Gossip is considered not only a virtue, but a duty. And so it was that Rebekah told Delilah, who then told me, that Adam had found Joy's necklace. Delilah said she had no idea where he'd found it. She reassured me that she still believed my sighting of Joy stepping onto a bus that day. It is a credit to me that I'd managed to contain that knowledge and demonstrate grace to the very man I might as well have shunned.

Yes, my decision had logic to it, and as if the gods themselves agreed, the lights dimmed, flickered and were gone. Undeterred, Delilah continued with her protracted syllables and random accompanying chords. Joshua slipped out through the kitchen door and moments later the lights came on again.

A smattering of applause marked the end of Delilah's set. I was on next and out of my side vision I could see that Juan was looking at me with raised eyebrows. I didn't shift my gaze. On my table, the last of the candles fizzled and popped and the flame was gone.

I was wondering if I'd get a chance to act when Adam left his seat. It was a moment of providence. He went through the bar to the kitchen, stepping aside to allow Joshua to re-enter the room. I followed close behind, closing the kitchen door behind me.

I addressed Adam with much concern in my voice. 'Adam, wait.'

He paused by the back door, and turned.

'The women's toilets are blocked too,' I said, going over to him and putting an arm round his shoulder. 'But the men's are clear, at least, last time I looked.'

He believed me. Why wouldn't he? I am Burton's plumber.

We walked together, out through the back door into a blast of cold air. As we cornered the side wall of The Cabin the wind pushed us on, pressing the legs of my trousers against my calves.

'Go on in,' I said. 'You were first.'

'Do you mind? I'm rather desperate.'

The moment he entered the cubicle I slammed my arm against the door, taking him by surprise.

Two hard kicks to the backs of his knees and he was crouched on the floor. He yelped. The hapless Adonis yelped.

The smell was acrid and I almost dry wretched as I opened the toilet seat lid. From there it was surprisingly easy to force Adam's face into the thick contents of Alf's stomach.

Leaning over him, I held down his head. His body writhed, hands flailing about scrambling for purchase of which there was none. I put a knee on his back, pressed his collarbone to the toilet bowl.

I had to shut my ears to the sound of his gurgling. But it was soon over. He was gone in seconds. Not even a minute. Unlike Eva.

And unlike Eva, that's where I left him.

I expected to feel relieved. The sacrifice complete. But where were the purifying waters? Instead I relented to a flaming upsurge emanating from my loins, and I opened my fly.

I took the hard shaft in my hand, leaned over Adam's body slumped over the toilet bowl, and I pumped.

The end was quick, the juices shooting high and descending like a little downpour onto the shirt on his back. My signature.

I stood, panting, letting the shaft soften in my grip.

I thought that might have been the end of my campaign but it wasn't enough.

I went to the mirror. I was a pitiful sight. I washed my hands and splashed my face with cold water. Then I left the toilet.

My vision had tightened. I was seeing down a tunnel. The wind hurled itself at me as I rounded the corner. I didn't take in the incinerator. Didn't think that the soggy reddened mess of flesh and bone in there had to be set alight.

Actions revealed themselves to me as things appeared in my line of sight. The meter box was first. I saw it as I made for the kitchen door. I opened the metal casing. It was hard to make out the switches and fuses. Then the clouds parted on the moon. Its ruddy light shone down on me. Its beatifying will swept through me in a sudden rush. I didn't know what to make of the feeling other than that I felt whole for the first time in my life. I knew, as if my mind were alight with lunar brilliance, that nature's will had aligned itself with my own little will, blessing my actions, sanctifying this night in a simple act of cleansing. And I was at once nature's master and its slave. I was no longer acting alone.

I flicked off the mains switch and removed the fuse, smashing it against the wall until I heard a crack. Then I returned it. A clamour rose inside The Cabin. I made out Cynthia's high-pitched wails. And Delilah's authoritative tone. I had to act fast. Joshua's utility was parked nearby. The tree had done a grand job crushing it. I found the wire cutters in Joshua's toolbox on the passenger seat. Delilah's wiring was as dilapidated as her plumbing. The mains cable was protruding from the wall below the meter box. A clean cut, close to the box, well hidden from quick eyes.

I threw the wire cutters into the dark on my way to the kitchen, entering as Joshua made his way through from the bar.

'It's no use,' I said, holding myself steady against the doorjamb. 'The power's out.'

'Might be the fuse,' he said and pushed past me.

'Might be,' I said and made my way into the room. I hadn't reached the table when he strode back in and closed the door.

'The whole town must be out,' he said on his way through to the bar. He paused and looked past me. Then he caught my eye. 'Good job Delilah's on gas.'

Good job Delilah's on gas, I thought.

And I knew what next to do. Joshua had handed me an idea as if it were a baton, as if that lunar will had passed through all of us, uniting us in a mission. The signs had been there all night. The outgassing possum in the chimney. Adam the maggot man. Everything made perfect sense.

The pale light of the blood-tinged moon filtered through the louvre windows, illuming the gas cooker.

There, contained in all those hoses and regulators and burners, was the solution.

In the bar, voices were raised.

'The night's over,' Delilah said above the others, as though she were reading my thoughts.

I turned each knob on full and opened the oven door. Fortunately, Delilah's oven had been designed long before anyone had given thought to safety features. I was confident the hiss would be inaudible in the bar above the ceaseless moan of the wind. And I gave thanks to the possum in the chimney.

'I can't see a damn thing,' said Juan.

'Leave it till the morning,' Delilah said.

'I'm not leaving my gear here,' Juan bellowed. 'Someone get me a light.'

Yes, yes, but not yet. Not quite yet.

'What do you think we're trying to do?' Alf said. 'You're not the only one in here in the dark.'

'Get me a light, you dumb fucks.'

I didn't allow myself a smile. The gas had become overwhelming. I left the stove and stood by the back door. It seemed that Juan was doing all the work for me.

'I can't find the torch,' said Hannah.

'It'd be useless anyway,' said Joshua. 'The batteries died.'

'Here's a candle.' Nathan sounded triumphant.

'Bring it here.' Typical of Delilah. Always the matriarch.

'What use is it without a match?' said David.

'Where are the matches?'

'I thought I put the spare box here,' said Hannah. 'Someone must have moved them.'

'I used them to light the incense.'

307

'So where are they?'

'In the grate. I used the last match a while ago.'

There was a groan of disappointment.

'You shouldn't have done that,' said David.

'There are others in the kitchen,' Delilah said.

I waited, poised to head out the door.

Then Cynthia piped up with, 'Where's Adam? He isn't in his seat.'

'He went to the toilet.'

'Someone should go and check on him.'

'For heaven's sake Cynthia, give it a rest.'

I made out Delilah's form in the doorway to the bar.

'I'll go and look for him,' I said, suddenly aware that she must have been staring in my direction. I buried a feeling of rejection that no one had noticed my absence as I slipped outside, pleased to breathe fresh air.

The last I heard was Delilah's voice saying, 'Found them!'

There was a long pause. I headed off, making for the car park. I didn't look back until I heard the blast.

It was a magnificent sight. The wind caught the smoke in its tendrils and hurried it away up the valley. I stood, feet apart, hands clasped behind my back, in awe of the achievement. Only an inferno could have cleansed the pestilence contained in The Cabin that night.

CHAPTER TWENTY

DELILAH

Complicity must involve premeditation. Collusion, however tenuous, a meeting of minds. No, I did not collude. But neither am I deaf. Above the commotion, as the patrons scrambled about in the dark and the wind and the rain thrashed about outside, I think I might have detected a hiss. But I was slow to take in what it was. The matches were already in my hand. In that moment, I succumbed to an urgent need for the lavatory. I hadn't been all night. For a woman of my age that's no small feat.

I did think of taking the matches with me, of making the patrons wait in the dark a short while longer. When I saw Hannah leaning in the doorway with that supercilious look on her face, I wanted to say, 'Here they are,' and hand them to her. Instead I yanked her to me and passed the matches to Joshua standing behind the bar. With a pointed finger, I indicated to him where I was heading. Yes, I handed Joshua the matches. I suppose I might have told him I couldn't find them. But then I would have lied. If I'm guilty of anything, it's opportunism. Maybe on a subconscious level I chose to save myself, and Hannah, over the lives of the others.

I was on the throne with my knickers round my ankles when the first explosion blasted through The Cabin. I stopped mid-flow, yanked up my underwear and bolted into my bedroom. Hannah stood there, useless. The only exit was through the window. She went first. I hadn't thought myself much of a climber but I was outside the next instant.

We headed straight for the gap in the Cyprus hedge that until then had broken the continuity of the screen and been a source of personal consternation. The gap was about my size. Once through, we scrambled down the embankment to Burton Road East.

On the verge, I was hot and shivering and panting all at once. Hannah was hysterical. I covered her mouth and spoke in her ear, 'He's still out here.' My remark confused yet quieted her. We'd escaped.

I'm good at escaping. It was a skill I acquired in childhood to avoid being alone with Father. A skill that had sharpened my instincts. Back then I became wily, wary, vigilant, all held beneath a cool indifferent exterior. I had the survival skills of a cat.

There I stood in the wind and I told myself I was alive. Hannah was alive. That child of hers was alive in her belly. It occurred to me I might just as well have left Hannah to burn alive with the rest of them. For I feared for that child, cursed with the sins of its father.

Yet I knew another was also alive, the cause of all this: Philip.

The flames were fierce. Smoke billowed this way and that, thick and black. Before long, a second explosion shook the hillside as my gas bottles exploded. My home was gone but there wasn't time to mourn the loss of The Cabin, the loss of my life and livelihood. No time to mourn the Sessions Benny had so tirelessly built up. Benny had always said he wanted to go out with a bang and while he slipped from us like silk, his sessions had exploded in a blast that must have been heard in Standlake.

I thought of Benny then, briefly. And what I thought was I'd done him a favour. Those goons who fancied themselves musicians would have made a hash of his legacy. I could just imagine the endless odes to him and the dreadful covers of his songs, when not even Lee Reece could manage Benny's chord progressions. For myself, I'd never touch the Muir song bag.

With Hannah firmly in my grip, I stood for a few moments longer watching the pyre of my life. I knew Philip was up there, watching too. Waiting. He could have had no idea we'd escaped. But I wasn't about to wait there in the storm to find out what he would do next.

I took Hannah by the arm and we hurried down Burton Road East, heading for the row of small cottages I rented out to art school graduates. One of them, Anna, had a short-wave radio. She'd asked me if I minded her setting up her equipment in the lean to out the back. It meant she would need to erect an antenna on the roof, she'd said. 'Not a problem,' I'd told her, happy to oblige.

Anna was away for the season. But I knew how to get in through a rear window.

I wanted him caught, wanted him punished, wanted him locked away, wanted to divest myself of the burden of three decades of suspicion in my heart.

Behind those innocent china-blue eyes had always lurked a shifty nature. Ever since he tried to smother his sister at the age of three I'd had my reservations as to the purity of his character. Suspicion is a curious phenomenon. It twists first here then there, gathering to itself all manner of potentialities. I wouldn't consider myself the sort of woman who would ferret, but in his case, I was ever alert.

He was born with a vengeful heart. When Aiden died, I told Dora I was convinced Philip had been involved, and urged her to be stern with him. I needn't have bothered for her grief took her over and punish him she did. As did my father, Pastor Makepeace.

Dora would complain about her son but she blamed herself for conceiving him out of wedlock. I told her that had nothing to do with it. He was bad seed. His was a makeup beyond sin, existing on the outer reaches where reality is cut to pieces on the razor wire of denial and lies. He was evil and just as he cloaked his malevolence in a smooth, well-groomed veneer, so I maintained my own pretence, agreeing with him, supporting him, defending him, keeping him close.

Perhaps I should have acted sooner, but it would have been pointless. There was never any evidence, let alone proof.

The law doesn't work before the fact. Perhaps it should. But there must at least be intent and that can be hard to prove. One cannot rely on the suppositions of others, for where would we be if that were so? We'd all be incarcerated upon the paranoid thoughts of others. Just because I supposed Philip to be a killer, didn't mean I could do a thing about it.

On reflection, I should have inspected the incinerator. I planned to do just that once the storm abated. Maybe that was negligent. But I didn't want to ruin my bun. Not after Rebekah had taken so long to create it. How was I to know what he'd put in there? Perhaps it could be said that the course of the entire evening hinged on me not wanting to spoil my bun. But that would be ridiculous. Wouldn't it?

In Anna's back yard, beneath the pink-tinged luminescence of the moon behind the thinning cloud, a curious feeling of loss mingled with a sense that justice had been served overcame me. Poor Eva. I recalled a moment earlier in the evening, when I'd sat with Philip and I'd filled him in on what the Cartwrights had said about her. That they thought she was strange, unhinged in some way, but we always knew that. Dora said she was obsessed with her brother as if she were his shadow. As if she were haunted by him. The Cartwrights said she suffered from poor concentration and flights of fancy. She would stand in a trance over a pretty overseas stamp. They'd kept her on for as long as they'd dared, but when Ruth caught her pocketing a postcard from the Seychelles they had no choice but to let her go.

I told Philip he had to take care of his sister, watch over her, think about a doctor, a psychiatrist, medication. We thought perhaps she hadn't recovered from the death of Aiden and then her parents. Philip had taken my comments well. He said she'd always blamed herself for their parents' deaths even though she'd had nothing to do with it. Perhaps that was at the root of it, we agreed, misplaced guilt.

I couldn't possibly have known what he'd done with her.

We went on to discuss the necklace. Thankfully

I'd told Philip that Adam had hidden it somewhere in the kitchen of his old church. Why I'd given him false information I have no idea. I felt protective, but of whom? All I knew was that Philip would be heading to the church to retrieve it and that he'd have to search a long time before he did.

The short-wave radio was battery powered. The moment I entered the lean to I switched it on.

END

Dear reader,

We hope you enjoyed reading *The Cabin Sessions*. Please take a moment to leave a review, even if it's a short one. Your opinion is important to us.

Discover more books by Isobel Blackthorn at

https://www.nextchapter.pub/authors/isobel-blackthorn-mystery-thriller-author

Want to know when one of our books is free or discounted? Join the newsletter at

http://eepurl.com/bqqB3H

Best regards,

Isobel Blackthorn and the Next Chapter Team

You might also like:
The Legacy Of Old Gran Parks by Isobel Blackthorn

To read the first chapter for free, head to:
https://www.nextchapter.pub/books/the-legacy-of-old-gran-parks

ABOUT THE AUTHOR

Isobel Blackthorn is an award-winning author of diverse and engaging fiction. She writes gripping mysteries, dark psychological thrillers and historical fiction. She is the author of *The Unlikely Occultist: A biographical novel of Alice A. Bailey.*

OTHER WORKS

The Drago Tree
Nine Months of Summer
All Because of You
A Perfect Square
The Legacy of Old Gran Parks
A Matter of Latitude
Clarissa's Warning
A Prison in the Sun
The Unlikely Occultist
Voltaire's Garden

The Cabin Sessions
ISBN: 978-4-86747-881-3
Mass Market

Published by
Next Chapter
1-60-20 Minami-Otsuka
170-0005 Toshima-Ku, Tokyo
+818035793528

28th May 2021

Lightning Source UK Ltd.
Milton Keynes UK
UKHW041024170621
385669UK00001B/65